# Prologue

22 November 1969
Defence Intelligence Agency Headquarters
Sena Bhavan, New Delhi
4.15 p.m.

He walked towards the washroom, his hands trembling in fear. His heart thudded rapidly, the sound reverberating loudly in his ears, drowning out the usual cacophony of clacking typewriters and shrill telephones around him. His hands, wet with guilty sweat, struggled to turn the knob, forcing him to grab it with both hands and wrestle it open.

He looked around, finding some self-control in the emptiness of the washroom. He took several deep calming breaths, releasing a part of his anxiety with each exhalation. He touched the inside pocket of his polyester suit jacket, feeling the reassuring weight of his equipment, his strength of purpose re-emerging from amid his muddled thoughts. He entered one of the stalls—the sound of the latch falling in place providing him with an additional sense of security.

He pulled out the pencil case, given to him for the purpose, and placed it gingerly on the now-closed lid of the pot. From his trouser pocket, he retrieved an immaculately clean white handkerchief and spread it next to the pencil case. Reaching into his pocket again, he gingerly drew out the papers that he had lifted from his supervisor's desk and laid them neatly on the handkerchief. His practised fingers slid open the secret compartment of the pencil case that contained the camera lens and activated the battery that powered the system. Carefully but swiftly, he photographed each page, the camera working soundlessly, as it had been designed to do by its American manufacturers. His work complete, he returned the papers to his breast pocket and reverted the camera to a boring pencil case, replacing it in his pocket.

While he hadn't heard the door to the washroom open, wanting to take no chance, he threw some water into the pot, trying to make it sound like someone was washing themselves after doing their business, before pulling the noisy flush. Opening the stall door, he strode to the basin and washed his hands, looking at his reflection in the mirror. He smiled sadly to himself: an honest man, forced to betray his country.

This small first step had just launched the journey of the most dangerous mole in the history of Indian intelligence—one who would rise to occupy the highest echelons of the system in India without being discovered for the next four decades.

# Chapter 1

15 December 1917
Petrograd, Russia
9.30 a.m.

The entire Roerich house was in chaos. How could it not be when the entire country had just been upended by the Bolshevik Revolution, a seismic episode that had torn through the very fabric of the Empire?

Nicholas sat in his rocking chair, still struggling to reconcile the defeat of the ruling elite at the hands of the working classes. Tall and gaunt, his striking blue eyes had sunk into his head from exhaustion; his wavy black hair turned white by the years of stress. He watched the chaos anxiously, encouraging everyone to hurry up at every opportunity.

Of an artistic bent, Nicholas had been encouraged to pursue his passions from an early age. Brought up in the privileged household of a high-ranking Tsarist government official, he had been able to pursue twin degrees, one in art from the Imperial Art Academy, and the other in law. He had no difficulty finding employment at the Imperial Society for the Encouragement of the Arts, where, across eleven years, he had combined his artistic talent with his love for archaeology to make his name as the nation's greatest painter of its glorious past.

He had enjoyed all the privileges—his fame and money allowing him to travel the empire with his friends, his charm enabling new relationships, both romantic and professional—wherever he went. During this time, he had noticed the decline in the Russian Empire, his intellectual curiosity leading him to dive deeper to understand why the changes were taking place. Over time, it became clear to him that the roots of unrest lay in the enormous strain exerted on existing societal structures by the emergence of factory life—the strain exacerbated by awful working conditions and desperately low wages, and stretched to breaking point due to the daily abuse of workers by the nobles who owned the factories.

As he had anticipated, strikes had broken out across Russia, bringing key industries to a halt. The Tsar, rather than addressing the root cause, compounded the problem by ruthlessly murdering hundreds of workers to quell this rebellion. The Tsar's actions transformed Nicholas from an intellectual spectator into an active player in the transformation of the empire.

Disenchanted with the Tsar and Tsarina, Nicholas had joined ranks with other members of the ruling elite who believed in a new economic model for the Empire, their group eventually forming a provisional government upon the abdication of the Tsar. Nicholas had played a vital role behind the scenes, leveraging his personal relationship with the Tsar and Tsarina to convince them to abdicate, promising their family's safety in exchange for the peaceful transfer of power.

But, soon after, the Bolshevik Party, under Lenin, emerged as the representative of the workers. Lenin, previously exiled by the Tsar, had returned to lead the Marxist revolution for the transfer of power to the workers. Nicholas's ideology clashed with Lenin's, the former believing in sharing power with the workers and the latter believing in putting power under the exclusive control of the workers. The men had clashed often, both in writing and in public debates, till the Bolshevik Revolution in 1917, in which the Bolsheviks had overthrown the provisional government and grabbed power.

Ruthlessly, the Bolsheviks had purged the new Socialist state of any opposition, with the dreaded secret police, the Cheka, arresting or making the leaders of the provisional government disappear. Recognizing the danger early on, Nicholas had begun to make arrangements to flee the Socialist empire. But, he had been too late, having failed to liquidate all his assets before learning that he was next on the Cheka's list.

It was thus that Nicholas's family had ended up packing in panic for their departure, today. Despite his opposition to Lenin, Nicholas still had many friends, including several in the Bolshevik Party, with whose assistance they were now executing a desperate departure. His wife, Helena, and her staff were packing what they could carry in the horse carriage, leaving behind the rest to be nationalized. The Roerichs, along with their young sons, George and Svetoslav, would make their way to the port, where they would board a steamer departing for Great Britain, hiding in the ship's cargo hold, away from the prying eyes of the Cheka. The family would, after resting in London for a few days, leave for India—both Nicholas and Helena having inculcated a strong interest in spirituality, inspired by their reading of Vivekananda, Rabindranath Tagore and the Bhagavad Gita.

They arrived in Bombay in the winter of 1917, enjoying the company of Nicholas's friends for the next several months. In June, they travelled to Kappar, the ancient capital of the Kullu kingdom, for a spiritual retreat and fell in love with the beautiful town, deciding to make it their home. By

September, they had purchased a house and moved to Kappar to start a new life.

While Helena watched the children, Nicholas explored India, his passion for archaeology taking him across the entire northern region, on a five-year expedition from Darjeeling to Kashmir. During this time, he produced dozens of paintings of the Himalayas that would eventually grace museums across the world. Helena, meanwhile, involved herself deeply in spirituality and mysticism, setting up the Oriental School of Spiritual Learning in Kappar. The boys struggled to adjust in an alien land, but, as children always do, eventually settled into their new lives.

The Roerichs established themselves comfortably in India, unaware of the part they were going to play in a game of international intrigue, a century later.

# Chapter 2

15 August 1975
Dhaka
6.30 a.m.

The room was pitch-dark, the thick green curtains blocking out the light of the rising sun. The mole lay quietly on the bed, smoking yet another cigarette and waiting anxiously for the phone to ring to provide him with the confirmation that the job he had planned had been completed.

His guilt at betraying his country had faded over the years, rationalized by the good that his relationship with the CIA had done for India. The rabbit hole had been deeper than he had expected, but once he had taken his first few tentative steps in espionage, he had accepted the impossibility of extricating himself from the relationship without finding himself behind bars for life, or, possibly, ending up dead. Having failed to confess before the damage was too great, he was now too far in to reverse course; the Damocles sword of being exposed by the CIA constantly hanging over his head.

He had planned the operation personally, every detail meticulously considered in the context of his knowledge of Bangladesh. Having been posted to the country in 1970, he had played a key role in securing accurate information about the military in East Pakistan for New Delhi; information that had allowed India to plan the military operation that had led to the bloody secession from West Pakistan and the birth of an independent Bangladesh. His contribution had not gone unnoticed, and he had been invited to be part of the Indian delegation that had met with Sheikh Mir Iqbal upon his return to Bangladesh in December 1971, as the head of the newly formed government.

Over the last four years, he had risen to lead India's intelligence services in Bangladesh, working closely with the Sheikh's government and his paramilitary force to maintain internal order. He had done what was expected of him as a friend of Bangladesh, fighting hard against Pakistan's Inter-Services Intelligence's—the ISI's—constant efforts to destabilize the government, keeping a close eye on dissension within the guerrilla resistance movement, Mukti Bahini, and battling the left-wing insurgency of the Gonobahini, the armed division formed by the student wing of the Bangladesh Awami League after it had split to form the Jatiyo Samajtantrik Dal, which had led to the assassination of several of the Sheikh's highest-ranking bureaucrats. As he protected the fledgling government, his reputation grew and he gained access to the government and nearly every important player in Bangladesh, making him one of the few people who knew everything that was happening.

Beyond reproach and with unlimited access, it had been relatively easy for him to plan the operation for the CIA. While he didn't agree with their assessment of the consequences of the operation and had advised them against it, the Americans had decided to move ahead anyway, believing that the installation of a puppet government would allow them to do both—keep the Indian influence in the South East Asian region at bay while also positioning them as a true ally of Pakistan that had rid them of the man who had humiliated them in 1971.

Finally, his phone rang. 'Good morning,' said the soft voice on the other end, the pre-agreed signal for the mission being a success.

The world would know soon enough—Sheikh Mir Iqbal was dead, assassinated in his home by carefully selected officers of the Bangladesh Army.

# Chapter 3

30 November 2009
Kappar, Himachal Pradesh
2.14 a.m.

Suraj had travelled a long way to reach his destination. He had flown from Jaisalmer to Delhi the previous morning and spent the day resting at a colleague's house, preparing for the long night to come. At 9 p.m., he had got into the nondescript car that had been organized for him and driven non-stop to Kappar, weaving his way between the thousands of trucks that moved busily on the highway in the night, arriving at the city's outskirts a little after his planned arrival at 2 a.m. He had stayed just below the speed limit, not wanting to provide any enthusiastic traffic policeman a reason to stop him or search his vehicle. He knew the precaution was likely superfluous, but he had nevertheless followed standard procedure to minimize the chances of the operation going awry.

He parked at the back of the public lot on the city's outskirts. Exiting, he placed his hands on his hips and rotated his torso, feeling the satisfying crack in his back as the shrunken muscle wrapped tightly around his backbone stretched out. He repeated the exercise for his neck, utilizing the opportunity to look out for anyone who may be taking more than a passing interest in him. He saw no one. The city was sleeping peacefully and, except for the sound of a truck grunting in its effort to climb the hill, all that Suraj could hear was the constant chatter of wildlife engaged in its nocturnal battle for survival.

He raised his hands above his shoulders and removed his sweater, the thick black t-shirt underneath complementing his black trousers. Reaching into the car, he removed his bag, locked the car and began his walk into the city, looking down occasionally at the device he wore on his hand—a GPS designed specifically for the armed forces. It ensured that the dial's glow, while clear to the wearer, did not escape its borders—the result of advances made by the Indian Defence Research and Development Organization. Dressed entirely in black, Suraj was nearly invisible, a flitting shadow on the margins of the route that he was traversing, his rubber-soled shoes muffling the sound of his steps. He hugged the shadows expertly, escaping the slivers of moonlight that filtered through the trees. He moved swiftly into the protective cover of a recessed doorway as a patrol car went by, waiting patiently while the vehicle moved ponderously over the paved road.

Fifteen minutes later, he was nearly at the rendezvous point, the 'X' on his display becoming larger as he got closer. Taking no chances, he walked a small circle around the point, his trained eyes piercing the darkness to spot any danger—an unnatural protuberance, a tree moving differently from those around it, the sound of a twig snapping under the weight of a living being unaccustomed to hiding in the forest. Spotting nothing, he moved towards the centre of the imaginary circle, his eyes identifying the silhouette of the man waiting for him at the exact point marked by the 'X'. The man, peering into his own wrist, noticed the movement out of the corner of his eye and stepped on to his toes with alacrity, ready to fight—the action born out of instinct.

Suraj whistled the opening bar to '*Nazar Ke Samne, Jigar Ke Paas*', moving forward when he heard the confirmatory response to his signal. The men, strangers to each other, finally stood eye-to-eye, sizing each other up as best as they could in the darkness, their ears still trained outwards, listening for any sound that did not belong.

The other man beckoned Suraj and began to walk purposefully but quietly ahead, Suraj following a few metres behind; their bodies tilted slightly in different directions to maximize the combined arc of their vision. The boundary wall, designed to keep animals out, posed no issue. Both men grabbed the top of the wall with their fingers, pulled themselves up and lay flat atop it, pointed in opposite directions. They strained their senses for any hint of the guards, who manned the building, passing through that section of the compound. Satisfied that the coast was clear, both men jumped down, the sound of them landing dampened by their shoes and the tuck-and-rolls they executed. They ran, half-bent-over, towards the building, slipping behind the large concrete columns that held up the massive structure to keep safe from the prying eyes of any guards that may come along.

Suraj's colleague used a key to unlock the door, which opened quietly on its well-oiled hinges. He squeezed through the narrow gap into the darkness beyond, waiting for his colleague to shut the door behind them. The men dropped flat on their bellies, out of the line of sight of anyone who may look in through the curtain-less windows, and slithered towards the desk in the centre of the room, their elbows and knees protected by pads sewn into their clothes. Suraj watched his colleague move behind the desk and open a hidden door—this one also sliding open quietly, on well-lubricated grooves—and followed him into the room beyond, pulling the door closed behind them.

Once inside, Suraj turned on a slim torch, a pencil-thin beam emerging from it. He aimed the torch in the direction that his colleague was pointing, the light briefly flickering over an ornate mantelpiece before settling on the objects they had come to steal. Suraj approached the paintings, taking in every detail and mentally preparing for the process of removing them from their frames without damaging them, and then replacing them with the two other paintings that his colleague would already have stowed somewhere in the room.

Suraj withdrew his rubber-padded equipment from the bag and got to work. Methodically, he loosened the screws that held the first frame shut and relieved it of its valuable contents. Holding the priceless painting gently, he pulled out a protective covering from his bag, neatly sliding the painting into it, sealing it shut and placing it back in the bag for safekeeping. He then repeated the process with the second frame. Once both paintings were safely in the bag, he took the first of the replacements that his colleague held out, placing the valueless replacement into the original frame and screwing it shut securely. Having performed the same task for the second replacement, he began to erase any obvious evidence of the screws having been tampered with. While his colleague pointed the torch at each screw in turn, Suraj applied a thin coat of silver paint, hiding the small scratches that he had inevitably made on their surface while loosening them. While he knew that the work would not stand expert scrutiny, it would certainly go unnoticed during any non-expert examination that took place, once the paint had dried.

His work complete, Suraj hung the frames in their original positions, placing them exactly as he had found them, using the dirty outlines on the white wall as his guide. Satisfied, he nodded at his colleague, who opened the door to the outer room, waiting for him to exit with his bag before locking it behind them. The two of them crawled back towards the first door through which they had entered, Suraj's colleague wiping the floor behind them to erase any trace of their presence.

Suraj opened the door leading out of the building a crack, keeping one eye on the opening and straining his ears for any indication of the guards. Upon seeing and hearing nothing, he opened the door just enough for them to squeeze out. He covered the distance to the column rapidly, holding up a closed fist to instruct his colleague to wait. Three seconds later, he dropped his fist and continued to keep watch as his colleague exited the building and locked the door. He pocketed the key and joined Suraj at the columns, both standing in heightened alertness and in the knowledge that they now possessed enormously valuable articles. Just as they stepped out from behind the columns, Suraj threw his closed fist up sharply, stopping his colleague dead in his tracks. They retreated behind the columns, listening as the sound that had alerted him grew louder as it came closer. A few seconds later, a guard ambled around the corner, his disinterested feet falling heavily on the gravelled surface, his radio blaring Kishore Kumar's '*Ek Ladki Bheegi Bhaagi Si*' at its loudest volume. Both men waited while the guard walked by, his torch pointing straight ahead of him, completely oblivious to the presence of the two men standing a few feet away.

They waited patiently for the guard to complete his insincere round of their side of the building, moving again only once he had turned the corner and the music had faded away. Being extremely fit, they scaled the wall easily, placing their hands on the top and vaulting over it and out of the compound. Back in the forest, Suraj's colleague took the lead again, walking confidently on the dark, uneven ground. At the border of the forest, the two men hugged briefly, the entire operation having been completed successfully without a single word exchanged between them.

Suraj commenced the long walk back towards his car, eager to start his journey back to Jaisalmer before dawn broke. He had a long day in front of him if he was going to get the paintings across the border and into the hands of his colleagues in the ISI before the day was over.

His colleague returned home, changed into his nightclothes and fell asleep. After all, he had to wake up early to return to work at the building he had just helped rob.

# Chapter 4

4 June 1946
Jammu
8 p.m.

The raja and Nicholas sat engrossed in their game of chess, Nicholas on the offensive with his white pieces. This time, Nicholas had opened with the Queen's Gambit and the raja had accepted the challenge that the opening offered. But the raja had made an early mistake, losing his rook to protect his advanced pawn at C4. Now, with his flank completely exposed and a piece down, he was desperately defending against Nicholas's ferocious attack, while trying to counter-attack the other flank, as the more gifted Nicholas deftly added additional stress to every move that the raja made. Finally, the tsunami of white pieces broke through the raja's defensive walls, forcing him to surrender.

'That's seven in a row if I count the wins from last time,' smiled Nicholas, amused by the raja's annoyance. 'You really need to read the theory if you intend to beat me. Or you could just give me your money and we could drop the pretence of playing.'

His Royal Highness, Raja Jai Kishan Singh of Kashmir, was not amused. He had played chess from his school days at Mayo, through his military training at the Imperial Cadet Corps and right up to the death of his playing partner, Ranvir Singh, whose passing away had led to his ascension to the throne. He believed he was significantly above average and grew increasingly unhappier each evening as Nicholas exposed his frailties. Nicholas had not mentioned his decade-long training under Russian grandmaster Nikolai Grigoriev. His natural curiosity had made him an excellent student, always willing to study various lines of play, but he had ultimately given up the game to pursue his passion for art.

Nicholas had first met the raja in 1931, when he had arrived in Jammu at the end of a five-year expedition, bearing an introductory letter from his friend Rabindranath Tagore. The letter had got him an audience with the raja, during which Nicholas had laid out the details of the excavation that he wanted to carry out at Kutbal, where he believed the Lalitaditya Muktapida—the civilization that had built the Martand Sun Temple—had ruled. The raja, a keen student of his state's history, had agreed to make available the funds and manpower that he needed for his endeavour. Nicholas had returned a year later, carrying dozens of terracotta heads that not only proved that the Lalitaditya civilization existed, but also demonstrated that civilization in Kashmir went back centuries before it was thought to have started. Despite the significance of his find, Nicholas had declined the rewards that the raja had wanted to shower upon him, requesting instead that a museum be built to house those and other treasures that may be discovered in Kashmir. The raja had happily agreed, appointing Nicholas to lead the designing and construction effort for the museum—a task that had taken two years to complete. During this time, the raja and Nicholas became friends, spending hours exploring the intellectual depths of one another. Over time, they began to share their most intimate thoughts and deepest frustrations, and seek solutions to their problems. The depth of their friendship had snuck up on them; the reality of it was brought to light on an intoxicated evening when the raja had shared the dark secret behind the death of two of his wives. Nicholas, while shocked by the raja's secret, had offered him the comfort he desperately sought to assuage his guilty conscience. Nicholas had returned to Kappar after the museum was inaugurated, the two continuing their discussions through weekly letters.

The raja's last letter had not arrived by post but had been delivered by hand. It had beseeched him to come to Jammu without delay to offer his counsel on a matter of such great importance that it had to be discussed in person. Nicholas had left straightaway in the company of the retinue that had conveyed the letter, arriving in Jammu on the afternoon of the second day after an exhausting journey. He waited the entire day for the raja to return from his meeting with the British government, taking the opportunity to visit the museum, which now had dozens more historical artefacts on display that had been unearthed in Kashmir by the museum's team of archaeologists.

With the game of chess now over, the raja and Nicholas walked out into the balcony, carrying their drinks. The raja sighed deeply as he looked at the city, worry etched into his face.

'I am at a loss, Nicholas. What shall I do?'

'About what, Jai?'

'About the future of the kingdom. Which side shall I join?'

Nicholas now understood the king's worry. To those not blinded by optimism, the writing on the wall was clear.

The British would soon have to grant India its independence. When that happened, there was no doubt that the country would be partitioned and a separate state would be carved out for the Muslims. Britain's policy of divide and rule, imposed for so long on the princely states, had unleashed the genie of Pakistan, which could no longer be put back into its bottle. When the partition did happen, Muslim-majority Kashmir, ruled by a Hindu thus far, would have to choose which side to join.

'What do you want to do?'

'I am unsure. We are a Muslim majority. But we have always been a secular state, ruled by Hindu kings. My council tells me that the people are undecided, unwilling to make the decision till they have to. For the first time in a long time, I am at a loss.'

Nicholas nodded sympathetically. The decision would have serious consequences for the kingdom and Jai did not have the room to make a mistake.

'Why not ask the people to vote?'

'I could. But should I? Would I be happy to accept their decision?'

'Why not?'

'Because they would be led by emotion, not logic. If they voted today, they would simply vote along religious lines and we would likely join Pakistan. But would they vote the same way if they got a chance to think about it rationally?'

'Let's forget the people, Jai. What do you want to do?'

'Honestly, I don't know. For now, I want to retain our independence. I want to see how both countries evolve and then make a decision. But, I fear, I will not have that luxury.'

Nicholas nodded. Situated between India and Pakistan, Kashmir would be strategically vital to both countries, no matter where the border was finally drawn. 'Jai, since you are asking me, let me give you my view. Kashmir has prospered not because it has a Muslim population and a Hindu ruler, but because its people are capable and its rulers have been good men who have enabled the population to be productive. Ultimately, in the long term, economics trumps politics and the markets always win. India is going to be the bigger market—for the sake of Kashmir's economic prosperity, I think you should choose India.'

The raja nodded. 'I understand that, Nicholas. But will my people believe that India will act in the interest of Muslims tomorrow? Economics is abstract—violence is not.'

'They will believe if you make them.'

With that, there was silence. Nicholas withdrew from the terrace gracefully, leaving the raja to ponder over his difficult choice.

# Chapter 5

12 January 1976
Tashkent
12 p.m.

The meeting had been running for over twelve hours. None of the attendees had expected to be called in on the previous night and so had gone about their evening like any other. Now, after having worked over twenty-four hours without a break, most of them were at the end of their physical limits. Despite their hunger, the food lay untouched before them on the table littered with dirty coffee cups.

At the head of the rectangular table sat Boris Medvedev, the head of the KGB, who had arrived earlier that morning from Moscow. To his left, sat Dmitry Ivanov, the head of Tashkent's police force. Viktor Shuvalov, the minister of external affairs for the Soviet Union and the leader of the Soviet delegation which was negotiating with India, sat on Medvedev's right, along with Boris Zubkov, the head of the medical department in Tashkent. In addition to the high-ranking Soviet officials, the only other occupants of the room were Rajagopalachari, the Indian chief of external affairs; Sumit Paswan, the Indian delegation's head of security, and two young intelligence officers—one masquerading as a liaison officer for the delegation and the other as a translator, but in fact representing the interests of the Research and Analysis Wing (R&AW) and the Defence Intelligence Agency—with their heads hanging sombrely.

The Indian delegation had arrived in the Soviet Union in the middle of the punishing Cold War between the USSR and the United States, the two superpowers of the world. India had not yet taken sides, despite both the US and the Soviet Union courting the strategically important democracy. The US was keen to have a military foothold in South East Asia, especially in a country that offered proximity to the Soviet Union on land, in the air and in water. The Soviet Union was even keener to incorporate India into its list of allies as it offered access to warm water ports—something the USSR had desired for years. The Soviets had maximized the opportunity that geopolitics had presented, providing the arms and ammunition desperately needed by the Indian Army in their war against Pakistan. America, having already cosied up to Pakistan, had little choice but to wait, hoping that the USSR–India alliance failed.

The Indian delegation had worked through the previous day, negotiating for assistance from the USSR. The very survival of the nation was at stake, the war with Pakistan in 1971 having pushed India to the brink of starvation and bankruptcy. India needed weaponry to continue to keep its hostile neighbours at bay, technology for the development of industry and power, and most importantly, food grains to tide over the shortages in that calamitous year. Given the importance of the negotiations, the delegation had been led by the prime minister himself.

Hours of negotiations, spread across several working groups, had ended only at 7 p.m. The tired delegation had returned to Hotel Tashkent to change into their finery for the evening. All of them knew that the banquet planned for them that evening was a deliberate ploy by the Soviets to drain the delegation of its last vestiges of physical and mental energy, and minimize the time available to them to strategize before the negotiations recommenced on the following morning. None of them was particularly perturbed by the punishing schedule, accustomed as they were to working long hours under their energetic prime minister.

The prime minister had arrived in the USSR riding a huge wave of popularity owing to India's victory in the war against Pakistan. Viewing the USSR as a better reflection of India's aspirations than America, he had chosen to negotiate first with the Soviets, citing America's relationship with Pakistan as a reason, to the significant public displeasure of the Americans.

He had been at his charming best before the Soviet leaders who had come together in Tashkent for the signing of the agreements with India, all wanting to be present when the historical moment arrived. Despite the accumulated exhaustion of the past two years, he had not made a mistake, addressing the Soviets by their correct ranks and designations, asking the right questions about their families, congratulating the right men on the birth of their grandchildren and duly offering his condolences to those who had recently been bereaved. Before the evening was over, he had resolved the few remaining disagreements, paving the way for the bureaucrats to translate what had been agreed to in principle, into nuanced agreements. His job complete, he had left before the rest of the delegation.

As the group assembled around the table had learnt over the course of the interviews through the night, the prime minister had returned to his suite at 10 p.m. and got to work, responding to the messages from India that had arrived during his time at the banquet. His attendants had, as usual, served him his warm milk with a pinch of turmeric, and retired to the waiting room attached to his suite, in case they were required. At about 11 p.m., they had heard a glass shattering in the prime minister's suite and run in to clean the mess, only to find the prime minister lying unconscious on the floor.

While one attendant had tried to revive him, the other had dialled the delegation's doctor on duty, who had arrived within a minute. Feeling no pulse, he had begun CPR, instructing the attendants to call for an ambulance immediately. The paramedics stationed in the lobby had arrived seconds later and carried him to the waiting ambulance, which had screeched away from the hotel and arrived at the Tashkent Hospital, four minutes later.

The paramedics had tried to revive the prime minister en route to the Tashkent Hospital, delivering electric shocks of increasing frequency to jumpstart his heart and even administering adrenaline straight into his heart. The chief of medical services for Tashkent had been on duty at the Tashkent Hospital and had been waiting at the Emergency entrance with his most experienced staff, to receive the prime minister. He and his team tried everything—even surgically opening up his chest to massage the heart directly. The prime minister was officially declared dead at 11.30 p.m., the message filtering back to an unbelieving delegation, part of which was at the hotel, while the rest were still enjoying the banquet.

Each member of the shocked delegation had been interviewed. The group at the table had pieced the story together from the bits and pieces they had heard from the delegation's members. All of them, on hearing the news, had instinctively moved towards the hospital, keen to get there as soon as they could. The chief of police of Tashkent had confirmed that his officers had denied entry to the hospital to everyone, except the prime minister's personal attendants and the Indian delegation's security team, and had escorted the delegation back to the hotel in police cars. The Tashkent Police had put a security ring around the hospital and locked down the hotel, ensuring that no one in it, not even the Indian delegation, could leave.

Upon the prime minister's death being confirmed, Sumit Paswan had called his home minister from the hospital, waking him to share the unfortunate news. He had then returned to the hotel and requested the external affairs minister to ask the entire delegation into the banquet room—they had filed in silently, still trying to recover from the shock. After seeking permission from the minister to speak and having no other way to ensure that his voice carried across the room, he had stepped on to a chair, noticing the silence in the group deepening.

'The prime minister is no more,' he had said softly, his voice audible to everyone through the silence. 'We don't know the cause of his death as yet. An autopsy will be conducted tomorrow, if the family permits.' The delegates had maintained their silence as they processed the finality of his statement. Finally, after what seemed like a lifetime, one of the negotiators had put up his hand hesitatingly and asked what they were expected to do now. Sumit had asked them to stay in their rooms and to remain available for the investigation that would follow.

He had then found Dmitry, who had already conveyed the news to the Soviet leadership. Dmitry had taken charge, requisitioning the hotel's conference room and making arrangements to have the Soviet external affairs minister and the head of the KGB join them. They agreed to first interview the Indian delegation, its members being the only ones with access to the prime minister's floor. While the interviews were ongoing, the two countries had drawn up a joint statement and issued it to the press, informing them of the unfortunate demise of the prime minister and the decision to postpone the negotiations to an undecided future date. Until then, the Soviet Union would provide the grain India needed, as a mark of respect for their departed friend.

Now, with the interviews done, the group had some decisions to make.

Medvedev turned to Zubkov, glaring at him accusingly, as if the death of the prime minister was his fault. 'Tell me again the cause of death?'

'A massive heart attack,' squeaked Zubkov, fearful in front of the head of the KGB.

'Was it a natural heart attack?'

'We do not know yet,' whimpered Zubkov. 'We can only know for sure after we get the toxicology report,' he added quickly, before Medvedev could speak again.

Sumit, quiet until then, now interjected. 'It had to be a natural heart attack. Only select members of our delegation had access to his floor. None of them would have poisoned him.'

'Are you suggesting that we poisoned the prime minister?' growled Medvedev.

'No, Boris. Of course not. All I mean is that, if it was poison, it could not have been anyone from our team.'

'How can you be so sure?'

'Because I know these people. I would trust them with my life. All of them loved the prime minister. It makes no sense.'

Boris smirked but held his tongue. Given the number of agents they had in the Indian system, and the number of agents they knew the Americans had, it was certainly possible that the assassin was someone from within the Indian delegation. However, it wasn't worth arguing till the toxicology report arrived. He would be responsible for investigating the murder, if that is what it turned out to be, and for that, he needed the Indian delegation to stay for the time being.

Medvedev said, 'Let's not debate this any further now. Let's wait for the toxicology report. Till then, I would suggest that all of you get some rest. Our team is tracing all those who were associated with the banquet. We will start interviewing them as well, if the toxicology report is positive.'

The men around the table nodded and left for their rooms. Most were too tired to sleep, but there was one who slept peacefully. He was the only man who had confidence in what the outcome of the report would be—after all, he knew that the poison that he had administered mimicked a natural heart attack and would not show up in a toxicology screening.

It wasn't the first time he had used the deadly poison.

# Chapter 6

20 February 2010
London
11 a.m.

The gleaming Bentley drove through the streets of London—a testament to the enormous wealth of the successful businessman. The car was making its way to the offices of Sotheby's on New Bond Street. Abbas Ali—unquestionably the richest Pakistani in England, and among the richest men in the world—sat in the back, lost in deep thought.

Abbas was about to undertake an unnecessarily risky transaction. As an expert in the business, he had argued vehemently that the transaction was a terrible idea and had the potential to destroy the business that they had so assiduously built. He had advised his superiors to postpone the initiative, begging for more time to generate the funds they needed. But he was fighting with his hands tied behind his back, for it was his colleagues who wielded true power over the business— ruthless men hardened by years of experience, who would not hesitate to replace Abbas as the head of one of their most lucrative businesses.

He had lost. Their chairman had decided that despite the risk, they had to proceed, as the date for the launch of the initiative could not be postponed. He had silenced Abbas's further efforts to argue, issuing the order that Abbas was now en route to execute. Abbas had returned from the meeting in Islamabad and made extensive preparations for the work that needed to be done. Now, with those arrangements finally complete with the help of his organization, to the extent he could be, he was ready to do once again what he had done for so many years.

The Bentley finally arrived outside Sotheby's. The beautiful vehicle was well-known to the doorman, whose pinstriped suit had been tailored especially for him at the expense of his employer, at Savile Row. This subtle display of exclusivity not only conveyed the right image to the extremely wealthy who constituted Sotheby's clients, but also ensured that the doorman's weapons were well-concealed, yet easily reachable, should someone be foolish enough to try and rob this mecca of the art world. The doorman ran to open the passenger door and smartly flicked open his Sotheby's-branded golf-sized umbrella as the client exited his car.

Abbas slid out gracefully from the warm vehicle into the freezing cold of a rainy February morning. A Pathan, he had the tall, broad physique and chiselled good looks of his tribe, an imposing six feet two inches, who, even at the age of seventy, worked out six days a week under a personal trainer to maintain his lean muscular body. His full head of hair, a graceful salt-and-pepper, complemented a beautifully proportioned face, a strong jaw and piercing green eyes that had driven scores of women into his arms over the years. The doorman hurried behind Abbas to keep the umbrella above him as he strode towards the entrance.

He was being expected. As the door swished open, James Mitchell, the global head of the department for art for Sotheby's, stepped forward to receive him. Thanking the doorman, Abbas permitted a fawning James to lead him to the Lodge—the luxurious private waiting room reserved for guests of the chairman and managing director of Sotheby's—a mark of respect for the man who now occupied the chair usually reserved for the chairman.

Abbas admired the room, appreciating the curated displays of wealth. He missed nothing, noticing the small changes since his last visit and the priceless new objects that had been added since. His eyes stopped searching the room only when the butler entered, carrying a silver tray, its handles inlaid with precious stones, elegant bone china cups resting on it. Abbas waited till he was served his usual beverage of choice—a thick concoction of tea leaves, milk, sugar, cardamom and ginger made in the style of his home—and the butler had left before he turned his attention back to James, who was waiting alertly for the real power in the room to speak.

'I have two paintings that I would like included in your auction on 10 March. I hope that won't be a problem?' asked Abbas, as usual leaving all pleasantries aside, fully aware that there was no question of being turned down, given the amount of business he had sent their way over the years.

'Certainly, Mr Ali,' came the expected response. 'Who is the artist this time?'

'Svetoslav Roerich,' replied Abbas, his eyes crinkling in amusement as James struggled to hide a combination of disbelief, happiness, greed and circumspection, behind a mask of professionalism. Not surprising, considering that no Roerich painting had been available for sale anywhere in the world for the past twenty-two years, all either hanging in private collections or public museums, or considered irrecoverable—their value rising exponentially each year as wealthy collectors clamoured for a piece of the legendary artist's legacy.

Finally regaining control of his overcharged emotions, James reverted to his professional best. 'Mr Ali, please accept my apologies for my impertinence. May I ask where you obtained these from? As you undoubtedly know, no Roerich painting has been available for sale for over twenty years, so there are bound to be questions about its provenance.'

'Twenty-two years, to be exact,' replied Abbas suavely, reaching into his breast pocket and sliding over a thick monogrammed envelope, bearing the seal of his house—two horsemen riding side by side on dark black stallions, their swords pointed forward in attack. 'I hope these are satisfactory. Both paintings have already been delivered to Sotheby's. Once your verification of the paintings and the documents is complete, we can discuss a base price.'

Abbas took a last sip of his tea and stood, signalling the end of the meeting. Taken by surprise by his abruptness and worried that his query had affronted the well-known art dealer, James stood up hurriedly, knocking over the tray, breaking the expensive teapot and spilling tea on to the exquisitely woven Persian carpet. Ever gracious, Abbas placed his hand on James's back and gently nudged him towards the door, through which the butler had discreetly stepped in, a dry cloth in his hand. The two walked over to the waiting Bentley, its engine purring to keep its interiors warm. The doorman hurried behind them, keeping Abbas dry even as James's left shoulder was left unprotected and consequently, sodden. Abbas shook hands with James and then with the doorman, sliding him a fifty-pound bill that had magically appeared in his palm and then just as magically disappeared into the doorman's pocket, before sweeping back into his car, which powered away to join London's morning traffic.

# Chapter 7

1 November 1947
Kappar
3.30 p.m.

Charan Singh arrived early afternoon via the train from Delhi. He had been stressed throughout the journey, eager to get the document entrusted to him by his master, Raja Jai Singh of Kashmir, into the hands of Nicholas Roerich.

Charan didn't know what the document said, nor did he know the meaning of the message that the raja had made him memorize, but he knew they were both important, given the circumstances under which he had been dispatched from Kashmir and the worry on the raja's face.

He assumed it had to do with Kashmir's accession to India. The raja had made it clear that Kashmir wanted to remain independent of both India and Pakistan and, when the partition arrived, he had remained a mute spectator, unwilling to take sides, even as thousands were murdered in his kingdom. From there, things had gone downhill fast. In the fires of Partition blazing throughout the country and the murders committed in Kashmir in the heat of Partition, an uprising led by Sardar Muhammad Ibrahim Khan had started in the Poonch jagir. The Poonch had a reputation for wanting to ally with Pakistan and the recent murders had allowed Ibrahim to whip up a revolutionary frenzy. The raja had ordered the kingdom's armed forces to quell the rebellion, which they had set out to do. Unfortunately, some of his officers turned, weakening an army that was already strained from trying to prevent further violence in the state. And then Pakistani forces had joined the revolutionaries, disguised as Kashmiri citizens to support the march to Jammu, bidding to overthrow Jai Singh.

Under grave threat, he had ordered the scattered remains of his forces to concentrate themselves on the route from Poonch to Jammu, to delay the advance by as much as they could. He had negotiated urgently with India for its protection, but India had refused till he signed the deed of accession as the other princely states had. As his shattered army retreated behind the last bridge providing access to Jammu, the writing was on the wall. He would either have to willingly join one country or the other, or Pakistan would snatch Kashmir away from him. He had finally signed the deed of accession with India, choosing to be part of a secular fabric that better reflected Kashmir's ideology, over a state founded on religious lines. As soon as Lord Mounten's representative had confirmed the execution of the deed of accession, contingents of the Indian Army were airlifted to Jammu to battle the invaders. The well-trained Indian armed forces eventually secured Kashmir's borders within the Union of India.

But what very few knew was that a second document was also signed between the raja and Mounten's representative, the two agreeing over a secret addendum known only to them,

Lord Mounten, the prime minister and the home minister. Given its sensitivity, the raja had insisted on a single copy, which would be retained in Kashmir under his protection. The others, keen to ensure Kashmir's integration into India, had reluctantly agreed.

Charan didn't know it, but this was the document that he had carried to Nicholas. The raja had decided that the document was not safe in Jammu, containing as it did a secret that both countries would desperately want. He had therefore handed the document over to Charan, his most trusted aide, who was scheduled to accompany Mounten's representative to Delhi to formally hand over the deed of accession. The second document, Charan was to carry secretly and deliver to the only person that the raja now trusted.

As planned, Charan had presented the deed of accession to the home minister in Delhi. He had rested for a few short hours at Kashmir House and then proceeded to Kappar to meet with Nicholas. Nicholas received him warmly, surprised to see him. The raja had been unable to forewarn Nicholas, suspecting that his lines of communication had been compromised, and unwilling to allow even a hint of the document's location leaking.

Salutations done away with, Charan produced the letter from the raja and recited the message he had memorized. The message was coded in some way and Charan had failed to make any sense of it. It was, however, clear from Nicholas's face that he had understood exactly what the message had meant and was not in the least pleased by it. Nicholas looked down at the envelope, suddenly heavier in his hands, the seal of His Highness's house—two elephants standing on their hind feet, the flag of Kashmir held proudly by both—staring back at him.

Charan, his assignment complete, asked permission to leave. Nicholas refused, insisting that he stay the evening before beginning the long journey back to Jammu. Nicholas was a gracious host, plying him with wine and regaling him with stories of the raja's antics when he was away from the eyes of the court. At some point, Charan's curiosity got the better of him, his tongue loosened by the wine, and he asked Nicholas what the document contained. Nicholas, drunk as he was, refused to answer, maintaining only that it was of utmost importance that no one ever learnt that the document was in his possession. Inebriated, the two dropped the topic, discussing instead the future of the newly founded republic.

Charan woke up late and just about made it on the train to Delhi, from where he would return to Kashmir. Once there, he stood waiting at the platform in Delhi, eagerly watching the train to Kashmir come in amidst the din of people that had started jostling past to grab a seat on the train. As he struggled to keep his balance, he felt two hands attach themselves firmly to his back and push him hard. Unable to resist the deliberate push, he tumbled headfirst on to the track just as the train arrived, instantly crushed under the weight of the iron giant.

Charan Singh, one amongst only three men to have known the document's location, could no longer reveal it to anyone. The loss of a trusted aide was a small price to pay for the security of the document.

# Chapter 8 •

13 January 1976
New Delhi
1.30 p.m.

The delegation returned from Tashkent to a country in mourning. Even the shell-shocked delegates could not help but notice the empty streets as they were driven back to their respective homes—it was almost as if the entire country was scared to sully the memory of a beloved leader by venturing out. Even the press had behaved with dignity, questioning the delegation with tact and sensitivity, addressing most of their questions only to the official spokesperson.

The assassin—was that really what he thought of himself as now?—had also been driven home. As he had after each betrayal in the past, he headed straight into his bathroom to bathe in an attempt to cleanse the deceit from his soul. He had then visited his puja room, praying fervently to the gods and begging their forgiveness for the awful crime that he had been forced to commit.

A simple man from one of the hundreds of unremarkable towns that dotted Uttar Pradesh, he could never have imagined that he would end up working to harm his own country. He had not been born into riches or power and had worked extremely hard to break into government service with the R&AW, which had been established just a few years before. He had complemented his natural gift of intelligence with hard work and in just eight years, had been promoted twice, and been marked as one fit to be groomed for a senior leadership role in the future. Everything had been going well till he had made a mistake—one that would haunt him for the rest of his life.

Young and inexperienced, while training in the US, he had allowed himself to enjoy some of the freedom that the country offered. He had met Pamela, a field agent for the CIA, at their training facility in Washington, where she was coaching the assembled agents from various countries in coding and code-breaking. Pamela was beautiful, with golden blonde hair, a slim body and a musical laugh that made its way straight through his heart. Smitten at first sight, he was in awe of her intelligence, helplessly falling in love with her. He had attended every class without uttering a word, watching Pamela weave her magic.

At the end of the week, he had finally gathered the courage to ask her out and had been thrilled when she had accepted. Deferring to her judgement, they had gone to Red Dragon—just far enough from the training facility to give them some privacy from their peers, without being so far as to be inconvenient. They had sat in an alcove, drinking wine and talking, barely touching the food. He had fallen head over heels in love during that conversation, delighted to find someone who was not only in a similar line of work but could hold a conversation on an array of subjects. She had obviously felt similarly, asking him out for another meal on the following evening. The relationship had progressed quickly, the daily dinner soon transmuting into intimacy. They had been at her house the first time they made love. He had been a virgin, inexperienced and nervous, and she had shown him the way, teaching him tenderly and without causing him embarrassment. After that first time, they were intimate often, ending almost every date at her house; him spending the entire night with Pamela cuddled in his arms.

He had never experienced such happiness, the halo of love surrounding them punctured occasionally only by the thought of his impending departure. By the time the end of the training approached, they had already begun to talk about their future and both of them had taken two weeks of personal leave to travel across America together. He had returned to India with a heavy heart, the two lovers having promised to find a way to meet again soon.

Little did he know that very soon, finding a way to meet each other was not going to be his biggest problem.

# Chapter 9

20 February 2010
New Delhi
11 p.m.

India's chief of intelligence, addressed always as 'CI', was a worried man.

Amitabh Mehta had been elevated to CI in 2008, from his position as chief of the R&AW. The position of CI had been created in 1998 to ensure inter-agency cooperation and consolidate inputs from all of India's intelligence services—a significant gap that had existed in the national security apparatus before this move. The agenda had been pushed hard by the Intelligence Bureau, India's primary internal intelligence and counter-intelligence agency, which had found itself handicapped without inputs from India's external intelligence agencies, especially as most threats were external.

Amitabh was of medium height and plump, and wore a quintessentially Indian moustache—black and bushy. His thick spectacles hid his eyes. His hair was neatly parted down the middle in the style of millions of men across the country, nondescript in its lustre, colour and cut. His complexion was the '*saanwla*' (wheatish) that Indians were well-known for, neither too dark nor too fair. He was the perfect spy—unremarkable, unmemorable and hard to accurately describe. The plainness that had plagued his early years had become his biggest asset in the world of espionage.

The hard-working ethic that had enabled his professional rise had been instilled in him at an early age by his disciplinarian father. Blessed with a formidable intellect, supplemented by endless curiosity, he had been an excellent student, regularly topping his school examinations. With limited employment options, he had, like millions of others, aspired to a government job. Unlike millions, he had cleared the civil services examination in his first attempt, winning the right to choose his service. Always keen on law enforcement, destiny cleared a path for him. One of the interviewers on his panel was the deputy chief of the R&AW, who noticed something special in the young man. He approached Amitabh after the interview and set up a meeting, following which he offered the patriotic young man the opportunity to serve his country in a more meaningful way. Amitabh jumped at the chance and joined the R&AW, where, as the deputy chief had expected, he shone bright, rising rapidly through the ranks.

As the years passed, he built his reputation by leading some of Indian intelligence's biggest successes, including his undercover infiltration of the Pakistan army. Amitabh had been so convincing in his role as a Sunni Muslim from Abbottabad that he had not only been recruited into the Pakistan army but had actually earned promotions to rise to the rank of major, after which he had been recruited into the Inter-Services Intelligence (ISI), the dreaded spy agency of Pakistan. He had caused tremendous damage to the ISI from within, providing disinformation that misled Pakistani strategy and thus was responsible, in part, for India's victory over Pakistan in 1971.

He had returned to India, and pretending to be Sikh, had penetrated the Damdami Taksal, led by the infamous Jarnail Singh Bhindranwale. As an insider in Bhindranwale's group, he had provided key intelligence that had allowed the Indira Gandhi government to launch Operation Blue Star. He had still been inside the Golden Temple when a miscommunication had resulted in the operation being launched ahead of time, only managing to escape because of the R&AW's intervention.

As his reputation grew, he was tasked with harder operations. He was sent to Bangladesh to support the Sheikh in snatching independence, and then to Bombay to procure the surrender of Chhota Rajan, the infamous mafia don and former Dawood aide; he extracted information from Rajan that allowed the Mumbai Police to break the backbone of the city's mafia. He was seconded to the Intelligence Bureau as its director, a post that he held for ten years. At the IB, he masterminded several additional coups, preventing an unfriendly government from coming to power in Sri Lanka, and stretching the ISI's resources by fanning the fires of genuine discontent in Balochistan. He maintained a file on every politician and every businessman of note, using the information as and when needed for India's security.

Today, he was more worried than usual. He had received information from Kanta—the R&AW's highest-ranking official in the ISI—that the feared Jaish-e-Mohammed were planning a significant terror strike across the world with the support of the ISI. Kanta had been in the meeting where the Jaish had discussed the strike—a plan so audacious that the combined efforts of the Hizbul and Lashkar would pale in comparison. To celebrate its founding on 6 April, the date coinciding with Eid this year, the Jaish would activate their sleeper agents in six countries—the

US, Great Britain, India, Iran, Iraq and Germany. The agents, working in teams of two, would simultaneously detonate dirty bombs in all six countries, the choice of location being left to each team so as to maximize civilian deaths and strike terror into the hearts of the populations.

Kanta, the deputy head of operations for the ISI's external affairs division—which was tasked with doing the dirty work that Pakistan needed, but in a way that the political establishment could plausibly deny—had been invited to the meeting to advise the Jaish on the logistics of sneaking the bombs into each country. The Jaish had asked for additional funds to purchase the bombs that had become available on the black market. Kanta knew, as did every other member of the ISI around the table, that the ISI did not have spare funds for this large an operation, either on their official account or off the books, its funds already having been allocated to other priorities. It was therefore to his significant astonishment that the chairman of the meeting, the highest-ranking officer of the ISI, had agreed.

Unwilling to query the decision in the presence of the Jaish, Kanta had waited for them to leave before asking where the additional funds would come from. The chairman had refused to answer, instructing Kanta to assume that the funds would be made available and to help Jaish plan the grandest celebration that he could.

The CI's concerns had, of course, lain with the innocents that would die, but he was even more concerned by the bigger picture. Of late, the Indian and Pakistani governments had reinitiated a peace process, and an attack of this nature, even if partly successful, would instantly bring the process to a halt, undoubtedly for a long time to come. Thousands more would die and thousands of crores' worth of scarce resources would be spent as Pakistan's unwinnable proxy war on India continued. He took the threat seriously, the Jaish already having demonstrated its ability to strike in India through its attacks on Indian airbases, the ambush of military convoys and, of course, mounting the audacious attack on the Indian Parliament that had nearly succeeded. The CI shivered at his recollection of the attack on the Parliament—if the Jaish had succeeded, India would have had to choose between sacrificing its entire political leadership or conceding to every demand of the Jaish, including handing over Kashmir. India would never have recovered from such an embarrassment and the CI had sworn never to let India land in that position again.

Unfortunately, other than the date, they knew very little. They didn't know the seller of the dirty bombs—a secret guarded closely by the Jaish and kept even from the ISI—or the target cities, let alone the specific locations in each city. If the attacks were to be stopped, they would have to stop the ISI from making available the additional funds. They had to find out where the funding was coming from and put a stop to it—no matter the cost.

Making up his mind, he made a call and initiated the protocol to ask for a face-to-face meeting with Kanta. He needed Kanta to find out more, even at the risk of exposure.

The stakes were too high to care for the life of one man.

# Chapter 10

29 July 1948
Mumbai
4.30 p.m.

'Help . . . help!' screamed Devika, her feet flying over Marine Drive as she ran for her life. Fear was cast on to her face like an iron mask. A few people took tentative steps to help her but turned away when they saw what she was running from.

Her sari caught the sea wind and billowed around her, slowing her down and allowing the goons to catch up. The leader of the gang ran up behind her and allowed his momentum to carry into the hard shove he gave her dainty form, bringing her crashing to the ground in an explosion of dust and noise. The gang surrounded Devika, closing in like a pack of wild dogs. She screamed for help and tried to push through the circle, but was hurled back into the centre by rough hands.

Their leader stepped forward, menace emanating from his scarred, rough features, a wickedly serrated eight-inch knife glinting in his right hand. 'No . . . please, no,' begged Devika as he reached out and hauled her up by her hair. 'Report us to the police, will you? Where are they now? Where are all your followers?' screamed the leader, drawing his right hand back and viciously driving the knife into Devika to its hilt, every ounce of stored fury contained within the strike.

'No!' screamed Devika, as the knife agonizingly pierced through her, bright red blood gushing out. She looked down in disbelief at her life oozing out of her body and grabbed the knife with both hands. She collapsed to the ground, holding on to the knife, looking up at the gang of men laughing maniacally. Her blood flowed on to the street as she closed her eyes and waited for death to come, the laughter ringing in her ears, a swansong from hell.

'Cut!' yelled the director, Asif Khan, as the entire set burst into spontaneous applause in appreciation of another masterclass in acting from Devika.

'Excellent shot,' said Asif excitedly, walking up to Devika and helping her up. 'This is going to make everyone feel like it happened to them! If there is even one person who leaves the theatre without crying, I am going to quit direction,' he affirmed, giving her a bear hug. A spot boy walked up and took the rubber knife dripping with tomato ketchup from Devika.

'Thank you, Asif, thank you all,' said Devika, bowing gracefully to the assembled crew. 'Shiva, you were outstanding! I wasn't acting—you actually made me fear for my life,' she said, turning towards the male lead of the movie.

'Don't be so modest, Devika,' laughed Shiva, taking her by the hand and walking her towards the trailer. 'Give us fifteen minutes to wash up and then let's meet for lunch, Asif?' said Shiva to the director as he opened the door to Devika's trailer and waited for her to step in before strolling towards his own.

Making themselves comfortable on the parapet on Marine Drive, the three shared their lunch while they discussed the schedule for the rest of the week and the upcoming shoot for the movie's climax in the hills of Kappar.

'We will take a small break after this week. After that, we meet on 15 August at the governor's house for the Independence Day celebrations. A lot of media is expected and we need as many pictures of the two of you together as we can get in the papers, from now on.'

Shiva and Devika nodded, having heard the sermon a number of times already.

'All of us leave for Kappar on the seventeenth of next month,' continued Asif. 'Your travel details are with your secretaries. It will take us a couple of days, so *inshallah,* we should be there by lunchtime on the nineteenth. We have a dinner with the district collector on the twentieth and then the shoot between the twenty-first and thirty-first.'

'Is the dinner really necessary?' asked Shiva.

'It's so boring,' agreed Devika.

'Yes it is and either of you can't even think about missing it,' replied Asif. 'The collector has given us permission to shoot in Kappar and will be providing police protection for the set. It won't be boring, I promise—he has invited the who's who of Kappar to meet both of you. And of course, if you do get bored, you can simply act as if you are enjoying yourselves!'

'Wonderful—we'll have to humour more than one person then,' sighed Devika. 'Asif, unless you want to reshoot any part of that scene, shall we call it a day? I'm tired and would like to go home and rest before tomorrow.'

'Of course. I'll get your car organized.' Asif got up, leaving Shiva and Devika immersed in their thoughts, staring at the fluttering sails of the fishing boats in the water.

'See you tomorrow,' said Devika, prettily smiling at Shiva as she saw her car emerge from around the corner.

# Chapter 11

13 January 1970
New Delhi
1.30 p.m.

He spoke to Pamela nearly every other day since his return. With both of them being caught up with work, the opportunity to meet refused to materialize, so they had to make do with regular phone calls, interspersed with letters filled with longing and promises about the future. Eight months later, she informed him that she would be unavailable for a few days, having been tasked with an assignment in Indonesia. A few weeks later, he read of the CIA's failed attempt to topple the Indonesian president and wondered whether this was the mission that Pamela had been assigned to. Having no way to find out, he continued to wait. A few weeks after that, when he had still not heard from her, he began to make inquiries, reaching out to his contacts within the CIA.

His contacts failed to find Pamela, running into impenetrable walls of classified information. He called her number every day, waiting painfully for the operator to connect the international call, but got nothing more than unanswered rings. He found himself at a loss and took time off work to visit her home in Washington, only to discover that her neighbours had not seen her in months. Assuming that the worst had happened in Indonesia, he returned to India, desolate. His dreams destroyed, he threw himself into his work, giving himself no free time to grieve.

In December, his friends introduced him to Neha, the daughter of India's ambassador to the USSR. Desperate to fill the void left by Pamela, he made himself fall in love again, telling himself that he could do worse than marry a girl devoted to him, having the right connections as well. By February the following year, they were married, the ceremonies attended by powerful friends of the ambassador's, including the incumbent and future prime ministers. One of the several wedding gifts organized by his father-in-law was his promotion to Senior Analyst, which allowed him to run his own team. His life was on track and although he still remembered Pamela sometimes, she became an increasingly distant memory, which dimmed daily as his love for Neha grew.

And then suddenly, it all fell apart with a phone call he received. Having reflexively answered the phone, he nearly dropped the receiver when he heard Pamela's voice. His happiness turned to dismay as he heard Pamela threatening him, unable to believe that this was the woman he had loved. She hung up before he could respond, confident that he would find a way to come to the States to meet her.

He hung on to the receiver long after the call was disconnected. He had not told Neha or her father about Pamela, and now he was stuck. He had no doubt that if Pamela acted on her threat and circulated either the sex tape that she claimed to be in possession of or the letters that he had written to her, his life would be over. Neha would leave him and his father-in-law would destroy his career.

Hoping to reason with Pamela, he flew to Washington on the pretext of meeting the CIA to set up an intelligence-sharing platform. Their meeting—no doubt, to reinforce the extent to which he was trapped—had been organized at her house. He walked in and saw Pamela, beautiful as always, but now with coldness in her eyes. She played the tape that showed them in bed, leaving no doubts about his identity or for their actions to be interpreted as anything but passionate sex.

Beseechingly, he looked up and was horrified by the haughtiness on her face. She needled him and asked him whether he had truly believed that she could love an insipid, ugly man from a Third World country like him. She laughed as she told him about the fun she had had reading out and responding to his passionate letters with her colleagues. He had wept silently, her words cutting him to the depths of his soul, anger replacing the space vacated by love.

He lost control when she asked him for what she wanted in exchange for her silence. He grabbed her by the neck, pinning her against the wall as he strangled the life out of her. She had been caught unprepared and once he had his legs locked with hers, there was no way for her to break out of the grasp of the much stronger man. Her eyes opened wide in terror as she realized that the gentle man she knew had changed into a trapped animal that was going to kill her to protect what he had earned. He cried as he strangled her, grief and anger combining to block out reason and the warnings of his rational brain drowning in the torrent of primal hormones flowing through him. He continued to squeeze long after she had stopped struggling, his fingers imprinting themselves on her squashed throat.

Eventually, he allowed her limp body to drop to the floor and sat on her sofa to catch his breath and collect his thoughts. He screamed when he felt a hand on his shoulder, but a blunt object crashed against his skull before he could even turn around. When he woke, he was tied to a chair. He looked around and found that he was still in Pamela's house, still facing the television on which he had watched himself having sex with her before.

But this time, it was playing the footage of the murder he had just committed.

# Chapter 12

20 February 2010
London
11.30 a.m.

James hurried back inside, anxious to see the paintings and examine the ownership papers. It would be an incredible triumph for Sotheby's and would certainly do his career no harm if they were to auction the paintings. He kept his excitement in check, knowing that it was unlikely that not one, but two genuine Roerichs could suddenly appear for sale when influential and extremely well-connected collectors and middlemen—including Sotheby's—had already spent years and vast sums of money trying to unearth the artist's works.

He returned to his corner office overlooking the beautifully manicured private park owned by Sotheby's and sometimes used to host social events and even, on occasion, auctions. He ignored the attempts by both his secretaries to seek his attention, walked past the tastefully decorated waiting room and opened the teak door to his private study, marvelling at the absolute silence in the room the moment the door was closed.

His feet sank into the thick carpet, muffling his footsteps as he walked towards his seat behind the intricately carved walnut desk. Settling into his luxurious chair, he eagerly reached for the envelope in his breast pocket, his hands trembling with excitement. He pulled out two photographs and two typewritten sheets, his breath catching in his throat as he gazed at the pictures of the two beautiful paintings that appeared to have been painted in the style of Roerich. His pulse rising, he held up the stapled typewritten sheets, his face crinkling in disappointment at the foreign language printed upon them. In hope, he flipped over the top sheet, his face breaking into a smile as he saw that Abbas had also provided a notarized translation into English. Appreciating his thoroughness, James began to read . . .

To
Abbas Ali
23, Everglade Terrace
London

Dear Sir,
It was very nice to meet you in Islamabad. As requested, I confirm that I have sold the two paintings (as per photographs) to you for 10 lakh rupees. I have received payment by cheque number 311083 dated 14 January 2010, from National Bank of Pakistan.
You had asked for an explanation as to how I had acquired the paintings. I hereby confirm that I purchased them from my friend Zakir Hussain. Zakir's family lived in Lahore and the paintings had been at his home. His grandfather had come from India during Partition and got

the paintings with him from India, and they have been with the family ever since. Unfortunately, Zakir died a few years ago. I tried to ask his wife for any further information that she may have had about how the paintings came to the family, but she was unable to provide any. She said that she remembered seeing the paintings when she had come to Zakir's home after marriage and that she thought they had always been there.

Please tell me if you would like me to provide more information. It was nice to host your esteemed self. Please allow us to host you when you come to Islamabad again.

Regards,
Rehan Shah
14, M.J. Road
Islamabad, Pakistan

James sighed and leant forward, his hands on his temples. As far as he could tell—and he was confident that he was correct—these paintings were certainly painted in the style of Roerich. Of course, the technicians would verify if they were indeed original works by Roerich. No stone would be left unturned to carry out this verification—after all, Sotheby's reputation was at stake and one could never be too careful. Why, only recently, the Louvre Museum had been sold a 100-million-dollar Da Vinci that had fooled even their experts and eventually been proved to be an extremely well-crafted fake.

Sotheby's had dealt with Abbas often and never had cause to doubt the authenticity of anything he provided. It was improbable that he would risk his reputation by trying to pass off a fake. So if the paintings were genuine, the next question was of their provenance. The chain of ownership that the letter from Rehan showed was fairly common in the art world, where people either had very little idea about the value of the art that they were parting with, or its true value would have appreciated only years, or even decades, after the transfer had been made. Most transactions were in cash, leaving no paper trail. To address this challenge, most of the art world had agreed on a twofold standard. The first step was to make every effort to interview as many previous owners as they could find, so as to establish as long a chain of ownership as possible. Of course, that didn't always work—often, a previous owner was dead or could not be found and the chain would be broken. The second step was to inform all leading museums, auction houses and experts in the field about the paintings that had become available, in an effort to generate any leads about their ownership—services for which the concerned experts were paid. Money often produced international cooperation on a scale that most international organizations could only dream of. If neither of these two methods resulted in a red flag, the auction house would go ahead with the sale, after clearly detailing the steps taken towards verification and providing potential buyers with all the information available to them.

James set about performing the necessary tasks for Sotheby's to go ahead with the auction. He called the head of the verification department and asked him to call in external experts to verify that the paintings were indeed original Roerichs, instructing him to expedite the process. Sotheby's own high standards additionally required the verification department to call in at least four experts to verify the genuineness of any article submitted to them. Experts, especially for some of the more exotic items that Sotheby's dealt with, were few, and while this often meant that verification took time, it did mean that a purchase from Sotheby's was a near-guarantee of the item's genuineness. Sotheby's also deployed the best available technology to verify authenticity, subjecting the paintings to a microscopic analysis, exposure to Wood's light, infrared reflectography and spectroscopic analysis. Once satisfied that the painting was genuine, they would then date the frame itself, by way of a final check. This would also be supplemented by a more subjective analysis, with experts judging whether the brush strokes were similar in direction, depth and fluidity of the strokes in other paintings by the artist. All of this would take time, but he could push the team to expedite the tests.

He then asked his secretary to connect him to Sotheby's representative in Pakistan—they employed at least one person in each country from where the artefacts generally arrived, exactly for the task that he was now about to allot. Once he had the clipped accent of the Oxford-educated Nizam Hussain on the line, he briefed him and instructed him to interview Rehan Shah that very day, promising to send over a scan of the letter shortly. Instructing his secretary to send the scan to Nizam, he turned on his computer and composed the email that would go out into the art world in search of leads. This email list comprised the who's who of the art world—a very powerful informally organized group that knew everything that transpired in this unexpectedly dark world. Over the years, the group had agreed on a template for all such inquiries and it took him only a few minutes to include a description of the paintings, attach the pictures and briefly explain the chain of ownership, as he knew it.

Having sent out the request for information, he composed an email to his chairman, providing a detailed update and seeking permission to include the paintings in the auction once the established procedures were satisfactorily completed. If the auction of these two paintings came through, it could mean a huge bonus for him. With that happy thought in mind, he decided to visit the preservation room to see the paintings for himself and stress again the importance of finishing the verification promptly.

# Chapter 13

2 November 1947
Kappar
11 a.m.

Nicholas had slept poorly the previous night, the raja's secret weighing heavy on him. Despite being inebriated, he had taken the time to hide the document in the middle of a book in his library, the previous evening. He had locked the doors, secured the windows, returned to his room and withdrawn a loaded pistol from his drawer, placing it under his pillow and resting one hand on its grip.

The unforgiving metal under his head, the dehydration from the vodka and the burden of the secret led to him spending the entire night wondering what to do with the document, without reaching a decision. He had woken before Charan and composed a message for him to take to the raja, using the same code, making sure that Charan had memorized the message perfectly, asking him to repeat it half a dozen times till it was exactly right. Satisfied, he had finally seen Charan off and retired to his library. It was then that he panicked, unable to remember the book that he had pressed the document into, the night before. As his search became more frantic, he tossed the books all over the room, paying little heed to the damage he was causing to some extremely valuable ones. He finally found the document buried in an atlas and retrieved it with relief.

Slipping the document into the pocket of his silk robe, he returned to the sitting room and contemplated where he could hide the document for a minimum of twenty years, as the raja had requested. He rejected dozens of hiding places—some too unsafe and others safer but still unable to offer the level of protection that the document demanded—before finally arriving at a solution. He disappeared into his gallery and locked the door, and gently made the arrangements to create the perfect hiding place. He emerged two hours later, the document safely hidden and well-protected.

All that remained now to be done, was to inform the only person he trusted about the location of the document, and to pass on the instructions for its eventual release or destruction. But that would have to wait till Svetoslav returned from his trip.

The raja had chosen, but it was too early for the world to know the secret that lay hidden in the now well-protected document.

# Chapter 14

21 January 1970
Washington D.C.
11.30 a.m.

Unable to turn away, the Indian officer continued to stare at the television, watching the life seep out of her. He began to shake and then cry as he vaguely comprehended what he had done, his emotional turmoil shutting out all thoughts of the ramifications of having been caught in the act on camera.

He saw a man step forward to retrieve the tape from the television as it was ejected and then leave through the front door with the tape in his pocket. Another man then appeared in his line of sight and spoke: 'Hi. I'm Martin. I am . . . or rather, I was a colleague of Pamela's. Can you understand me?'

He continued to snivel, trying to come to terms with having ended a life he had loved. Eventually, he nodded, his fuzzy brain regaining a semblance of control and finding meaning in the words being spoken to him.

'That was a terrible thing you did. It was hard to watch. Strangling is a really deliberate way to kill someone, isn't it? Hearing them struggle for breath till you hear that final gasp before they give up on even trying to breathe. And here I was under the impression that you loved her.'

The officer was quiet for a long time, replaying the images from the television over and over in his head. Every word that the man spoke struck home, and hard—that was exactly how it had felt as he had strangled her with all his strength.

'Who are you?' he finally asked.

'I just told you, I'm Martin. You can think of me either as the friend who keeps you out of prison or the law enforcement officer that guarantees you spend the rest of your life in it. It's really up to you.'

'How?'

'How do you stay out of prison? That's quite simple. All you need to do is share some of the information that comes your way, with us.'

Instinctively, the intelligence officer shook his head. 'I can't betray my country.'

'I would have been really disappointed if you had said anything else. Pamela did always speak very highly of your patriotism. But I do believe you are mistaken. Our interests are more aligned than most people think, but I'm sure you already know that. I'm not asking you to betray your country—I'm just asking you to share some information regarding the Chinese.'

'What sort of information?'

'Things that we don't know quite as well. How do they fund unrest in India? What is the extent of their support to Pakistan? Who are the Americans that are spying for them? The kind of things that you will know better than us, but which we can use to slow them down, if not muzzle them altogether. In exchange,

I will not only allow your freedom but also provide you with information about your neighbours which you will find quite useful, and which will, I daresay, help your career. Especially about the troublesome ones in the north. I mean it—you won't work *for* us, but *with* us.'

The officer struggled to keep up, the cacophony of emotions drowning out his rationality.

Martin recognized the confusion. It wasn't the first time he was seeing a brilliant man struggle to bring his mental engines up to speed. Knowing that the Indian officer needed time, Martin left the room, promising to return shortly to hear his answer, but leaving behind two armed colleagues to keep an eye on him.

He sat there, trying to calm himself. It was clear to him that he was not willing to go to prison and at freedom, he drew his line in the sand. A necessary corollary of that decision was that he would have to work for—no, that wasn't quite right, as Martin had said, he would have to work *with* the CIA. These decisions made, he spent the rest of his time tied to that chair convincing himself that working for the CIA was in everyone's best interests. If not him, they would certainly find someone else, who may not be as keen to protect India as he was. And certainly, there could be no better partner than the CIA if his country's interests were to be protected. With him still in the picture, it would be easier to leverage their strengths while keeping under control the information that was shared with them. And certainly, at some point, he would extricate himself from the situation.

Martin returned an hour later and was delighted at the officer's positive response. The two men shook hands and Martin promised to get in touch soon to set up communications protocols between them.

He had become a spy for the CIA, falling, as he would eventually find out, into a rabbit hole. He hadn't known it then—or maybe some part of him did and didn't want to acknowledge it—but he was now in the inescapable clutches of the most ruthless organization in the world: the tape, an omnipresent death warrant which became increasingly potent every time he betrayed his country during his journey up the ranks in Indian intelligence.

# Chapter 15

22 February 2010
Islamabad
7.30 a.m.

Colonel Abdul Hussain was returning home after a long night. He had been in office, supervising the Lashkar-e-Taiba's infiltration of five freedom fighters into Kashmir. Infiltrating India had been getting harder with its growing economic strength; India, now able to spend more on defence, had fenced nearly the entirety of Rajasthan's and Kashmir's borders. They had also added technological defences, installing hidden infrared cameras and providing its border security force and army with night-vision goggles. The colonel also suspected that India had stationed one or more satellites above the Pakistan border to keep an unerring eye on its most vulnerable region at all times.

The infiltration was planned through the Mandrake Gully in the Dras sector—the dozens of tunnels carved into the Himalayas by the streams that ran through it. Most tunnels had been identified and sealed by Indian forces that kept a constant vigil over them, but there remained undiscovered tunnels that were known to only a handful of the ISI's senior staff—Colonel Hussain being among them. The three tunnels not only passed under the electrified fences but also offered protection against both the infrared cameras and satellites. Invaluable to the ISI for this reason, they were used only for key operations and the current infiltration was among them.

The infiltration had commenced at 2 a.m., the time carefully selected with India's patrolling schedules in mind. The five men's passage was supported by heavy shelling by Pakistan's Border Action Team, the shells exploding across the entire Dras Sector, thus hiding the men's exact point of entry.

Colonel Hussain, with his maps spread out before him, had guided the five men to the hidden entrance of the tunnel. As expected, they had lost communication once the men were inside, the signals having been blocked out by the mountain's rocks. They had waited impatiently for the team to emerge on the Indian side, nervously watching the monitors for confirmation that contact had been re-established. Their microphones, supplied by the Pakistan Army, had captured the audio from their efforts as they made the arduous descent from the cliff. He thanked the Almighty once the team made it safely to ground, the first phase thus successfully completed.

Everything had gone to plan and he encouraged the infiltrators to rely on their GPS trackers to guide them through the nearly impenetrable jungle as they made their way through the thick forests of Kashmir towards their rallying point. They had selected the thickest part of the forest, aware that the area was lightly patrolled as it was considered to be inaccessible from the Pakistani border.

And then, suddenly, everything had fallen apart. The radio was suddenly filled with gunfire—the unmistakable sound of

AK-47s on automatic fire. He heard the team leader yell instructions to his men, asking them to adopt defensive positions. Once his men were organized, the leader provided a situation report. The group had been pinned down by a BSF patrol, with fire coming in from all sides, cutting off their retreat. The leader whispered that their only option was to break through one of the flanks, hoping that the patrol did not have enough men to cover all sides adequately. Colonel Hussain agreed and granted permission. He heard the roar of gunfire as his men mounted their charge, grenades exploding, voices yelling in both Urdu and Hindi. He sensed when the pace of fire dropped, one side no longer fighting with the same ferocity. Finally, the Urdu ceased completely and was replaced by Hindi on the still-live connection between him and the either deceased or captured leader.

He broke the connection, careful not to provide the technical wizards of the Indian armed forces with any access to their network. Paying no heed to the lateness of the hour, he dialled another number, and reported failure to a waiting General Liyaqat, conveying that the operation had been foiled by some tremendously bad luck with the BSF patrol. General Liyaqat, disappointed but pragmatic, had simply asked Colonel Hussain to file a report before they met later that day with the leadership of the Lashkar, promising to inform them of the unfortunate news himself.

Colonel Hussain knew he would not be blamed. This happened often enough—sometimes because the infiltrators were spotted and other times because information would be leaked to one of the many members of India's spy network, and yet other times, through sheer bad luck. There was never any way to know with confidence why things had gone bad and he was certain that this would be another instance where the inevitable internal inquiry that would follow, would come to no concrete conclusion. Of course, he would still have to demonstrate his utmost professionalism in his report and with that sole objective in mind, he stayed back to write it up.

He finally called it a day at 7.15 a.m. on the next day and left for home to get a few hours of sleep before he had to return to face the disappointment, and possibly the fury, of the Lashkar. Half asleep in the back of his chauffeured vehicle, staring listlessly as the beautiful city passed by, he jerked awake at the sight of a particular TV antenna, which was pointing in the opposite direction to its usual orientation.

He noted this but soon retreated into his near comatose state, remaining in that restful position till the car halted outside his home. He headed straight to the washroom to wash up and change, whilst his manservant prepared his breakfast. He half-opened the bathroom's window shade before taking a long, satisfying piss, brushing his teeth, washing his face and changing into his kurta pyjama. And then he dug into his breakfast.

Colonel Hussain had acknowledged the signal conveyed to him by the altered antenna. Having delivered yet another blow to Pakistan, he was now looking forward to the conversation that the antenna had thus requested.

# Chapter 16

30 November 1947
Kappar
12.15 p.m.

The congregation walked sombrely through the marble arch entrance to the cemetery. A cool breeze caused the temperatures to drop nearly to zero, the men and women rubbing their hands together and stamping their feet in an effort to keep warm. The pallbearers—Svetoslav among them—trudged over the uneven ground, making their way to the top of the slope where a grave had been dug for Kappar's legend.

A tranquil silence permeated the cemetery, almost as if the cemetery itself was paying its final respects to the great man. The mahogany coffin reflected the bright sunlight, blinding those who caught its rays, forcing them to turn their heads away sharply to escape its fierceness.

The coffin was lowered gently into the ground, its brass handles creaking in protest against the pressure suddenly brought to bear heavily on them. Ropes attached to either end of the coffin held it in place while the priest spoke, remembering fondly the legendary Nicholas Roerich and the indelible mark that he had left not just on Kappar, but on the world at large.

Nicholas had died of a heart attack on the previous day, having accomplished in his sixty-seven years more than most men would in multiple lifetimes. Just as he had wanted, he was being buried in the plot he had selected for himself. The wake to follow would be held in his own backyard, a place where he had spent so much of his life painting the Himalayas, getting deeply involved in horticulture and hosting summer evening parties that were the pride of the city.

With his wife Helena having passed away two years previously, Svetoslav was the only family member present at Nicholas's funeral. His brother George had studied in Great Britain along with Svetoslav, but had married a British girl and decided to settle in Great Britain itself, much to the disappointment of the family. Svetoslav had earned a bachelor's degree in architecture and then a master's, but unlike George, had returned to be with his ageing parents.

Over the years, he had taken over the mantle from Nicholas, emerging as the family's most gifted artist. He had learnt from his parents, interpreting their stories and art through the lens of his own experiences. As he painted, his reputation grew and he soon became the heir to his father, a king of art. His reputation opened to him the doors of the Indian elite. He was well-known to almost everyone in Kappar and, in turn, knew everyone who mattered, enjoying an active social life, even in this small Indian outpost.

His fame had also brought him some fortune, allowing him to purchase his own property and move out of his parents' house, though he had continued to live a five-minute walk away from their cottage. He had bought Sommerville House from a colonel of the British Army, who had decided to liquidate his holdings in India before its independence became a reality. He also inherited the trained staff that had manned Sommerville House under the colonel and who now worked to make his life comfortable.

Svetoslav was distraught at the loss of Nicholas. The father and son had shared a wonderful bond and had done several things together. Life had deprived them of more time with each other, with both having to live away from home for considerable periods of time—one to pursue his passions and the other to complete his education. They had often painted together and Nicholas's influence was evident in Svetoslav's work—and would continue to be so for the rest of his life. From the time he had received the news of his father's death, he had been unable to function. Nicholas's butler, having been with the family for nearly thirty years, had taken over and made the arrangements for the burial.

The coffin was finally lowered into the ground. Svetoslav, lost in his memories of his father, mechanically followed the priest's instructions. He had not yet been able to cry—grief had not yet sunk in. He stood wordlessly as scores of people filed by, whispering commiserations and messages of support to him.

When the ordeal was finally and mercifully over, he returned to Sommerville House, asking not to be disturbed till he instructed otherwise. He opened a fresh bottle of vodka and started drinking, finally letting the tears fall.

Svetoslav spent the next month in drunken purgatory, refusing to meet anyone. He made one exception for the district collector, his dear friend Rajesh, whom he met to gift his parents' house to the district administration, provided it was used to create a museum to commemorate them. As he gradually came to terms with his father's loss, he began to paint again, his melancholy and memories shining through in the art he created. Unable to muster the energy to travel to Delhi to purchase new canvases for the volume of art that he was creating, he raided Nicholas's house for canvases and frames that his father had left unused.

His grief lasted a long time, alleviated only by an obscure article appearing in a newspaper, many months later.

# Chapter 17

10 September 1970
New Delhi
2.30 p.m.

The intelligence officer had returned to work with blood on his hands and was now reporting to two masters. The CIA never reported the crime and instead made Pamela's body disappear. Of course, they retained copies of the tapes and his DNA, taken from the body and knew that the evidence was enough to destroy him at a time of their choosing.

At the CIA's insistence, he joined the Gurukamal Ashram in Delhi. The ashram accepted followers from across the world, each of whom came seeking the guidance of Guru Kamalakantji to find their inner selves. Surviving solely on voluntary donations, the ashram had built a reputation for being a world-class institution for spiritual learning, meditation and yoga, as it indeed was for its followers.

For some others, however, it offered the perfect hideaway. Given its global following, people from every nationality came and went as they pleased, some staying for years, others for just a weekend, raising no eyebrows either way. The ashram offered spaces for people to interact in privacy and help each other along their spiritual journeys. For the CIA, it was manna from heaven, providing them with unquestioned access to India and the opportunity to meet their newest recruit regularly.

The newest recruit struggled to come to terms with his crime. He had considered confessing to his superiors but had rejected the idea, concluding that they would see him as a threat to Indian intelligence and would, at best, expel him. So instead, he had thrown himself into his work, excelling more than before, the CIA's inputs helping him deliver analyses that could predict events accurately. The CIA had got what they wanted—a rising star in Indian intelligence who was sure to occupy a senior leadership role in the years to come.

While he had started hesitantly, it had got increasingly easier for him to work for the CIA. He enjoyed the success and fame that their inputs brought him, the scars from his time in the US fading over time. For now, he found their relationship to be beneficial and the value of the CIA's inputs far exceeded the value of what he was offering them. While he knew that the CIA would demand its pound of flesh when the time came, the tenuous foundations of their relationship were plastered over by the immediate gains.

It was, therefore, more with anticipation than with trepidation that he had arrived at the ashram that morning. He had willingly participated in the morning programme, having begun to enjoy the benefits of meditation and yoga, especially in times of stress. Over lunch, he had met with 'Mike', who had just arrived from the US, where he was a 'forensic consultant' to the US Government. Despite being shuffled constantly over the years, this was the same story that each new contact narrated when they met him, thus subtly identifying themselves as CIA agents. Sitting in a quiet corner under a beautiful banyan tree, its falling roots providing privacy, he disclosed India's intention to move closer to the Eastern Bloc and the ongoing negotiation of a friendship treaty with the Soviet Union. 'Mike' had absorbed the information, memorizing the details rather than jotting any of it down on a piece of paper.

Mike reciprocated with information about a Communist spy in R&AW and the dangerous information he was relaying to the KGB—information that severely compromised India's security. The CIA was certain—having verified the spy's existence from their sources within the KGB—that the payout had been received in the guise of a generous scholarship awarded to the spy's son for his higher education in the US. Mike had asked the young officer to investigate, pointing him in the directions where he could search for the truth.

The officer had looked in the dark corners to which Mike had pointed him, confirming everything the CIA had claimed and painfully putting together the dossier that would expose the Communist spy and catapult his own career to the next level. He had just earned a secondment to the Defence Intelligence Agency.

# Chapter 18

22 February 2010
Islamabad
11.30 a.m.

Colonel Abdul Hussain's bad night had transformed into an even worse day. He had slept for only a couple of hours before his cell phone started ringing wildly, the ringtone unique to the person who was calling. Having no choice but to answer, he had woken quickly to take the call from General Beg, the chief of the ISI.

General Beg was not happy. He had been briefed by General Liyaqat on the failed infiltration and had read Abdul's report. Nevertheless, he was keen to hear about the events in the colonel's own words, to ensure that no snippet of information had been omitted from the written report. Abdul knew General Beg well and knew him to be extremely sharp. He had to be, to wear the crown of thorns that characterized the position of the ISI chief. Abdul had narrated the events of the past two weeks, sticking as closely as he could to his report. The general had listened without interruption, the sound of his breathing the only sign that he was still there. When he finished, General Beg said just one thing, but that simple statement sent shivers down the colonel's spine.

'We have been betrayed, colonel. See me today at 2 p.m.' Order issued, General Beg hung up, leaving no opportunity for Abdul to ask how he had arrived at that conclusion. He dressed, thinking back over the operation to analyse whether he had missed something that could be traced back to him. He could appreciate that General Beg had his suspicions, but could not fathom why he thought that they had been betrayed. Abdul wondered if the general suspected him, but had that been the case, wouldn't he already have been picked up and questioned? In this situation, there was no honour among thieves.

'*Que sera sera*,' he said to himself. In any event, what choice did he have? His wife was still in the army hospital, where she had been ever since a bomb had exploded outside the US embassy, eight years ago. Planted by the Jaish in retaliation to the US drone strike that had killed their northern commander, the bomb had failed to kill a single American, but had caused the death of twenty-two Pakistani nationals and injured another 127, including his wife. Among the dead was his young son, who had accompanied his mother for their visa interview, only for his life to have been snuffed out in an instant. The twin misfortunes had destroyed Abdul's belief in the Pakistani establishment and shattered his faith. He had taken a leave of absence and travelled to London to spend time with his relatives, where he had met Amitabh.

Amitabh was introduced to him by a common friend and had been sympathetic to Abdul's loss. As their friendship grew, Amitabh began to suggest that Pakistan's strategy of destroying India with a million cuts was destined to fail. In any event, if it meant that Pakistan was not only unable to put down its rabid dogs, but exercise even a modicum of control over the monsters, was it really worth it, allowing the devils to live in the hope that they could destroy India? Abdul, his belief system upended by his loss and with a thirst for vengeance, had, over several conversations, come around to accepting this point of view. Only then had Amitabh revealed that he worked for Indian intelligence and offered Abdul the opportunity to exact his vengeance by spying for India and causing more damage to the Jaish and Lashkar from within the system than he could ever do from the outside. Thus Abdul had turned and Pakistan had only itself to blame.

As for now, he decided to stay the course. He would go meet General Beg and if it was meant to be, he would not return. With that morbid thought, he entered his car and was driven to the army headquarters, where he was ushered into a room where General Beg, General Liyaqat and the Lashkar's local commanders were already seated. General Beg asked him to take a seat and to once again narrate the sequence of events, the assembled panel of terrorists listening to him carefully. Finishing his account, Abdul sat ramrod straight, waiting for accusations to be hurled at him, mentally rehearsing the lines he had prepared during the drive.

He was barely able to contain his relief when Colonel Beg had asked for his views on the identity of the traitor. His senses on high alert, he identified that this was a trick question. If he suggested a name, thus implicitly agreeing that there was a mole, Beg could have concluded that Abdul was the mole, for whatever it was that the general knew, the information was unavailable to him.

So instead, he deferentially suggested that the operation had failed due to sheer bad luck, not openly opposing the general, but making the point to show that he did not believe there was a mole. General Beg nodded, almost in relief, as he heard the answer he had hoped for, rather than the answer that would have led to Abdul's arrest.

'The BSF has never patrolled that area on a Friday,' replied Beg. 'Trust me, I know,' he added, sensing the question that Abdul was about to ask.

Abdul nodded. Of course, General Beg had his own spies within the Indian security establishment, who no one but he had access to.

'So if they chose that very Friday to patrol that particular area, there is obviously a mole in our midst.'

No one spoke.

'I want you to find the mole, Colonel. And fast. Liyaqat will make available whatever you need. Dismissed.'

Abdul stood, saluted both generals smartly and left. He now had the impossible task of hunting himself down.

He returned home, in need of time alone to think carefully. He could not disappear, not without leaving Salma behind, so he would have to play the game to the end. It would have to look like a genuine inquiry was underway and that it was making progress, but it could never come close to unearthing the identity of the mole. It would be dangerous, with no margin of error.

At 9.30 that evening, he logged on to a chat platform used only by the most hardcore fundamentalists in the world. He logged in as 'Pakistani Patriot' and waited to be contacted by Muhammad Fidayeen, the alias of the Indian CI. His computer pinged and the message 'D 25 7 U' flashed on his screen.

The meeting was set, the pre-agreed code was clear to Abdul. His eye was drawn to the 'U'—whatever it was that the CI wanted to speak about, it was of utmost urgency. Good, thought Abdul, maybe Amitabh could help him hatch a plan for how he should handle the inquiry.

Logging off, he began making his travel plans for Dubai. After all, General Beg himself had just given him the perfect reason to fly there.

# Chapter 19

15 August 1948
Mumbai
9 a.m.

Devika and Shiva stood side by side, their backs straight, their chests puffed out and their hands tucked smartly into their sides, looking straight at the tricolour fluttering proudly before them. The sea breeze tugged at and eventually drew a few strands of hair out of Devika's bun, whipping them playfully against her face, tickling her nose. As much as she wanted to put her hair in its place, she waited for the ceremony to finish, very aware that a number of eyes were focused on her and would notice the slightest transgression.

As the last bars were played out by the military band, the thousands assembled at the magnificent bungalow on the coast of the Arabian Sea broke into spontaneous applause, energy coursing through the crowd as it celebrated India's Independence Day. Each of them had experienced the horrors of the British Raj and several had been key contributors to the political movements against foreign rule. For them, just standing in the house of an Indian governor for the state of Bombay, with the tricolour flying freely in the wind, was enough to stir up a storm of emotions. Some hugged, some chanted 'Vande Mataram' and 'Bharat Mata Ki Jai' while others saluted the tricolour—each person celebrating the historical moment in their own way.

Devika and Shiva walked up to the governor, smiles on their faces, their hands folded in greeting. The governor, his moist eyes still glued to the triumphant tricolour, failed to notice them until Shiva coughed politely to get his attention. Tearing his eyes away, Governor Rajagopalachari turned towards the sound, his weathered face breaking into a smile as he saw the couple before him.

'Thank you for coming today,' he said, turning towards them. Waving away the polite responses that they were beginning to mumble—both in awe of the legendary freedom fighter who had not only spent years imprisoned by the British Raj, but also lost his entire family to the fight for India's freedom—he signalled them to turn around for the assembled media.

The gaggle of reporters burst into a cacophony of excitement, photographers from leading publications jostling with each other for the best angle to click the perfect photograph of this moment—India's biggest female superstar with one of its most iconic freedom fighters—to encapsulate in one frame, India's newfound freedom on many counts. The seasoned stars, with easy, well-rehearsed smiles on their faces, stood on either side of the living legend, who smiled uncomfortably at the posse. Pictures taken, the photographers scurried away, eager to get them into the hands of their editors in time for the next edition of their newspapers.

Little did one of them know that the picture that he had just captured would be of consequence to dozens of lives in the decades to come.

# Chapter 20

23 February 2010
Islamabad
9.30 a.m.

Colonel Abdul had asked for, and received, an appointment at short notice with General Liyaqat. Obviously, the importance of his task and of the man who had allotted it to him, had already been made clear to the general's staff. He had drawn up his strategy the previous evening and it was, therefore, with confidence that he marched to the general's office.

He detailed the first steps that he wanted to take to find the mole. He had already activated the ISI's agents in the R&AW, IB and Military Intelligence, asking them for any leads. He now needed permission to travel to Dubai to activate their most important Indian asset—the infamous Dawood Ibrahim—who still knew more about events in India than most, his tentacles reaching deep into the Indian system given his constant connection with some of India's most powerful politicians, businessmen and law enforcement officials.

Dawood's rise was a legend in the ISI. He had been raised in Dongri, in what was now Mumbai, as one of twelve siblings. The family had lived in poverty; his father, a police constable, unable to provide for his large family. Forced to drop out of school because his family could no longer afford the fees, Dawood and a bunch of other similarly placed boys in Dongri had formed a gang. This gang had begun small but managed to make their mark with the elimination of Baashu Dada, the reigning king of Dongri. The D-Company, as they would come to be known, was born on that day.

In the years that followed, the D-Company shaped the real estate in Bombay, using violence to clear land and evict tenants on behalf of various real estate businesses, which were often fronts maintained by corrupt politicians. Left unmolested by the police due to his political patronage, Dawood had expanded his influence through smuggling, bringing the D-Company into conflict with Haji Mastan, the then king of the Indian underworld. The Bombay Police stood by idly during the violent gang war that followed, allowing the gangs to weaken each other in their quest for dominance. The D-Company eventually seized control of the Bombay underworld, and believing themselves to be invincible, turned on the very interests that had nurtured them, extorting money from the same builders they used to work for. They went too far and the Bombay Police, finally let off the leash by its political masters, reopened an old armed robbery case against Dawood—perceived by Dawood as a betrayal; one that would haunt India for decades to come. By the time the Bombay Police moved to arrest him, Dawood had already fled to enjoy a life of luxury in Dubai.

The move to Dubai, rather than hurting Dawood, had accelerated his growth. The D-Company partnered with Afghan warlords and European arms dealers to smuggle their narcotics and illegal arms into India. The vast surplus cash allowed Dawood to become an important cog in the hawala system, standing as a guarantee for payments across the world. This brought him into contact with the senior leadership of Pakistan, which was always on the lookout for means to smuggle their ill-gotten wealth out of the country. Dawood had obliged, depositing euros and dollars in various '*benami*' bank accounts for his Pakistani friends.

In Pakistan, Dawood also found a natural enemy of India. He facilitated the serial bombings in Bombay in 1993, an act that made him the world's most wanted man, hunted by dozens of countries. Fearing for his life, he fled to Pakistan, from where he continued to operate with impunity, living under the fake identity created for him by the ISI. The Pakistani military provided him with protection, while the civilian government denied sheltering him on the world stage.

Abdul was not privy to the truth either and was unaware that Dawood was on Pakistani soil. He had, however, worked with Dawood before on behalf of the ISI, and knew how to get a meeting. If there was anyone who could find out how the infiltration had been compromised, it was Dawood, and General Beg would have expected Abdul to tap into this invaluable resource. The colonel had simply moved the meeting further up in his priority list to make the appointment with the CI in Dubai—the 'D' in his chat message.

Abdul asked for the meeting with Dawood to be set for Dubai on the following day. In keeping with the protocols for Dawood's protection, no place or time for the meeting was intimated. Abdul was aware that Dawood's men would keep an eye on him from the time he arrived in Dubai and at an opportune moment, take him to Dawood once they were confident that he was not being followed. Intending to give them as much time as possible, he booked himself on the first Pakistan Airlines flight out of Islamabad and spent the rest of his day planning the remaining steps that he intended to take to demonstrate that a genuine inquiry had been made, hoping to discuss his plans with Amitabh.

The flight to Dubai was uneventful. He landed at 11 a.m. local time and hailed a taxi to his hotel. He had looked for but failed to spot Dawood's surveillance team which was undoubtedly keeping an eye on him. To make it easier for them to pick him up for the meeting, he had stayed outdoors, roaming the streets of Dubai, walking purposelessly in a straight line, so they could check if anyone was tailing him.

After an hour, just as he decided to stop for lunch, a car pulled up next to him, the men signalling him to get in. He was blindfolded and placed between two men in the back, and sat thinking through his questions for Dawood, making absolutely no effort to quiz his escort about their destination or try to keep track of the direction they were heading in. He had been expertly searched for a weapon by hand and then with a wand, to ensure that he was not bugged in any way. He was impressed with the thoroughness of the men, who had examined every inch of his body, even taking off his shoes and putting them through a rigorous examination. Though the drive took an hour, the driver made so many turns—whether to confuse him or to identify tails, he could not be sure—that they could be anywhere in Dubai. He was politely escorted out of the vehicle and led to a chair, where his blindfold was removed and he was offered cold water and refreshments.

Dawood arrived a few minutes later, grinning widely at Abdul. After a brief hug and briefer pleasantries, Abdul detailed the sequence of events and the instructions from General Beg. Dawood listened without interruption and asked Abdul to provide him with the names of those involved in the operation, which Abdul did from memory, including, of course, his own name. Dawood promised to make inquiries and thanked Abdul for bringing the matter to his attention—after all, any spy in the ISI put Dawood's own existence at risk.

By the time Abdul was dropped off at the hotel, it was late afternoon. He used his key card to enter his room and found the CI lounging comfortably in a chair in the corner, reading something on his phone.

'Dawood says hello,' joked Abdul.

'That's not funny,' replied the CI. 'I assume you have no idea where to find him.'

'None whatsoever. But he still looks like the sketch that you are using, so at least you will recognize him if you ever find him.'

Abdul's words rankled Amitabh. The Indian government's inability to bring Dawood to justice irked the CI each day, made worse by the fact that he was so well-protected that India had not even been able to mount an attempt to capture or kill him. Meanwhile, Dawood had continued to exert his influence over Mumbai and the political leadership; his businesses in extortion, smuggling and narcotics growing each year, wreaking economic havoc on India in the process.

Cutting into the CI's chain of thought, Abdul spoke. 'Your message came at just the right time. I needed to speak to you. The ISI knows there is a high-ranking mole in the system.'

'How? Running into the patrol was a coincidence.'

'Apparently not. Your geniuses in BSF forgot to inform you that they never patrol that area on a Friday. Somehow, Beg knew that and you didn't. He, of course, concluded that there was a leak and is now hunting the mole.'

'Relax, Abdul. There is no way to trace it to you. It could have been anyone in the chain of command.'

'There is always a way, Amitabh. You know that as well as I do. All they need is my computer. I am sure the ISI can crack the encryption or get the Chinese to do it. And then what answer will I give for the strange chat messages that I receive?'

'We will think of something. Those messages are gibberish—they could mean anything.'

'Thanks,' replied Abdul sarcastically. 'You start thinking of an explanation anyway, but for now, I have taken care of it.'

'How?'

'I am in charge of hunting the mole.'

Both men laughed—a privilege neither enjoyed frequently.

The CI was suddenly excited. 'You have just made my life simple. I was going to ask you to do something very important, which may have put you at some risk, but this hunt alleviates that risk.'

'You need me to find out where the money is coming from.'

The CI nodded. 'We need to stop the bloodshed. Both countries have been held back because we have been unable to make peace. But now we have a real chance, under the present leaderships, to finally end this proxy war. The Jaish know that and will try and stall it. We cannot let that happen—too many lives depend on it.'

'Of course, I know that, Amitabh. But I am not part of the group planning the strikes. I am only providing logistical support. How would you have me find that out for you without exposing myself?'

'I have an idea,' said Amitabh, laying out a plan for Abdul. When he finished, Abdul found himself spellbound yet again at the genius of the little man in front of him. It was a good thing India wanted peace—with people like Amitabh in their corner, Pakistan was never going to win this war.

They fine-tuned the plan, arguing back and forth, identifying pitfalls and means of circumventing them. At 7 p.m., they finally agreed on a plan that Abdul was happy to pursue.

'Hope Salma is better?'

'Still in a coma,' replied Abdul.

The CI shook his head sympathetically, opened the door and left. Abdul would, no doubt, kill him if he learnt that the medical staff had kept Salma in a coma on Amitabh's instructions.

# Chapter 21

18 August 1948
Sommerville House, Kappar
11 a.m.

Svetoslav lazed in his garden, sipping his tea and watching the steam rising from his cup into the nippy morning air. As he did every day, he had just returned from an hour-long walk on the town's hilly terrain, allowing his creativity to roam freely in search of new ideas.

He had been thinking about his next painting for a while now and during his walk, the last few pieces of the puzzle had fallen into place, bringing him clarity on the treatment he was going to adopt while painting the landscape he had decided on. Satisfied with the morning's work, he happily unfurled the Mumbai edition of the *Times of India*, especially brought up to Kappar for him, albeit a couple of days late, and absorbed the news from the real world far removed from the calm of his home.

Whistling tunelessly as he scoured through the paper— full of news about the steps being taken by the fledgling state of India to become a federal republic—his eyes were drawn to a picture of a woman standing next to a striking gentleman and the governor of Bombay. Roerich was instantly enamoured by her striking beauty and the more subtle signs of confidence in her relaxed posture and the tilt of her head. Roerich read the article, learning that she was Devika Rani, the doyen of Hindi cinema. His heart filled with anticipation as he read of her impending visit to Kappar to complete the shoot for her latest movie.

Finishing the article, Roerich leant back into the cane chair made especially for his gaunt frame. His artistic mind fixated on Devika's picture, tracing every inch of her face, appreciating its symmetry, understanding and absorbing its angles, the distance between its various features, the different hues of its components, the thickness of her eyebrows, the length of her eyelashes, the shape of her eyes and the colour of her irises.

Finishing at the taut skin of her neck, he made two resolutions. The first was to paint a portrait of her from memory and the second was to have it ready in time for her arrival in Kappar, for he already knew that he would make sure he got the opportunity to meet her.

Roerich laboured out of his chair and purposefully strode into his studio, tucked away at the back of his house. The portrait, created from his memory of that grainy picture, would eventually come to be known as his greatest work.

# Chapter 22

25 February 2010
Islamabad
12.30 p.m.

Abdul had returned from Dubai on the twenty-fourth, utilizing the additional day there to execute Amitabh's plan. He had written up another report for General Liyaqat, detailing the steps taken to date to find the mole, the information he had found and the steps he intended to take in the coming days.

As per Amitabh's brilliant plan, a BSF intelligence officer had reached out to Abdul through a contact in Dubai, asking for a meeting to provide information that would prove invaluable to the ISI. The approach would not be questioned as everyone in Indian intelligence knew of Abdul's role in the ISI. Abdul attended the meeting in Dubai, during which the BSF officer offered information regarding an Indian spy in Pakistan, in exchange for 2 million dollars—the amount selected carefully so it was significant, but still within the limit that Abdul could approve directly. Abdul, as the head of the failed operation, was expected to be smarting from his recent loss to the BSF and keen to get even, and thus, could decide to pay the money without being questioned. The information he received was worth its weight in gold—the BSF's spy was a senior member of the Jaish, who had warned the BSF about the impending infiltration. The information not only shifted the needle of suspicion firmly in the direction of the Jaish, but also empowered Abdul to question every member of the Jaish, including those who had attended the meeting with the ISI to seek additional funding.

Liyaqat had granted him permission to interview members of the Jaish and so Abdul had arranged interviews with several of them on the previous day and today, hiding the fact that his interest lay only in those who had attended the meeting regarding the funds, by including several other plausible names.

In the course of his questioning—the Jaish cooperating on orders from General Beg—he had come across the information that Amitabh had been looking for, from a member who was keen to prove his innocence by describing the work he was actually doing with the ISI. Not being high enough in the hierarchy to know the full details, he could only reveal that the funding was being arranged from London. He didn't know how exactly, but he swore that he had heard about an artist in London arranging for the money.

Abdul logged into the chat platform at 9.30 p.m., leaving a single message for the CI: 'Artist in Love'. He now sat lost in thought about how he could find out more, knowing that Amitabh would soon ask for a lot more than the location from where the money was coming.

# Chapter 23

20 August 1948
District Collector's Residence, Kappar
7 p.m.

Rajesh Kumar was parked on a comfortable chair on his porch, fondly watching his wife yelling last-minute instructions to their staff in preparation for the dinner that evening.

As Kappar's district collector, he occupied the colonial bungalow that had once been the official retreat of the British viceroy in India. The bungalow was perched on top of a hill surrounded by acres of immaculately manicured gardens. He admired the sight before him—a quiet town in the valley below and an endless sky above, lit by a billion stars. Lamps lit the estate gardens, complementing the luminosity of the stars. It was quiet with only the sound of crickets breaking the silence—and his adrenaline-fuelled wife, of course!

He smiled, watching his wife brandishing her arms in the air before a hapless servant, trying to explain the exact arrangement of flowers at each table. After finally managing to get him to understand, Vishaka turned her energies on Rajesh, charging up the driveway towards him, her dupatta fluttering behind her.

'Stop sitting there with that idiot look on your face and go get ready,' she hissed at Rajesh. 'The guests will be here any minute and we cannot have the host greeting them in his robe.'

'Relax, Viku. It's only seven and we are not expecting anyone before eight today. Must respect the timings of the Bombay crowd after all—even if they are the ones coming to Kappar.'

'Just hurry up, Rajesh. It's getting late and I need you here when the first of them arrive. I cannot believe Devika and Shiva are joining us for dinner!'

Rajesh beamed indulgently, aware of Vishaka's love for movies and her curtailed access to them after he was posted to Kappar. It was one of the reasons he had wanted to host this dinner when the crew requested permission for the shoot— not that breaking the monotony of life in sleepy Kappar wasn't reason enough.

'Don't worry, Viku. I'm pretty sure Devika is as excited as you. After all, how often do you get to meet the boss of the highest authority in town!' Laughing to himself, Rajesh finished the rest of his drink and went in to get ready.

# Chapter 24

27 February 2010
London
10 a.m.

Everything seemed to be moving in the right direction in James's life. After multiple attempts, the IVF therapy had finally paid off and Janie, his wife of twelve years, was now in her third month of pregnancy. They had paid off the mortgage on their house and their bank accounts showed a healthy surplus, not quite enough for them to retire, but more than enough to live on comfortably for at least a few years. Janie had just been promoted as a partner in her law firm and his career too was progressing well, with the upcoming sale of the Roerichs promising to provide another boost. The chairman had already promised him a promotion to the position of CEO after the sale, a position that James felt he had deserved for several years now—not to mention there would be a fat bonus from the sale itself. Janie had always wanted to spend a few weeks in Italy and perhaps he would actually take a couple of weeks off and take her before she was prohibited from travelling.

His day had ended on a high with the report from Nizam in Pakistan. Nizam had traced Rehan Shah using his contacts in the army, the small bribe paid for the information proving a worthwhile investment. He had questioned Rehan as best as he could and confirmed to James that Rehan had not deviated from his story. Nizam had spoken to Zakir's wife as well but was convinced that she was clueless. In Nizam's opinion, with Zakir dead, there was no way to verify whether or not Rehan's story was true. For what it was worth, it was his opinion that there was more than an 80 per cent chance that Rehan was indeed telling the truth. As far as James was concerned—and most of the art world would concur—that was good enough.

The bright sunshine reflected his happy mood as he ambled out of the underground and towards his office. He glanced through the mail on his desk—mainly catalogues of various auctions across the world—while his computer booted up. He entered his password and checked his email. While he waited for them to load, he disposed of the physical mail, marking appropriate instructions for his secretaries. He turned back towards his screen to begin responding to his emails.

His eyes crinkled with happiness as he saw the revert to his email inquiry about the paintings from his good friend Jonas, the head of the Roerich Museum in New York and the foremost expert on Roerich in the world. He clicked on it and began to read:

Dear James,
I thought of calling you, but decided it was better to reply formally, given what I have to say.

Firstly, I must apologize for the delay. I have been away from New York for my annual vacation (you know how cold it gets here in February!) and have had absolutely no access to emails till earlier this morning.

While I have no concrete proof, I do suspect that further inquiries need to be made before you proceed with the auction. I assume that you have verified that the paintings are indeed original, else you would have withdrawn them by now.

What truly concerns me is the chain of ownership. We have on record a couple of photos taken by two art grad students during their visit to India. They had come across these paintings, and to their credit, had had the presence of mind to snap the pictures. As per them, the paintings were displayed at the ICAR Centre in Kappar. I googled it and it turns out that ICAR stands for the Indian Council of Agricultural Research, which is a department under the Ministry of Agriculture of the Government of India. This centre is based in a hill town called Kappar. These pictures were clicked in 1994, so we know that the paintings were there till that date, at least.

I have very limited experience with the Indian government, so I am not sure whether they could have sold or given away these paintings. However, what is worrying is that I have never heard of them changing hands. At the risk of sounding immodest, as you well know, I do get to hear one way or another whenever a Roerich is moved. Of course, it is possible that the chain of ownership is entirely honest, but I would strongly urge you to make further inquiries.

I'm really sorry about the delayed response, especially with your auction being scheduled for the 10th. While I will try and make independent inquiries for you, our Indian representative has recently quit on us, so this may take me some time. I suggest that Sotheby's also reach out to the Indian government to ensure that there are no issues with the ownership at a later date.

I am attaching copies of the aforementioned photographs. I am also attaching the descriptions that we have on record for both paintings.

Please do pass on my regards to Janie and tell her I look forward to her meatloaf.

Warm regards,
Jonas

James's smile had turned into a frown as he read through this, recognizing that Jonas's email was, in the art world, the equivalent of an air raid siren in London at the peak of the Luftwaffe's carpet bombing. Though Jonas had categorically stated that he could not be sure, his email cast serious aspersions on the chain of ownership. There could be no question of proceeding further with the auction without making inquiries at the ICAR.

He replied to Jonas, thanking him, promising to see him the next time they were in the same city and committing to making further inquiries of the Indian government. He forwarded the email from Jonas to his chairman, adding a note reassuring him that he would do his due diligence.

He summoned a secretary and asked her to find the number for the ICAR Centre in Kappar, India. While he waited, he could not help but wonder if the paintings had been stolen—it happened more often than the art world liked to acknowledge, after all. The photographs from Jonas clearly showed the paintings on display and on the back of each photograph was written the date and the location. The students had no reason to lie. So the paintings were, in fact, on display at the ICAR. How then did they find their way out of there?

His computer beeped. The chairman had responded quickly, given the stakes, asking James to follow standard procedure, considering the information at hand. This meant that he wanted James to make reasonable inquiries of the Indian government and give them as much time as he could, until up to a week before the auction, to furnish any evidence of their claim to the paintings. With the auction scheduled for the tenth of March, this meant that James could give the government time only till the second of March, merely three days away, which was hardly adequate for a notoriously inefficient bureaucracy to produce results. Failing to acquire adequate evidence, Sotheby's could still go ahead with the sale after disclosing the information that had come into their possession—not that any buyer would be remotely deterred. Of course, if they did receive the evidence from the Indian government, he would have to withdraw the paintings from the auction till the matter was resolved.

His secretary returned with a printout which she handed to him. Glancing through the list, he was pleased that his secretaries had not only pulled out the contact details of the ICAR Centre at Kappar but also the contact numbers of the entire chain of command. He waved the secretary away, her shapely figure turning around smartly, hips swaying with each step as she walked out of the room.

James went through the list and wondered whom he should call. No one could accuse him of not doing his job if he called the centre itself and informed them. But if the Indian government was anything like their own, it was unlikely that he would get an answer from a local centre without approval from their headquarters. James had not risen to his position by doing what most others would. Given the short timeframe and the enormous value of the paintings, he decided to reach out straight to the top of the hierarchy, hoping that the person occupying that position would be far better placed to respond to the gravity of the situation.

He wondered whether he should inform Abbas but decided that any such intimation at this stage would be premature. For all James knew, the ICAR had never owned the paintings or had sold them or would not revert before the deadline, in which case there would be no reason to bother Ali. He would wait for India's revert before he decided what the next steps would be.

He had sent an email to Abbas in the morning, attaching descriptions of the paintings prepared by their creative department for inclusion in the catalogue, requesting Abbas's feedback on them. He had heard back within the hour—Abbas had approved the descriptions with a few minor changes for James's consideration. James had smiled at the use of language which suggested that he had an option, when he didn't. A few minutes later, his handheld rang, 'Unknown Number' flashing on the screen.

'Good morning, James. I wanted to congratulate you on the stellar work you have done. I'm glad that I brought this to Sotheby's,' said Abbas, getting straight to the point.

'It is our honour to conduct this auction, Mr Ali. We will, of course, incorporate your suggestions and send back the final descriptions for your approval,' replied James.

'Don't embarrass me, James. You are the expert. Please go ahead as you deem appropriate. Shall we discuss the base price?'

'Certainly, Mr Ali,' he replied calmly, despite his excitement at discussing what mattered most to Sotheby's and to James, personally. 'We have discussed this internally and we believe that a base price of 10 million pounds each would be appropriate.

That would encourage more bidders to participate, which should be the case for a discovery of this nature. Of course, the more the bidders, the higher the final price will be.'

There was silence as Abbas digested James's suggestion. Even if the paintings sold at the suggested base price, the 20 million pounds would be higher than what his masters had demanded. But he had protected the knowledge of these paintings for a lifetime now and was keen to maximize their value. A few moments later, he spoke, 'James, your logic is sound, but I think it undervalues the paintings. No Roerich painting has been available in the last two decades and it is unlikely that another will appear within our lifetime. You and I both know that there are scores of buyers out there looking for a Roerich for years and would pay well for one. We don't need more bidders. On the contrary, we only need those who really want these paintings to participate. Get those twelve or fifteen people into one room and you will discover the real price. I have already had some informal conversations and there is a lot of excitement about them. We need to go higher, to at least 20 million apiece.'

'That's too high,' said James, regretting his lack of finesse immediately. 'I'm sorry, Mr Ali. I didn't mean that. I only meant that it is our opinion that an amount of that nature may discourage several serious bidders as well. Of course, these are your paintings, and it is ultimately your decision,' James carried on, trying to recover from his impertinence.

Abbas thought again about what James had said—he was the expert after all—before making a final decision. He had not got this far by playing it safe and he wasn't going to play safe now, especially with these paintings. 'Thank you, James. I appreciate your opinion but I think we will stick with 20 million each for these.'

'As you wish, Mr Ali,' replied James. 'That only leaves the matter of whether we can expect to receive our standard 2 per cent from this auction.'

Abbas smiled at James's attempt at nonchalance about what mattered most to him personally and professionally. 'I think not, James. Given the value, I think 1 per cent is more than fair.' As James began to protest, Abbas spoke again, cutting him off. 'I am not negotiating. I am telling you what I am willing to offer, given our long-standing relationship. If Sotheby's is not happy with it, I will take them elsewhere. Of course, the decision is yours,' said Abbas, mimicking the words that James had uttered only a few seconds ago.

'I understand, Mr Ali. Unfortunately, I am not authorized to accept a reduced fee but I will pass on your message to the chairman.'

'You do that, James. If I don't receive a contract from you by end of day, I will assume that Sotheby's is not interested.' His ultimatum issued, Abbas disconnected the call.

'We have no choice,' thought James, quickly typing out a text message to the chairman to seek his approval, which he received a few seconds later. He asked his secretary to call the head of the legal department and issued instructions for the necessary paperwork to be drawn up and sent to Abbas Ali. Lastly, he forwarded the email from Abbas to his creative department, instructing them to incorporate all the suggestions into the final write-up for the catalogue.

As he took a moment's break, he wondered whether these paintings could break the 100-million-pound barrier that had been broken by so few paintings before.

# Chapter 25

20 August 1948
District Collector's Residence, Kappar
8.20 p.m.

The dinner was in full flow. The police band sat on one side, decked in full regalia, their instruments rendering credible versions of Western classical tunes. The guests talked over the band, their chatter flowing out into the thin night air of Kappar.

The entire bourgeoisie of Kappar had shown up—an invitation from the all-powerful district collector and the lure of rubbing shoulders with Hindi movie royalty had ensured full attendance. As Rajesh looked around, he smirked at how the people had distributed themselves into groups—the men standing near the bar and the women huddling around a set of *sigris*. The hierarchy of power was evident in each of the smaller groups, one or the other senior representative of the bureaucracy held centre stage, surrounded by a retinue of hangers-on relying on the largesse of the government representative to advance their own businesses or administrative careers.

Rajesh was already bored of the mundane conversations all around. He was also getting increasingly frustrated at the late arrival of Devika and Shiva, who were the central attractions of the dinner. He was leaning against a pillar, listening to Vivekananda Raju, the director of the ICAR, droning on about the latest advancements in seed research, his eyes glued to the main gate in waiting for the impending arrival of his star guests.

He finally smiled when he saw Svetoslav Roerich walking up to him. 'Good evening, Mr District Collector,' said Roerich in a voice made husky by smoking, a cigarette inevitably dangling from his lips.

'Good evening, Svet,' replied Rajesh. 'Glad to see you haven't finished all my liquor yet.'

'I only just got here, Your Excellency,' smirked Roerich. 'Bear with me a little!'

The men shook hands and hugged effusively. Roerich then turned to Vivekananda Raju to give him a warm handshake and a hug as well. As the men sipped their drinks and chatted, Rajesh heard a motor car drive up to the house.

Thinking—correctly—that it must be the guests from Bombay, he signalled to Vishaka to join him, the two of them heading out to welcome the film stars.

Devika and Shiva walked in, their entourage surrounding them. Intimidating bodyguards, clad in black uniforms, carved a path for them through the admiring crowd and made their way towards the centre of the assembly, where the hosts were waiting. The entourage stopped once they reached Rajesh and Vishaka—the hosts were surrounded by their own entourage, their status made obvious by the humility of the guests around them.

Rajesh stepped forward to introduce himself and the bodyguards parted to allow him access to Devika, Shiva and

Asif. Instinctively, he reached out to Shiva, the most imposing of the group, to shake his hand firmly as he introduced himself and then Vishaka. Shiva turned to Asif and then to Devika, introducing each of them by turns. Vishaka, starstruck, laughed nervously as she was introduced, finding it hard, despite her station, to believe that she was not only standing in the presence of movie royalty but actually having a conversation with them. With nervous energy flowing through her, Vishaka walked over to Devika and guided her gently by the arm to the corner table reserved for them, the men following.

Once seated, the liveried bartender—requisitioned for the evening from the city's only notable hotel—appeared at Rajesh's side. Walking around the table, starting with Rajesh and finishing with Vishaka, he took everyone's orders before disappearing behind the bar to prepare their drinks. While they waited, uniformed waiters, their spotless white gloves contrasting splendidly with their red uniforms, began to appear, bearing plates of *hors d'oeuvres*, each carefully selected by Vishaka in honour of their esteemed guests. The head waiter announced each dish as it was presented while the waiters waited to serve the food till after its introduction was complete.

The conversation stuttered forward between the strangers. Vishaka was a pale self-conscious shadow of her generally exuberant self, barely managing to keep a conversation going and just about managing to keep at bay the giggling schoolgirl who threatened to ooze out of her every now and again. Rajesh had no interest in movies and had organized this evening mostly for Vishaka's benefit. The stars from Bombay were unfailingly polite but had no real interest in striking a friendship or making any more effort than was required to get through the evening.

Thinking that Vishaka would be far more comfortable in the company of just Devika, Rajesh asked Asif and Shiva to join him as the three gentlemen excused themselves from the head table and walked towards the bar. The crowds parted, aware that they would need to be invited into this group and could not risk intruding.

After the men had claimed a bar stool each, Rajesh ordered a fresh round of drinks. He pulled out his cigarette case and offered it to both guests. A waiter emerged, bearing a lighter and puffs of smoke billowed into the air as the three men lit up and took their first drags with deep satisfaction.

The three chatted politely, coming to an informal agreement on what the movie unit needed from the district administration and likewise, what the administration expected from them. While the written permissions would only follow later, Rajesh, keen as always to ensure that everything was in place, listened with professional interest, interjecting occasionally with questions and ensuring that his guests were clear on the rules they were required to abide by.

As they concluded their discussion, Rajesh was bemused to see Roerich strolling up to them—undoubtedly the only man present there on that evening who had the courage to break into that closed circle without invitation. Catching his eye, Rajesh invited him to join, introducing him to Shiva and Asif.

Roerich was at his charming best, narrating stories about the Himalayas and the Himalayan people, interspersed with hilarious anecdotes about the foibles of the Kappar elite, taking care to disguise their names even while providing a clear idea of the type of person he was referring to. The men were glued to every word, laughing loudly at the narrations, seeing the parallels between the elite of their own world and the rich of Kappar.

Thus the ice was broken by the chain-smoking Roerich, who was, inevitably, invited to join the high table at which Devika and Vishaka sat chatting. Accepting the invitation, Roerich signalled for another round of drinks as the group stubbed out their cigarettes and returned to the waiting ladies.

Roerich beamed as he was introduced to Devika and took the seat next to her. He was mesmerized by her beauty—he had, of course, expected that the grainy picture would not have done her justice, but even his gifted mind had fallen well short of being able to imagine all the subtle nuances of her beauty.

Despite his awe, he maintained his composure, using his artistic insight to make meaningful contributions to the discussions around the shoot, suggesting angles and ways of using natural light and shade to create imagery that would leave the audience inspired. As he spoke, the table listened, recognizing the genius in his words. The group continued to discuss and debate as only passionate experts can, exploring the myriad ways of bringing alive Kappar for the Indian audience, most of whom would never visit the pretty hill station.

As the conversation progressed, Devika became increasingly drawn to Roerich, so confident of his abilities that he was not afraid to discuss movie production with three of India's leading experts in the field; so sound in his knowledge that they found it difficult not to consider his ideas seriously. His charm was infectious and it enveloped the entire table.

Rajesh and Vishaka, having little to contribute to the niche topic, excused themselves to attend to their other guests and ask for dinner to be served. Shiva and Asif used the opportunity to excuse themselves to use the facilities, leaving Svetoslav and Devika alone for a few minutes.

Devika, keen to know Svetoslav better, took the lead. 'How do you know so much about shooting a film?'

Svetoslav laughed. 'I know absolutely nothing about shooting films, Devika. But at its core, a film is just visual art in motion, a series of images ordered in a way that strikes a chord with the people who watch it. That is no different from my art—of course, I get to show only one still image to convey my message.'

'The things you have said today—you have a god-given gift for direction. Have you ever thought about joining our industry?'

'Thank you, that is very kind of you, but I am very happy in Kappar, doing what I do. Painting is essential to who I am—I wouldn't compromise on that in any way for anything at all. In fact, to be completely honest, I haven't seen a movie in years.'

'Not even mine?' she asked flirtatiously.

'Not yet, but now that I have had the opportunity to meet you, I intend to watch them all.' Looking straight into her eyes, he continued, 'I'm sure you are as wonderful an actor as you are beautiful.'

Devika blushed at the forward compliment. Before she could respond, Asif and Shiva had returned and the four of them resumed the previous conversation, diving deeper into artistic interpretation for cinematic films, their throats lubricated by the ever-vigilant bartender, who promptly replenished everyone's drinks as soon as their glasses were empty.

Rajesh and Vishaka returned to join the group for dinner and the conversation moved on to nation-building, on which everyone in newly independent India had a view.

Dessert was brought out immediately after dinner. Protesting vociferously against this further assault on their already distended stomachs, the six of them nevertheless cleaned their plates, firmly declining seconds. Coffee was offered but was declined by everyone, given the lateness of the hour.

That marked the end of the evening. The district collector, his wife and Kappar's foremost artist escorted the guests from

Bombay back to their cars. Devika and Roerich hung back a little, not really saying anything to each other, but walking side by side in electric silence, each keen to know a lot more about the other, but unsure of the appropriateness of asking for the other's time to do so.

Having arrived at the two waiting vehicles with their engines idling, the film icons thanked their hosts for a wonderful evening. Roerich stooped to open the door for Devika, holding her hand as he helped her into the car. He held it open a moment longer while signalling to someone who came and handed him a package. He opened the front passenger door and gently placed the large package, covered in brown paper, on the seat.

'What is that, Svetoslav?' Devika asked.

'A small gift. If you like it, I do hope to have the opportunity to make up for this plebeian effort while you are in Kappar.' Smiling, he stepped back from the car and the vehicles exited the district collector's compound as the hosts and the artist waved goodbye.

'Thank you for a wonderful evening,' said Roerich. 'I do hope you will organize at least one more dinner, perhaps a smaller one, before our guests from Bombay leave.'

'Stay over, Svet,' said Vishaka. 'It is too late to walk back now.'

'You are very kind, but I must get back tonight. If I could borrow one of your guards, I too would like to take your leave'.

'Of course,' spoke Rajesh. 'Ram Singh, please take Vipin and escort Mr Roerich home. Goodnight, Svetoslav, and thank you for entertaining our guests tonight.'

The friends parted. Rajesh and Vishaka headed back into their mansion while Roerich, Ram Singh and Vipin began the long walk back to Sommerville House; Roerich whistling all the way.

# Chapter 26

26 February 2010
New Delhi
12.30 p.m.

The CI was in his armoured car, heading to the National Security Council (NSC) meeting called at his behest. He had seen the coded message from Abdul last evening, and had been racking his brains ever since on how the money could possibly be coming from an artist in London.

After reading the message, he updated his team on this latest intelligence from Pakistan and tasked them with unearthing the source of the money. Experts on the ISI were also called up and asked to pore over their records that evening itself to discover the missing link. The CI had then personally called the heads of the other intelligence departments and briefed them, instructing them to initiate inquiries within their set-ups. The entire intelligence community had been woken up to deal with the threat and asked to activate their networks across the world for any information that could lead them to the source of the funds.

The CI had also called up the national security advisers of the five other countries on the Jaish's radar and explained the urgency of the situation, asking them to provide any leads on the ISI's sources of funding in London if they wanted to stop the imminent nuclear attacks on their cities. He was frustrated as no agency had so far been able to provide a link between an artist in London and the ISI or Jaish. With the attack planned for 6 April, there was very little time for them to act. Considering the way the Jaish operated, the sleeper cells in the six countries would be under the vigil of dozens of people across the world, with layers between these actual decision makers and the terrorists that would actually conduct the strikes, and no one other than the Jaish leadership would know who the members of the sleeper cells were. Sure, they may find one or two, but unless they could find a way to stop the funding, the catastrophic attacks would certainly follow.

The CI entered the anteroom of the prime minister's office, the customary venue for the meetings of the NSC. The NSC had been created on the recommendation of the Parsheera Committee, set up in the wake of the attack on the Parliament. The committee had identified that fragmented intelligence about the planned attacks had been available to the R&AW and Military Intelligence, but India had failed to prevent the attacks due to grave lapses in coordination between the agencies. The NSC—consisting of the prime minister, home minister, defence minister, cabinet secretary, the CI, the heads of the intelligence services and the chiefs of the armed forces—was therefore set up to protect India's internal and external security by ensuring coordination between the intelligence services.

Since its formation, India's security had tightened considerably. While isolated attacks had still occurred, they had been limited to small attacks on the armed forces, generally repelled with minimal damage. Civilian casualties from terrorist attacks were down to their lowest numbers in Indian history, a remarkable achievement, given that the efforts from across the border had never been greater. Even as the government was lambasted by the media for the attacks that did occur, it remained silent about the attacks that it had prevented, for if the Indian people ever learnt of the threat that they lived under each day, they would find it hard to leave their homes.

Having already briefed the chiefs of the intelligence services, the CI now briefed the rest of the NSC, highlighting the expected casualties numbering in lakhs and the dent that would put in the people's confidence in the government. The enormity of the threat was not lost on the political establishment, and unsurprisingly, it was the prime minister who spoke first.

'Do whatever it takes, Amitabh. All of you. This attack must not take place. The resources of India are at your disposal. The country's future depends on us putting a stop to this. We are counting on you.'

'Thank you, prime minister. I would like to ask all of you to do what the chiefs of intelligence are already doing. Reach out to your contacts, shake every tree, look under every rock and detain anyone you need to. Focus first on finding the source of this funding, then on finding the seller of the bombs and only then on finding the sleeper cells, if you can.'

'All offices will work 24*7 till we find the artist in London. All chiefs will report to me and I will keep the PM informed. Nothing is too small to discuss, nor too unrealistic to ask for. Let's get this done.'

The group nodded. The prime minister dismissed the meeting—the biggest intelligence operation in the country had just been flagged off.

# Chapter 27

21 August 1948
Kappar
5 p.m.

The shoot had started early that morning. The movie's climax showed Shiva's character following Devika to Kappar, with the final scene showing the two grappling with each other at the edge of a picturesque waterfall, before tumbling to their deaths.

The day was spent shooting surround content around Kappar, ensuring that the leads were in enough shots for the editors to be able to create the impression that large parts of the film had been shot there, even though nearly the entire movie would be shot in Bombay. Asif had driven the unit hard, working with the writers to envisage the shots that might be required later and ensuring that Shiva and Devika delivered a series of different expressions in each of those shots.

Devika had been preoccupied the entire day and had to reshoot several scenes far more times than her average. She had returned to her room, tired after dinner on the previous evening, and then gone straight to her dressing room to freshen up and change. As she had washed her face with the face cleanser imported specially from England, she had recollected the events of the evening, the charming Russian coming sharply into focus.

She had definitely been charmed—given her experience with the hundreds of men that regularly tried to weasel their way into her heart, she had recognized that what she had felt this time, was different. She thought about what it was about him that she found attractive—certainly not his looks, which were, at best, average. It was his humour, she had thought, which had allowed for such vibrant conversation. It was also his confidence; the confidence of a man at peace with himself, not requiring the approval of the rest of the world. Those qualities were hard to find and certainly called for further investigation.

What was it that he had said as she was leaving? Something about the gift he had given her . . . The gift! Where was that package he had so gently placed in the front seat?

She had slid out of her chair, passing through the delicate lace curtains that separated her dressing room from her bedroom and opened the door that led to her sitting room with the intention to ask her attendant to fetch the package. She swallowed the instruction as she entered the sitting room—the package had been resting comfortably on the floor, propped up against the sofa, still in its brown packaging held together with red twine.

Taking a seat in the middle of the sofa, she had picked up the package gingerly and propped it against the armrest. She had gently undone the twine and removed the packaging, eager to see what lay underneath.

Her eyes had widened in incredulity as the painting had been revealed. She had been the subject of many portraits, but no one had captured her essence quite like Roerich had. She had felt as if she was looking into a mirror, one that ripped away all pretence and bared the reality of the person looking into it, exposing their desires and insecurities. She had scrutinized every inch of the portrait, mesmerized by the detail. He had got almost every angle, every crevasse and every shade right—the very things that make each person unique. She had recognized the traits that were only known to her—the boredom in her smile, the impatience in her eyes and the annoyance in the tilt of her head.

Questions had poured forth from her subconscious, clambering over each other for her attention. How was this possible when he had never met her until that evening? How could he possibly have captured her subtleties without having known her? Who had he spoken to? Where had he seen her? When had he painted this?

She had no answers—the only person who could give her the answers she wanted was Roerich. She had to meet him again.

Now, while she waited for her next shot, she thought back to the things she had done earlier that morning. She had written a thank you note for Svetoslav on her personal stationery, trying, as best as she could, to express her appreciation for his art. She had asked her attendant to deliver it by hand to Sommerville House, which she had discovered was his home. She had also been direct—maybe even brazen—in requesting Roerich to join her for dinner tonight if he was free. Her attendant had returned during her second set of shoots to confirm that Roerich had accepted her invitation and would join her for dinner at 7 p.m.

Her excitement at the prospect of meeting him again had kept her distracted today and the resulting retakes were now causing her to run late. Eager to not keep Roerich waiting, Devika requested Asif to call it a day, promising to make up for lost time tomorrow. While Asif wasn't particularly keen, with the light fading, he decided to heed her request, dismissing the entire unit with instructions to reassemble at 8 the following morning.

Devika and her attendant rushed to her car and left immediately, ignoring the daily debriefing. Devika, a little guilty at this digression from routine, already had her script with her and knew which scenes from today would need to be reshot and the new scenes that were planned for tomorrow. She knew that she needed to meet Roerich first if she wanted to be able to deliver her scenes properly tomorrow. It was, in a way—she told her guilty conscience—in the interests of the entire unit that she left early.

She arrived at her hotel a few minutes later and not even waiting for the doorman to open her door, she pushed it open and leapt out, propelled by her excitement and deaf to the doorman's greeting. She ran up the stairs to the lobby and straight to her suite, which was located strategically at the back of the property, cut off from the rest of the hotel, with a magnificent view of the valley.

She entered her suite and called her staff to attention, issuing instructions to prepare for the dinner with Roerich. The attendants scurried out of the suite, returning with various members of the hotel staff, who stood before her, notepads open to take down her instructions. Starting with the chef, who needed the longest time to prepare, she designed a menu that not only ensured they would spend a fair amount of time enjoying the meal but also guaranteed privacy, requiring minimal service from the staff. She ordered three bottles of wine, one for each course, and asked for a bottle of whisky and a bottle of vodka to be arranged for her guest. Food and beverages organized, she then turned to the head of housekeeping, asking him to follow her into the balcony.

She picked out the area where she wanted the table to be organized, positioning the chairs such that they would both be able to enjoy the view and also look at each other without having to turn around. She asked for a tall candlestand to be placed on their table and smaller candles for the area where the food would be left for her to serve. A table would be used as a makeshift bar, housing the correct glasses, ice, soda, water and tongs.

She finally turned to the general manager. Explaining her need for complete privacy, she asked for the food and liquor to be laid out in advance and for the staff to be instructed to stay away unless they were called. As her last instruction, Devika asked him to personally escort her guest to her suite. Nodding, the general manager left to ensure that the evening went off impeccably.

Devika, buzzing with eagerness, looked up at the clock, her face showing panic at the realization that it was already 6 p.m.— she had less than an hour to get ready for the dinner that she was looking forward to, something she hadn't experienced in years. Her attendant had already begun assembling her outfit as per their discussion in the car. Devika had decided, after much deliberation, to wear her black pleated skirt and blue chamois silk top, matching it with the violet shrug gifted to her by Lady Mounten and the diamond earrings from Jamshedji Tata. Deciding on the footwear had taken considerably longer as she had travelled light to Kappar—of the three pairs available to her, they agreed that even though it was far from ideal, she had no choice but to repeat the pair that she had worn to the district collector's dinner.

Taking a calming breath as she slid into the lavender-scented bath that had been drawn for her, she allowed the warm water to melt away the stress from her body. After drying off and wrapping the thick hotel towel around her, she sat before the dressing-room mirror, thinking about her make-up, deciding that anything more than *kajal* and a light lipstick would feel jarring against her ensemble. Her practised hands applied the simple make-up and she got dressed, admiring herself in the mirror—she knew, like most beautiful women do, that she was beautiful, and saw it as a gift from god. Yet, even she was taken aback by the glowing woman smiling back at her, her excitement shining sensually. She asked her attendant to comb her luxuriant hair, deciding eventually to wear it open, flowing down her back. Finally, she put on her earrings, slipped her feet into her shoes and pirouetted in front of the mirror to take one final look from every angle. Her attendant's satisfied nod confirmed her own assessment. She was ready for the evening.

Gliding out into the balcony, she nodded appreciatively at everything having been readied as per her instructions. A bottle of red wine had already been uncorked by the well-trained hotel staff, giving it enough time to breathe before the guest arrived. Devika poured herself a glass, lit a cigarette and sat in the chair she had chosen for herself. With a little time to spare, she began organizing her thoughts. Given how she felt, there was a lot she wanted to learn about her dinner companion, but it would be remiss of her to ask those questions in an uncouth, direct manner. She would need to steer the conversation in a way that would allow him to tell his story at his pace.

# Chapter 28

27 February 2010
Delhi
3.30 p.m.

Kamal looked up in exasperation from the file he was reading, at the annoying intercom that was beeping persistently.

'Yes, Sandeep?' he asked his secretary, answering the intercom, his irritation evident from his tone.

'Sorry to disturb you, Sir. There is a call from London coming for the fourth time. They say it is very important.'

'Who is it?'

'Sir, I am not sure. It is James from a company called Sotby.'

'Sotheby's! What do they have to do with the ICAR?'

'I don't know, Sir. He is saying something about paintings.'

'Tell him I am in a meeting and ask him to write to us formally,' said Kamal, putting the intercom down.

The high-backed leather chair creaked in protest as Kamal leaned his considerable bulk on it. He looked around the dank office allotted to him as Secretary of the ICAR, Ministry of Agriculture.

His eyes were drawn to the steel cupboards, overflowing with files in their mouldy cardboard covers and fading red laces that once promised so much, but now lay there neglected by a creaking bureaucracy. He smiled to himself at having noticed how this image reflected his own reality—a once-blossoming career, ruthlessly stalled by a vindictive ruling party that begrudged his work for the previous leadership and transferred him to this dead outpost. He wondered again at the injustice of a decision that punished him for simply doing his job, despite his twenty-five years of honest hard work, notwithstanding the credit that the previous government received for the implementation of those policies.

Shaking his head and sighing deeply, he clicked his mouse and brought the computer screen to life. The screen glowed brightly as he put on his glasses and peered into it to check his official email. Amongst the useless forwards from various bureaucratic groups, his attention was drawn to one email with the subject line 'Sotheby's: Your Cooperation'. He clicked it open and began reading.

Dear Mr Maheshwari,

Good afternoon.

I tried reaching your office several times earlier today, but was informed that you were held up in meetings. Your secretary asked me to reach you via email if the matter was urgent. The matter is indeed of utmost urgency and I do hope to hear from you today.

As you may know, Sotheby's is one of the world's most reputed auction houses, specializing in paintings, fine art, antiques and jewellery. Our headquarters are in New York and our operations span several countries.

Our reputation is built on our willingness and ability to verify the authenticity and ownership of the articles that we auction.

On 15 February 2010, we were approached to include two paintings by the legendary artist Svetoslav Roerich, in our auction scheduled for 10 March 2010 in London. These paintings are known as 'Silent Night' and 'Valley of Flowers'—pictures of both along with descriptions are attached herewith.

Once we had verified their genuineness, we conducted a provenance check, which included a reference from the Roerich Museum in New York, the leading authority on the artist. We have finally heard back from them today, which brings me to why I have been trying to reach you.

According to the museum's experts, photographs available with them show both paintings on display at the ICAR Centre in Kappar, at least until 1994. The museum and indeed, the rest of the art world, have no further information about the fate of these paintings after 1994, but based on the attached photographs, it does appear that the paintings were previously in the ICAR's possession.

Could you please confirm whether the paintings were indeed owned by the ICAR and whether they have subsequently been transferred to someone else? If that is the case, may we please also request your support with all details relating to the transaction that are available with you to help us track the ownership chain?

Please note that the paintings have already been included in the auction on 10 March 2010 at a base price of 20 million pounds each. Unless we receive proof of the ICAR's continued claim over these paintings before 3

March, we will continue with their auction after providing the necessary disclosures required under applicable law. We look forward to hearing from you.

Regards,
James Mitchell
Head – Department of Art
Sotheby's, London

Kamal sat back shocked, his legs shaking vigorously as they always did when he was thinking deeply. A base price of 20 million pounds was over 200 crore rupees! For both paintings, that meant that the ICAR—if it was indeed the owner—stood to lose at least 400 crore rupees, considerably more than the department's annual budget! He pulled open the top drawer of his desk and rummaged amongst his personal papers for his cigar and matchbox. Lighting himself a cigar—the one luxury that he, a father of three college-going boys, permitted himself despite his limited budget—he sighed in pleasure as the first mouthful of the fragrant, heavy smoke swirled around his tongue.

He could just ignore the email for now and respond a few days later when it was too late—it would shock no one that the Indian bureaucracy had lived up to its infamous standards. That would teach these nasty politicians a lesson as well, busy as they were in lining their own pockets while sidelining honest men like him who made cheating taxpayers inconvenient. The rebellious thought brought a smile to his face, which vanished as the next thought asserted itself firmly that in spite of everything, he was not the kind of man who would allow his personal frustrations to get in the way of his duty.

'I have no choice,' he said out loud to himself. Ignoring the ashtray, he stubbed the cigar in a dustbin already stained with burn marks and buzzed for his secretary.

'Yes, Sir,' said Sandeep, as he walked into his boss's room with the standard-issue notepad and ballpoint pen.

'Have you read the email?' asked Kamal, adopting the tone that he reserved for underlings in the bureaucracy.

'Yes, Sir.'

'This is a very serious matter. You are not to talk about this to anyone else. Is that clear?'

'Yes, Sir. Absolutely, Sir,' he replied, swallowing nervously and looking down at his feet.

Fifty years old and the third-most powerful man in the department as the doorkeeper to the Secretary, Sandeep was always immeasurably frightened of his current boss, feeling, as he always did, like a little boy who had been called into the headmaster's office.

'Good. How long have you been at ICAR?'

'Almost ten years, sir.'

'How do we verify if these paintings are ours?'

Sandeep paused for a moment, ordering his thoughts, before replying. 'Sir, each centre has to maintain a register of all assets. This is updated when a new asset comes or an existing asset is taken out of the centre. We will have to check the register at Kappar, Sir, to see about these paintings.'

'Such expensive paintings—would such an expenditure not have to be approved by us?'

'Not necessarily, Sir. Each centre has an annual discretionary budget. They can spend as they like but have to comply with procedures of recording expenditure.'

'Such as recording assets purchased in their register?'

'Yes, Sir.'

'And if there is no record in the register or if they have not maintained a register?'

'Not possible, Sir. The centres are audited annually. Auditors would have reported if there was no register or if any asset in the centre was not listed in it or if an asset mentioned in there was no longer at the centre.'

'Have they made any such report?'

'No, Sir. Such reports lead to departmental inquiries. There is no inquiry pending against Kappar. I will check records, but I am sure there is no such report.'

Kamal got up and relit his cigar. Based on what Sandeep was telling him, unless the auditors were in cahoots with the officials at Kappar, every asset, including the paintings, would be listed in that register. It was unlikely that the auditor would file a false report—the risk of being blacklisted aside, he would almost certainly go to jail on very stiff criminal charges, if discovered. But if the paintings were worth 400 crore, perhaps the auditor had decided that his share of the take was worth the risk. Deciding that the auditor's role was secondary, he first decided to find out whether the paintings were indeed listed in the asset register.

If they were, then they should either still be hanging in Kappar or there should be documents showing what happened to them. In either event, it should be easy enough to establish whether the ICAR still owned them. If they were not in the register, then given the mail from Sotheby's, a far deeper inquiry would be required because then either ICAR didn't own them—in which case, why were they hanging at the centre?—or if ICAR did own them, why were they not listed in the register? Was it because the auditor was involved? Had there been an oversight? Was something more sinister at play? Or could it be . . .

'Would a gift to the ICAR also be recorded?'

'Yes, Sir. Every asset has to be recorded.'

However he looked at it, the first step was to take a look at the register. 'Check the records and tell me in ten minutes if there is an inquiry pending against Kappar.'

'Yes, Sir,' said Sandeep, leaving the room and shutting the door softly behind him, leaving Kamal alone in his office.

While Kamal waited, he composed a reply to Sotheby's, using, like most of his generation, just his index fingers to type.

Dear James,

Thank you for your email and for bringing this to our attention. We do not have an answer to your queries at the moment, but given the urgency, we have initiated an inquiry and will get back to you as soon as we can.

However, based on the pictures you have provided, we agree that it prima facie appears that the paintings were indeed owned by the ICAR. Accordingly, we take this opportunity to assert the claim of the Government of India over the paintings and request you not to auction them.

Yours sincerely,
Kamal Maheshwari
Secretary, ICAR

Kamal, legs shaking rapidly, read the email again, wondering if there was anything else he needed to add. There was a soft knock on his door.

'Come in.'

Sandeep walked in with a file under his arm and stood by the desk.

'Don't just stand there. What did you find?'

'Nothing, Sir. There is no inquiry. I have seen the auditor's reports till 2009 and there is no mention.'

'What about 2010?'

'Sir, the audit happens in April and the report is submitted in early May. The 2010 report will come then.'

Kamal nodded. 'How long will it take to bring the register from Kappar to Delhi?'

'The assets register, Sir?'

'No! The register of births in Kappar,' snapped Kamal at the stupidity of the question. 'Of course, the assets register! To be clear, I need the assets register from the ICAR centre in Kappar, here in Delhi. How long will that take?'

'Three months, Sir,' stammered Sandeep, shivering slightly after the outburst from Kamal.

'Three months!? We don't need to walk from Kappar! It can be flown here this evening itself! Why would it take three months?'

'Sir,' said Sandeep, his voice quivering, 'As per rules, to take the register from the centre, we need permission from the Board of Administration of the ICAR. The board meeting is in three months—it is on your calendar.'

'What a stupid rule! We don't have ninety days. Tell me a faster way.'

'We will have to go to Kappar, Sir.'

# Chapter 29

21 August 1948
Kappar
7.05 p.m.

Devika's thoughts were interrupted by her attendant, who excitedly informed her that her guest had arrived and was being escorted to her room by the general manager. Devika felt her heart beat a little faster and her face flush with excitement. Her attendant left to welcome Roerich at the door, while Devika, unsure of where she should be positioned when he walked into the balcony, looked around frantically, imagining the various places she could stand and how each would play out. Eventually, she decided to simply time her entrance into the suite for it to coincide with Roerich's walk towards the balcony.

She walked back into the room when she heard the attendant return, and held her hands out to greet her guest. Each took in the other, noticing the effort they had made to dress and groom. Roerich smiled widely, his delight apparent at seeing the world's most beautiful woman again. He held her extended hands with his long, slender fingers, and pecked her on both cheeks in a traditional Russian greeting. Her heart fluttered again as she felt his touch, and she blushed despite her best efforts to conceal her excitement. Roerich had a wonderful scent, somehow both manly and gentle at the same time. The greeting complete, he stepped back and waited for Devika to take the lead.

She dismissed her attendant and asked Roerich to follow her into the balcony. Both of them walked out, Devika taking her seat and Roerich sliding into the other.

'Thank you for this invitation,' said Roerich, once again smiling widely, wearing his interest in Devika on his face.

'What choice did you leave me after that magnificent gift?' replied Devika flirtatiously. 'I have been painted dozens of times, and yet, a man who has never met me does a better job than all of the others put together. Having dinner with you seemed like the very least I could do. What did you even base the painting on?'

Roerich explained that a picture had caught his eye and he decided to paint the portrait and give it to her. 'Thank god you liked it. I am not very good at anything else and my confidence as an artist would have been severely shaken if you didn't like this first effort,' said Roerich, laughing.

'First effort?' asked Devika. 'Are you going to paint another?'

'Only if you permit it. Now that I have met you, I know this portrait doesn't do you justice. It doesn't bring out the person you have hidden underneath this charming exterior. I want to bring out the real you, but I can only do that if you agree to model for me.'

Devika knew, instinctively, that she was going to accept, since it would give her more time with this man. But his words had piqued her curiosity—he was hinting at a truth about her that only the people closest to her knew. And that too, after having met her only once before. If Roerich had actually been able to see through her, then she needed to get to know him even better. 'I think I would like that, but let me think about it and see if I can find the time,' she replied. 'For now, may I offer you a drink?'

As they sipped their drinks, both delved deeper, trying to get to know the other better. Their first instincts about each other had been correct. They were two souls, born on different continents, brought up worlds apart and pursuing different career paths, and yet they had more in common than members of most families do. As the evening progressed, Devika forgot all strategy and asked— even shamelessly pried—into every aspect of Svetoslav's life.

Dinner was left untouched as the conversation flowed. The spell was finally broken when Devika's attendant discreetly coughed at the balcony's door, utilizing the pretence of getting the food heated to remind her that she had an early start tomorrow. Both Devika and Roerich recognized that it was time to bring the evening to a close and while neither was thrilled about it, they both already knew that they would be seeing each other again—there would be time to continue the conversation from where they were leaving off today.

More out of politeness than hunger, they ate a little of the cold food, finding no joy in the meal that had been so carefully thought through by Devika and meticulously prepared by the chef. Declining Devika's offer for a nightcap, Roerich thanked her for a wonderful evening and took her leave.

'I do hope that you will find the time. But, more than that, I hope that we can meet again soon. I imagine your schedule is packed, so I will wait to hear from you.'

'Thank you, Svetoslav. I cannot remember the last time I enjoyed a conversation as much as today. I do have a couple of busy days, but I promise you that we shall meet again soon.'

Devika pecked him gently on both cheeks and walked him to the suite door, where the attendant waited to escort him. Roerich, bowing deeply, thanked both of them again, insisted that he would find his way out of the hotel himself, and left, his long strides echoing against the walls of the now sleeping hotel.

Devika, feeling light with happiness, changed and got into bed. The only way for her to spend a lot more time with Roerich was to finish her scenes at the earliest. She would need to confess to Asif to get him to move the shoot schedule around, and also to Shiva, who would need to work harder for the next few days to finish all the shots in which they featured together. She knew that they would both pretend to vociferously protest, but would eventually accommodate her request. They respected each other enough to know that no such request would be made without extremely good reason. With that final thought, Devika sank deeper into her mattress and wrapped the duvet tightly around her. She dreamt the whole night, smiling, after years, through the night.

# Chapter 30

4 March 2008
London
12.30 p.m.

The mole had come a long way from his humble origins in Uttar Pradesh, his understanding with the CIA, and, in no small measure, his ability and perseverance, paving the way for his ascension through the ranks of Indian intelligence.

Following the assassination in Bangladesh as he had planned it, he submitted the report that he had meticulously authored, with inputs from the CIA, in anticipation of their success. The report left no doubt that the plan had been hatched by Pakistan as a final token of their unending hatred for the leader who had cost them an entire country, and was accepted as the truth by the Indian establishment—their own hatred for their neighbour making it easy for them to accept their ruthlessness. No one had suspected that he could have had a hand to play in the ordeal and he remained a firm friend of Bangladesh's.

His outstanding work in Bangladesh earned him a promotion to the Soviet desk at R&AW. There, he was chosen to be part of the delegation to the Soviet Union in 1976, purportedly to help negotiate the arms purchase agreement with the Soviet Defence Ministry. The events that followed had shocked the world but came as no surprise to him, the former prime minister's choices having made him some very powerful enemies, including the CIA. Already an Indian hero, albeit an unknown one, he was never a serious suspect so the inquiries that followed the death of the prime minister exonerated him, as expected. His career continued to flourish, as he worked to further Indian interests— at least till they turned out to be in conflict with those of his paymasters in Washington.

While the world would never know it, he was responsible for some of India's greatest strategic wins—in Fiji, where local Indians were being persecuted by their nationalist prime minister Sitiveni Rabuka, he had almost single-handedly built the alliances with Australia, New Zealand and the United Kingdom, that had together launched the unofficial operation to oust him from power. In Afghanistan, while the Taliban fought the Russians, he had whisked away a top Afghan politician, an ally of India's, from under the Taliban's noses, and brought him to India via land, through the same tunnels that Pakistan consistently used to infiltrate India. As the deputy head of the intelligence services, he had embedded an R&AW agent into the Damdami Taksal and had created and run the infrastructure of dead drops which the agent used to communicate invaluable information that facilitated Operation Blue Star.

But by 2006, approaching sixty, the hard work and lies had taken their toll on the mole. His body, once lithe and firm, had turned soft and plump; his hair, once thick and black, was now thinning and needed to be dyed, the middle parting a faint reminder of its glory days. His blood pressure, which had always rested at 120/80 had spiked to a consistent 170/100 over the last few years, the increased pressure causing frequent headaches and, on occasion, debilitating migraines that brought on unending waves of nausea and made it impossible for him to work. Under pressure from his family, he finally decided to semi-retire, using his relationships within the government to be appointed as the Chief of Counter Intelligence at India's National Security Council, a job that he had expected would offer all of the comforts that he was accustomed to as a high-ranking bureaucrat, without any of the pressures.

As luck would have it, soon after joining, he was asked to lead an investigation into a suspected spy within the council and he eventually unmasked the naval officer who had been forced to work for the British after being honey-trapped by them in Colombo. The irony of one double agent exposing another was not lost on him and he had decided then to stop tempting fate and fully retire from the world of spies. The CIA had reluctantly agreed, if only because a tired old man was prone to making mistakes that held the potential to undo years of good work.

He had sought an appointment with the prime minister, who reluctantly allowed him to vacate his post, but only on the condition that he accepted one last position, meant as a political statement by the prime minister to MI6 in Britain, following the discovery of their agent.

It was thus that the mole found himself serving as the Indian ambassador to the United Kingdom.

# Chapter 31

27 February 2010
London
5.30 p.m.

Abbas, true to his nature, was working hard to ensure a successful auction. He had been on his phone most of the day, calling buyers from across the world, who he knew would be interested in the Roerichs.

Most were legitimate, well-known and respectable and represented a multitude of clients across three broad categories. The first were unimaginably wealthy individuals who bought art for their private collections, locking away some of the most magnificent examples of human creativity for the pleasure of a chosen few. The second category comprised multinational corporations that looked at art in three ways—as an investment that could offer a significant return; a means of making an investment that could be treated as business expenses to reduce their tax liability; and lastly, as an adornment for the walls of their offices in a not-so-subtle display of their wealth and power. And the last category comprised museums, which invested public money in purchasing art for universal enjoyment and for protecting these important cultural achievements.

But not all of Abbas's clients were legitimate. Several, including the buyer codenamed 'Jupiter', whom Abbas had spoken to last, were but fleeting shadows, visible only occasionally in the real world—their existence known to only a select few outside the best law enforcement agencies in the world. They owned or represented wealth that could never appear on a balance sheet or a tax form—wealth that had invariably been generated from some zero-sum game by hurting others, whether through narcotics, smuggling, human trafficking, terrorism or by corrupt leaders looting their own countries. They were a different kind of elite—as wealthy as those whose names featured on the lists of the world's 100 richest people but obscure to the general public. Abbas didn't care about their backgrounds as they were also some of the world's biggest art buyers, using innumerable shell companies in overseas tax havens to purchase whatever they desired.

Abbas knew that an auction by Sotheby's would appeal immeasurably to this second set of buyers, as it would guarantee that the authenticity and chain of ownership would never again be questioned—after all, Sotheby's mere agreement to auction an item was considered a gold standard of authenticity and legitimacy, accepted all over the world. As cool as he had played it with James, Sotheby's participation had been vital to his attempt to sell the Roerichs given that their ownership claim was corroborated by the tenuous paperwork that he had submitted to Sotheby's, which included signed statements from poorly educated nationals of a Third World country.

Abbas understood the rules of demand and supply. Well aware that very few Roerich paintings survived, and the few that did were unavailable for sale, he directed his efforts at ensuring a two-stage bidding war, first between the legitimate buyers and the group of obscures, and then between the competing interests within this second group of the world's biggest criminals. The higher the price, the greater the likelihood of the honest buyers dropping out, and the dishonest getting what they wanted, as they almost always did. He adored the shameless greed of the art world—it enabled the practice of opaque buying, which required no proof of identity of the buyer while also offering legal protection from forced disclosures to the representatives of these buyers, thus guaranteeing buyer secrecy. It was also because of this unabashed greed that people like him could extract a heavy price from people who treasured their privacy more than art—after all, how else could anyone sell stolen merchandise at a public auction?

But, not everything was sunshine and roses. Abbas knew exactly the process that Sotheby's would follow, being one of the members of a group of art traders that was often called upon for information into the antecedents of an item that was trading hands in the art world. As expected, Sotheby's had reached out to the art world, asking for any information about the ownership of 'Silent Night' and 'Valley of Flowers'—he had seen the email, forwarded to him by several of his friends.

Abbas knew that the paintings had never changed hands. From the time his parents had told him about their existence, they had been hanging, their value unknown, in the same place for the last six decades. He was hopeful that because they had never changed hands, the art world may not even know of their existence. In that best-case scenario, by the tenth, his organization would have had all the money it needed to execute its most audacious plan yet. But Abbas hadn't got to where he was without planning for failure.

It was not impossible that someone somewhere had heard of the Roerichs hanging at the centre. And if the person knew of their existence, they would certainly be on Sotheby's mailing list and would undoubtedly raise the alarm when they received the email from Sotheby's. Unfortunately, there was no way for Abbas to know who this person could be, or else he would have ensured that his organization took the necessary steps to guarantee the silence of the person who could put their plan in jeopardy. Accounting for this probability, he had deliberately approached Sotheby's as late as possible for inclusion into the auction on the tenth, minimizing the time for their inquiries, without arousing any suspicion.

If James received no objection, as was most likely, his precaution would prove to be unnecessary and would go completely unnoticed. If, however, he did receive an objection, he would undoubtedly waste no time in writing to the likely owners of the Roerichs. There was nothing they could do about the Indian government receiving this communication from Sotheby's, but his organization had every confidence, given their experience in India, that the combination of a lazy bureaucracy, decentralized governance, a crumbling record-keeping structure and a notoriously incompetent political establishment, would combine to ensure that the government would be unable to move with the necessary alacrity to register their claim of ownership.

Abbas had planned how to protect his cover. He had worked hard to build his legend as a reputed art broker known for delivering the most unique of works, sourced mostly from the Indian subcontinent, but occasionally from other parts of the world as well. The antecedents created for the paintings were not foolproof but could not be disproved as long as Rehan stuck to his story, which Rehan would have to do, given what was at stake for him. Even if ownership was contested, his cover would not be blown. He needed to keep working if the Jaish was to have enough funds to win its holy war against India. His masters at the ISI would have it no other way.

# Chapter 32

28 August 1948
Kappar
8.15 a.m.

Devika had woken up exhausted. She had been working nearly nonstop for the last six days. As expected, Asif and Shiva had protested at her desire to speed up parts of the shoot schedule but had agreed once she had explained her motivation. Both of them had since been remarkable in their support, Asif reordering the entire unit into a different sequence of shoots and Shiva not only doing his scheduled shoots for the day but also learning the lines for and shooting the additional scenes with Devika.

Like Shiva, Devika too condensed every two planned days of shoots into one. She started shooting early every day and went on till daylight permitted. She then joined the daily debrief that Asif was absolutely insistent on for the entire unit. A light meal and a bath later, she spent hours with Shiva, rehearsing lines for the next day—Asif joining in when he could—to bring as many scenes close to rehearsed perfection as they could, thus minimizing the time spent on retakes the next day.

The entire crew was exhausted but had soldiered on, till finally, late last evening, Asif had yelled the 'Cut!' that marked the end of the shoot to which Devika was essential. In appreciation of their efforts, Asif organized a party at the hotel after winding up for the day, and gave the entire unit the next day off to recharge their batteries and enjoy the city, confident that they could finish the remaining shoot in the time they had left before they had to return to Bombay.

Devika's sheepish request for the evening off was firmly denied by Asif, who asked her to attend the party to show her gratitude for the crew's sacrifices. She did not argue and attended the party, a smile pasted on to her face, forcing herself to be charming as she went around the group, spending some time with each member of the unit.

She drew energy from what awaited her. She had sent a message to Roerich yesterday, informing him of the completion of the shoot and asking him to meet today. The messenger returned with an invitation to lunch at Sommerville House, which she accepted. While plans had been made for just one lunch, she had no doubt that she would be spending the rest of her time in Kappar in Roerich's company. That thought propelled her through the exhaustion on the previous evening, her mind clinging on to the happy thought during all the banal conversation.

The evening mercifully ended at 11 p.m. She returned to her room and fell asleep immediately, not having the energy to even change out of her sari. She slept deeply, waking only when the sunlight shining into her room had grown strong enough to pry her eyelids open. Rising groggily, she smiled, as it dawned on her what the new day marked.

She freshened up and emerged from her room to find her tea laid out on the balcony, just as she liked it, a shawl draped over her chair in case she felt cold. She looked out over the valley, blooming in all its glory under the rising sun and sipped her tea contentedly. After a leisurely breakfast, she began getting dressed.

She was fully dressed by 11 a.m., but with Sommerville House being just ten minutes away, she had to wait and whiled away the time reading newspapers and catching up on unit gossip with her attendant. Finally, she asked her attendant to arrange for her departure and took one final look in the mirror, pushing back the few strands of hair that had come undone from her assiduously made ponytail.

Ten minutes later, she was driving into Sommerville House, awestruck by the beauty of the small estate and how meticulously it was kept. Another peep into Svetoslav, she thought. She reached the end of the driveway, where Roerich, who had been lounging in an unusually long chair, got up to welcome her. He waited for the car to pull up, holding open her door as she stepped out. Under instructions from Devika, the driver left straight away to park at the spot near the estate's entrance which she had identified.

Roerich and Devika smiled; the pecks on the cheek were followed, this time, by a warm embrace relieved at the end of longing. Peeling himself away, Roerich led them into the garden, where their table had been set up under a large peepal tree which permitted enough sunlight to allow for a cheery setting, without the midday heat. Devika appreciated the effort put into thinking about the placement of their table—it did not seem to her that Svetoslav made this kind of effort often, and the thought of him working to please her brought an involuntary smile to her face.

'Thank you, Svetoslav. This is absolutely lovely. But before we sit, may I see the estate?'

'Of course, Devika. But wouldn't you like something to drink first?'

'Not at all. I left the hotel not ten minutes ago. I'd love to see first what it is about this property that gives you the peace you need to create your work.'

Roerich smiled, delighted that she wanted to see his home. He walked her around the estate, finishing at the gallery where he painted—his special place where he permitted no one else. Devika took it all in with a keen eye, recognizing that the honest effort of the staff was missing the directions of a lady of the house. She could see that with just a little work and a few decorative additions, Sommerville House could outdo any home in Bombay. The art gallery had not impressed her—it was untidy and smelled of paint and wet rags. It looked like it hadn't been swept in weeks, if not longer. She surmised, correctly, that this was Roerich's shrine and access to it was severely restricted, perhaps only to himself. Not wanting to embarrass him, she refrained from asking him questions about it, focusing instead on the marvellous art that lay strewn about. While Svetoslav had made the effort to frame a few pieces, most were simply scattered about without any regard. She saw an empty canvas resting on an easel, awaiting his masterstrokes, and wondered whether he had set it aside for painting her.

Svetoslav had been watching every expression on her face, correctly interpreting most. As she turned towards him, he nodded gently, confirming that the canvas was meant for her. Seeing her hesitation, he thoughtfully added, 'Whenever you are ready', before taking her by the hand and escorting her back into the garden.

The conversation took off from where they had left it, almost as if it hadn't been disrupted by a week-long break. As before, she enjoyed the intellectual interaction and listening to his views on a variety of subjects. They continued talking over lunch, served discreetly by his staff, and took more pleasure in the meal this time as they relaxed even more in each other's company. Finding in him a kindred soul, Devika opened up about her life, like she had to almost no one before, even telling him about her disastrous marriage to Himanshu Raichand.

It was only when the sun had retreated behind the mountains, taking away its warmth, that they realized it was getting cold. Neither wanted to end the day, but they knew that they had to. Devika, on the precipice of falling in love and eager not to let any opportunity to spend time with him pass her by, took the lead.

'I must meet my team for dinner.'

'Yes, of course,' replied Roerich, asking his butler to have Devika's car brought in.

'But, if you have the time, I would like to come back tomorrow.'

'I would enjoy nothing more. Perhaps you would like to join me for lunch again?'

Nodding happily, Devika pecked his cheek gently, got into her car, and left.

# Chapter 33

28 February 2010
Delhi
6 a.m.

Kamal looked out of the window of his business class seat on a Jet Airways flight as they took off for Kappar. He was already annoyed, the early start having forced him to cancel golf, an essential part of his daily routine and the only exercise he got. He had waited fifteen years for a membership of the prestigious Delhi Golf Club (DGC) and looked at each day without golf as a missed opportunity to make use of the lush green facility sprawled across 150 acres in the heart of the capital. As he looked down at the concrete jungle of Gurgaon, he could not help but compare its arid wasteland to the green oasis of the DGC.

He turned towards the front and began to prepare for the meeting with the director of the Kappar centre, opening the report that Sandeep had prepared. The director, Abhijeet Singh, was a career scientist, whose limited ambition had ensured that he had already risen to as far a level as he would ever go. Having started out as a junior researcher in Tonk, Rajasthan, he had risen steadily, if unspectacularly, to occupy various unimportant positions in the Rajasthan government. He was deputed to the centre in 2005 and had been stationed there for just over five years, performing as per expectation, with no achievements, and perhaps more importantly, no controversy to show for his term.

It was very unlikely, thought Kamal, that such a bureaucrat would ignore any government formality, no matter how trivial, or allow any omission to go unreported. It was even unlikelier that he would have the imagination, leave aside the gumption, to participate in the disappearance of government assets. His mood lightening at the expectation that he was going to find the register in the boring hands of Abhijeet and have his answer before the end of the day, he beckoned the stewardess to order his breakfast and sat back to plan his round of golf for the following day, once he returned.

Kamal landed an hour later, managing to take a refreshing nap. He switched on his iPhone to check his messages as the airline made the numerous annoying announcements that not one person listened to, and which served no purpose other than forcing people to talk louder over the noise. With the seatbelt sign finally switched off, he collected his overnight bag and waited impatiently for the stairs to be attached to the plane so that he could deboard.

A cramped—but thankfully brief—bus ride later, he walked through the tiny terminal, handed his bag to the driver holding a placard with his name and squeezed himself into the backseat of the dented Ambassador that had been provided to him for the duration of his stay. His nose crinkled in disgust at the mixture of smells in the car, a noxious combination of sweat, stale food, damp cloth and something that smelled like a dead rat. Realizing that it was pointless to rebuke a driver who had probably been allotted randomly to the best car available at the centre, he swallowed the sharp taunt that had risen to his lips.

He rolled down his window, breathing the cold, clean, fresh air that swept into the car, in deep gulps. Instructing the driver to take him to the ICAR guesthouse on Kaulagarh road, he sat back and checked his email, his eyes instantly drawn to the reply from Sotheby's that had arrived late last night. He clicked it open.

*Dear Mr Maheshwari,*

*Thank you for your prompt response. We appreciate your effort in trying to resolve this issue at the earliest and look forward to the results of your inquiry.*

*However, I would like to point out that in accordance with British law, we are entitled to continue with the auction of any property brought to us unless a claim of ownership, supported by adequate documentation, is made by a third party. Accordingly, in the absence of adequate evidence from you by 3 March, we will have no choice but to continue with the sale after making the disclosures that are required of us. We trust you understand our position.*

*Regards,*
*James*

'What a condescending, entitled prick,' thought Kamal. Well, this made it imperative to find the register of assets and send a copy to Sotheby's before the day was out. However, as a career bureaucrat, it was now also apparent to him that he needed to ensure that the blame for the loss of the paintings, if that is what it came to, did not fall on him. If the media caught wind of it—as was likely, whether or not it was deserved—there would be a public crucifixion, first on television and then in print media. Any hope of transfer to a ministry that mattered would then be washed away by the tsunami of uneducated and emotionally charged public opinion. Galvanized by the need to keep clear of the fingers that would wag at him all too willingly if news broke, he forwarded the emails to his minister to keep him abreast of the fast-developing situation and included a brief note on the developments since the previous afternoon, requesting his instructions. Deciding also that a legal dispute with Sotheby's and the party claiming ownership over the paintings was possible, he forwarded the emails to his ministry's legal wing, including a detailed note on the events that had led him to Kappar, highlighting the potential financial loss to the government from this violation of the Antiquities and Art Treasures Act, and seeking their legal opinion, in view of the position that Sotheby's had taken.

Satisfied but feeling carsick from typing on the mobile in his moving car, Kamal looked out of the window. He had not been to Kappar since the late 1990s, and while he had heard of the large-scale ecological destruction that this once marvellous hill station had been subject to, he was shocked to see it first-hand. Where there had once been thousands of trees lining the roads, there were now as many concrete buildings. Clouds, cold and wet to the touch, that had once floated at street level had now disappeared. The silence for which the town was once revered, was now constantly ripped apart by a cacophony of car horns, which jostled with steamrollers, motorbikes, pedestrians, animals, cycles and food vendors for space on the narrow roads. Hoardings of political leaders and consumer brands were plastered on every available surface, hiding behind them any beauty that may have remained after a population explosion and the inevitable corporate and political greed had irreversibly altered the face of the city.

What was the point of having a research centre in Kappar any more? The whole idea of locating a centre here had been to be where research was not affected by overpopulation, chemical use or pollution. Based on what he could see, all those laudable reasons had well and truly fallen by the wayside—the centre may as well have been in Delhi for all the good it would now be able to do here in Kappar. Resolving to initiate a discussion on the relocation of all ICAR centres away from cities, he made a mental note to put up a discussion paper for the consideration of the minister upon his return.

Fifteen minutes later, they arrived at the ICAR guesthouse, attached to the ICAR's Research Centre. As they drove through the high wrought iron gates that guarded the entrance to the centre, the gate opened hurriedly by two *chowkidars* at the sound of the Ambassador's horn, Kamal felt like he had been transported back in time to the Kappar of old. Hundreds of trees lined the gravelled driveway, the gravel crunching under the vehicle's weight as the bald tires struggled to find a firm grip on it. The temperature dropped noticeably and the air became lighter and cleaner. The thick canopy blocked out large swathes of the weak morning sun, sunlight filtering through the foliage intermittently, casting thin alternating strips of light and shadow. Located at the edge of a cliff, the centre painted in a *sarkari* yellow, stood out against the background of the rugged brown Himalayas. All his worries about the centre's location melted away as he saw that the centre had remained protected against the advances of time.

An unusually large reception committee awaited him under the high ceiling of the patio set in the middle of the circular driveway. The door was pulled open from the outside and a multitude of hands reached in, almost manhandling his bulk out of the vehicle in their eagerness to be the first ones to ingratiate themselves. He folded his hands in a humble namaste, managing to include the entire reception party in the greeting at once, his eyes seeing an amalgam of brown faces and shiny teeth, rather than individuals.

The leader, a short, fair man, dressed in a shiny silver suit matched badly with a yellow tie and blue socks, stepped forward to welcome him to the centre. On cue, a lady dressed in a dark green sari with an intricate yellow border magically appeared, bearing a large brass thali that held the paraphernalia for a *tika* ceremony, her thin hands quivering under the weight of the thali. Silver-suit grabbed the marigold garland from the thali and stretched upwards to garland Kamal, a task made possible only by Kamal bowing to allow the short man to reach. The tika was applied on his forehead and he was led to breakfast by Silver-suit, the entire reception party in tow.

The standard government breakfast buffet was laid out on the veranda attached to the reception. The veranda was built on thick wooden planks supported by iron girders, three of its sides stretched out over the cliff, providing breathtaking views of the valley. An ugly plastic table covered with a dirty chequered cloth sat in the middle, an eyesore in contrast with the spectacular view. Soggy samosas, cheese sandwiches and ghee-soaked jalebis were heaped on the table in large bowls, flies swarming around them. Kamal's stomach churned at the sight, but not wanting to disrespect his hosts, he accepted a cheese sandwich and a cup of steaming tea, wincing as the sugary concoction burnt his tongue. Finishing his tea as fast as he could, he excused himself so that the rest of the group could dig into the free breakfast without inhibition.

As he walked back into the reception, he signalled to Silver-suit to follow him.

'Abhijeet?' asked Kamal.

'Yes, Sir,' said Abhijeet.

'Thank you for making all these arrangements at such short notice. The matter is pressing and I needed to find an answer quickly.'

'I understand, Sir. How can I help?'

'Have you heard of a painter called Roerich?'

'No, Sir. I can't say I have.'

'Do we have any Roerich paintings at the centre?'

'I don't know, Sir. We have several paintings, but I don't know if any are painted by Roerich, Sir.'

'Hmmm . . . You maintain a register of assets, correct?'

'Yes, Sir, we do.'

'That would list all our assets, including paintings and their artists?'

'Yes, Sir, it would. But if we do not know who the painter is, then it would only list the painting with a description.'

'Why would we not know? Almost all paintings are signed by the artist. Why not just take down the painting and look for the signature under the frame or at the back?'

'We used to do that, Sir. Then in 1971, one painting was damaged while being removed from its frame. Experts had to be called in from the National Museum in Delhi to fix it. After that, the ministry ordered that no paintings were to be handled without experts from the National Museum. The correspondence and order are on file, Sir. I can show it to you if you like.'

'Not now. Have a photocopy sent to my room, I will take it to Delhi with me. But if that is the case, then why haven't experts been called from Delhi to help list paintings that we bought or received after the policy was issued?'

'Sir, I have seen the register. It does not list a single painting as having been purchased by us. I don't think we have ever had the budget for such luxuries. I cannot speak for before I came here, but since I have arrived, we have tried several times to get experts to come in and evaluate the paintings we have been gifted. Unfortunately, their schedule has always been full.'

'How long ago was the request placed?'

'Four years, Sir,' said Abhijeet, disgust in his voice.

Recognizing his frustration at bureaucratic inertia, Kamal made another mental note to have all paintings across the ICAR

centres evaluated and listed by the National Museum. Patting
Abhijeet gently on the back, he promised to intervene and
ensure that the experts came to Kappar soon.

'Thanks, Abhijeet. I am going to freshen up. I will see you
in your office at nine—please make sure the register is there.'

'Of course, Sir. I can bring the register to your room if you
like. It is not an issue at all.'

'No. I'd like to see the centre and take a walk around to meet
the staff—get an update on what you are doing here.'

'Of course, Sir. I will send someone to escort you.'

Shaking hands perfunctorily, Kamal walked away, escorted
by two members of the guest house staff, both eager to show him
to his room. He walked down the long corridor to the corner
room allotted to him, stopping intermittently to look at the
photographs displayed on the walls on either side. Amateurly
clicked and badly framed, someone had made an effort to
compensate for the dearth in quality through volume. Dozens
of pictures, mostly of flowering plants, but also of events at the
centre, narrated the story of the centre over the past five decades,
a small plaque under each explaining uninspiringly each event in
some detail. He dismissed both staff members outside his door,
waving away their fervent offers for breakfast and tea.

Opening the door to his room with trepidation, expecting
to find more of the smells that had overwhelmed him when he
had first entered the Ambassador, he was pleasantly surprised to
find a clean, spacious room waiting for him. He drew back the
curtains and admired the view—the entire valley was on show
from the private balcony. He withdrew his half-smoked cigar
from his bag, picked up the matchbox placed thoughtfully on
the bedside table for him, and fell on to a *moodha* in the narrow
balcony. Lighting his cigar, he thought of what he had learnt
from Abhijeet.

If the Roerichs were received before 1971, they would be listed in the register of assets along with the artist's name. Abhijeet would have had no reason to look at the names of the artists, or he may have forgotten them, which didn't matter either way. If they were received after 1971, then they would, at least, be described in the register and he could compare their description to Sotheby's, to check whether the paintings were the same. There was no question that the paintings had been at the centre, given the photographs James had sent him. If they were indeed displayed here but were no longer here, then what happened to them? 'There's only one way to find out,' thought Kamal, making a considerable effort to pull himself out of the comfortable moodha.

Smoke billowing around his face, he returned to his room to retrieve the file containing the emails from James. Peering through the thick cigar smoke, he sifted through the printouts till he found the detailed descriptions of the paintings. He took off his shoes, lay on the bed and began to read:

### 'Silent Night'

Very little is known about the antecedents of this painting. As per Roerich's personal diary, he completed the painting in August of 1947. Photographs available with the Roerich Museum in New York show that the painting was displayed at the Indian Council of Agricultural Research's Centre at Kappar till at least 1994 (and possibly later).

Roerich describes 'Silent Night' as his 'personal experience of peace manifested in the magnificent silence of a moonlit heaven on earth'. The Roerich Museum has provided a more detailed description as below:

'While we have not physically examined this work, we have examined photographs, some of them taken close up, of "Silent Night", which is a magnificent example of Roerich's later work. The painting is oil on canvas and measures 3'x3'. It represents the artist's spiritual experience while looking down at a small hill town from on top of a mountain. The painting shows the side of the artist's mansion in his peripheral vision, but its primary focus is on the valley, completely dark except for bright moonlight streaming through thin wispy clouds. Roerich's genius captures a silence undisturbed by man, the sounds of nature delicately brought out in the breeze rustling through the trees, the dogs howling their ode to the moon and a river bubbling its way down the mountain, the shimmering mountain itself a dark sleeping giant.

'Broad brush strokes capturing the beauty of nature are complemented by thin strokes that detail the nocturnal sounds, the combination allowing the viewer to experience the peace that the artist experienced while capturing the sight.'

### 'Valley of Flowers'

Much like 'Silent Night', very little is known about this painting. As per Roerich's personal diary, he completed the painting in May 1947. The 'Valley of Flowers' was also on display at the Indian Council of Agricultural Research's Centre at Kappar till at least 1994 (and possibly later).

Roerich describes 'Valley of Flowers' as his 'attempt to capture nature's genius in presenting life as a mixture of colours coming together during spring'. The Roerich Museum has provided a more detailed description, as below:

'While we have not physically examined this work, we have examined photographs, some of them taken from close up. The painting is oil on canvas and measures 6'x3', the additional length likely chosen by Roerich to accommodate a panoramic view. Like a lot of Roerich's work, the painting focuses on a single element, in this case, the rugged beauty of a farmer's simple wooden hut, and effortlessly blends the beauty created by man into the backdrop of nature's own beauty, without either overpowering the other. The wooden hut, utilitarian and sturdy, stands next to a mountain stream, surrounded by lush green grass and grazing animals. The simplicity of the scene is complemented by thousands of colourful wildflowers stretching up towards the sun, dozens of insects dancing around them in their hunt for nectar.

'The use of only thin brushes has allowed Roerich to capture the life force of each element. It is, to the best of our knowledge, the first work in which he has drawn the outline of each element before painting it in, the colouring book style that he would later perfect and elevate to art.'

Despite never having been an art lover, Kamal was surprised that a written description had left such a vivid imprint on his mind, enabling him to imagine clearly what each painting looked like. Feeling well-prepared, Kamal laboured off the bed, stubbing out his cigar in the glass ashtray. He struggled to put on his brown Oxfords, grunting with effort as his ample stomach impeded his effort to bend low enough. Finally succeeding in squeezing his unnaturally broad feet into the pointed, size twelves and breathing hard, Kamal combed his hair and left the room, the emails from James back in the file which was now tucked under his left armpit.

# Chapter 34

28 February 2010
Kappar
8.55 a.m.

The staff assigned to him by Abhijeet was waiting outside Kamal's door, squatting comfortably on their haunches, as only people from rural areas can, and jumped to attention as soon as he opened it. Instructed to escort him to Abhijeet's office, they scurried down the corridor, looking back repeatedly to make sure they were neither going too slow nor too fast for the *bada* sahib from Delhi to keep pace. They walked out of the guest house, took a left at the end of the small walkway leading up to the front steps of the guest house and walked a few hundred metres down a gravel path till they arrived at the entrance to the centre, where the same lady who had held the thali before was waiting for him. On learning that she was Abhijeet's secretary, Kamal dismissed the two men and followed her through a maze of corridors till they reached Abhijeet's office in the southwest corner of the building, with sweeping views of the centre's agricultural lands on which its experiments and research were conducted.

Abhijeet, still in his silver trousers, his jacket now off, rose from his desk and came forward to receive Kamal, leading him to the separate area in the centre of the office earmarked for meetings. His secretary appeared a moment later, carrying three thick registers, her arms now shaking under the weight of their yellowing pages. She placed the registers on the table and left to arrange for refreshments for her boss and his boss.

Once alone, Kamal asked Abhijeet to explain how the records of assets were entered and maintained in the registers. Abhijeet pointed to the relevant portions of the register as he answered: 'As you can see, separate entries are maintained for each year in these two registers. The third register is the consolidated account of all assets under our control. Whenever we obtain an asset, it is entered into the year in which it was acquired and also in the consolidated register. As I told you, Sir, if the name of the asset or its creator is unknown, then just a description is inserted. A specific code is created for each asset by the general administration department and that code is then painted on to the asset. Each new entry on the annual and consolidated registers is signed by the general administration department and the director of the centre for confirmation. Similarly, if an asset is sold or written off, an entry is made in the annual register next to the asset, stating the date and details of the transaction. This is also signed by the general administration department and the director, and the details of this asset are struck off the consolidated register so that the centre always has an exact list of all the assets in its possession.

'The final step is part of the audit by the ministry's external auditors. As you know, the auditors look into our accounts in April each year. As part of their audit, they also look into the register for assets acquired during the preceding financial year and the consolidated assets register, and then physically verify that all assets listed in the registers are indeed present at the centre and carry an asset code. This is also tallied against our revenues and expenditures. If the auditors find any discrepancy, they include it in their report to the ministry's finance department, which then opens an investigation. I am happy to report, Sir, that there is no pending investigation at our centre as of 31 March 2009.'

Finishing his explanation, Abhijeet took a deep breath and sipped water from his glass, waiting for Kamal's reaction. Kamal was lost in thought. He had already decided that the Roerich Museum's evidence established that the paintings had indeed been on display at the centre—after all, they were the world's leading authority on Roerich and if they were wrong, then he was on a wild goose chase. The paintings were obviously not at the centre—they couldn't be if they were about to be auctioned in London. That could only mean that the paintings had once been with the centre but no longer were, which left only two possibilities. Sandeep had already confirmed what Abhijeet had just told him—there was no adverse audit report. He had also realized that the auditors were unlikely to have facilitated the disappearance of the paintings by manipulating records, so he moved on to the second possibility—the paintings were not owned by the ICAR at any point in time and were therefore not listed in the registers. In that case, their auction was immaterial to ICAR, as they had no claim over them. Why they were hanging at the centre if they were not owned by it, would be interesting to discover from an academic standpoint but had no real-life impact on the situation at hand. At this point, it was imperative to establish whether the ICAR did indeed own the paintings as per its records—the rest could come later.

His decision made, he looked at Abhijeet, who was waiting expectantly for instructions. Reaching into his file, he pulled out the descriptions of 'Silent Night' and 'Valley of Flowers' and asked Abhijeet to read them, hunting through the file for more documents while he did so. 'You have been here for several years. Have you seen either of the paintings described in those notes?'

Abhijeet's brow furrowed as he tried to compare the mental images he had created based on the descriptions of the paintings, with those that he remembered seeing at the centre. Finally, he shook his head.

'See if these help. They were taken at the centre,' said Kamal, handing over printouts of the photographs that James had sent him. The photographs showed the two paintings from different angles—three were close-ups, showing only the paintings themselves; the fourth showed them hanging above and on either side of a shelf piled high with government files; the fifth, taken from a more obtuse angle, had captured the edge of a thick wooden door in addition to the shelf and the paintings themselves; while the last of them, taken from straight ahead, showed two ancient wall lamps on either side of the painting along with the edge of a ceiling fan at the top.

Abhijeet nodded enthusiastically, pleased at being able to be of some assistance. 'I have never seen the paintings, Sir. But I do know this room! It is the librarian's office. I've been there only once but I know it is the only room in the entire building that has a fan!' he trilled excitedly.

'So two of the world's most valuable paintings had been relegated to the complete obscurity of a librarian's office in a forgotten outpost of a small department in an enormous ministry,' thought Kamal. 'How incredibly typical!'

'I'd like to see the room,' he said.

More than happy to oblige, Abhijeet hopped on to his feet with alacrity. 'Please come with me, Sir.'

'Actually, it would be better if your secretary escorted me. I need you to check on something else. Obviously, the paintings were in that room, no question about it. But how did they get there? Could you please check the registers and see if they describe how the paintings got here? Start from the time the centre was set up and go right up till March 2009, and pull out all the details that you can. I'll be back soon.'

Taking his seat reluctantly, Abhijeet buzzed his secretary in and passed on the necessary instructions. Once Kamal had left, he pulled the consolidated register on to his lap and began to thumb through the entries. 'Did the ICAR actually own these paintings?' he wondered.

# Chapter 35

10 December 1948
Bombay
9 p.m.

Devika and Svetoslav stood side by side, smiling for yet another picture with a guest who had stopped to extend his congratulations.

After months of courtship—the happiest of their lives—Svetoslav had finally proposed and Devika had unhesitatingly accepted. Roerich met her parents in Bombay and while they had decided to go ahead irrespective, it was to the delight of the couple that Devika's parents had loved Svetoslav.

With their blessing received, the preparations for the nuptials had begun and everyone worked together to resolve the complications arising out of the union of two different religions and plan the various ceremonies that would need to be organized. With the Christian faith not requiring the wedding to be organized on any particular date, Devika consulted a Hindu priest, who first drew up the astrological charts for Roerich, then matched his chart with Devika's, before finally announcing 10 December as the auspicious date for their wedding. They settled on a small Christian wedding in the morning, to be attended only by immediate family and close friends, followed by a Hindu wedding, later that evening. The functions in Bombay would be followed by a grand reception in Kappar.

Invitations were designed and despite every effort to keep the guest count down, over 1500 invitations were sent out. The news, known only to a very few of their closest friends until then, spread like wildfire, leaving in its wake dozens of broken hearts. The media set up camp outside Devika's house, perpetually hunting for a photograph that they could publish or a quote they could use. Calls poured in from across the country to congratulate the happy couple. Even the prime minister, a friend of Svetoslav's father's, called up to bless the couple. The family dealt with the limelight gracefully, accommodating as many callers, journalists and well-wishers as they could. They heaved a sigh of relief when the wedding day finally arrived, marking the end of the incessant telephone calls and social visits.

The Christian wedding and the intimate brunch that followed at Devika's house had gone off flawlessly. The wedding party, tired after this first round of celebrations, had struggled to get ready in time for the Hindu ceremonies in the evening, reaching the venue half an hour behind schedule. Contrary to tradition, they had insisted on being married before the guests arrived, so as to allow Devika enough time to mingle with the attendees who came in the evening, as most of the guests in Bombay had been invited by her.

Everyone who mattered in Bombay had accepted the couple's invitation. The entire film fraternity was present, faces of the country's best-known actors, producers and directors spread out across the room. The business community was well-represented too, comprising as it did of a number of Devika's fans, a lot of whom knew her personally. Where there was money and glamour, there was also the political class and bureaucracy—no less than the governor of Bombay, the mayor of Bombay and the chief of police were in attendance.

The Taj Mahal Hotel had left no stone unturned in decorating the room to befit the stature of the wedding. Decorative pieces had been handpicked from the homes of the wealthy and various museums in Bombay, and flowers had been brought in from all over India on Jamshedji Tata's personal airplane. Cooks had been flown in from across the country to lay out a feast that celebrated the diversity of the new India. Service by India's leading hotel was, no doubt, excellent.

Devika and Svetoslav sought out Asif and Shiva, drinking together at a corner table with their group. Introductions were made between the couple and Asif's wife Nagma and his brother-in-law Nazir, Shiva's wife Savitri and their son Rohan. Devika and Svetoslav thanked them profusely for the sacrifices in Kappar that had allowed them to come together and made them promise their attendance at the celebrations in Kappar.

The celebrations carried on late into the night, fuelled by endless bottles of liquor and the energy of the happiest couple in India. The two of them were still dancing when the last two guests took their leave, only the hotel staff left behind to watch them holding each other tenderly.

# Chapter 36

28 February 2010
Kappar
9.30 a.m.

Kamal followed Priyanka, who had marshalled the courage to introduce herself. Admiring the various pictures, beautifully framed, adorning the walls of the centre, he mechanically trailed behind Priyanka, his long strides easily keeping up with her short steps, made even shorter by her sari.

He walked through a thick wooden door as she held it open, and found himself in a spacious library. His eyes wandered around the enormous room, absorbing its details, pausing at each painting, his breath halting momentarily in expectation, even though he knew that the paintings could not possibly be there. Unexpectedly clean, the library was fully stocked with reference books, periodicals and journals, all addressing various topics related to agriculture. Long wooden tables occupied the centre of the room, enormous, high-backed wooden chairs on either side. Various people, all men, some in spotted lab coats over formal trousers and collared shirts, and a few clad casually in trousers and t-shirts, were scattered around the room, diligently poring over the literature. The silence would have graced any library in the world, disturbed only by whispered coughs, the occasional rustling of turning pages, the scratch of pencils on paper and chairs scraping lightly on the floor as their occupants shifted their weight about to alleviate the ache in their muscles.

Priyanka navigated her way through the shelves confidently, obviously having traversed this route several times before, her lithe form gliding across the floor. They walked quietly till they reached a corner occupied by a handsome, well-polished, semi-circular mahogany table, behind which sat a bespectacled young man busily typing on his computer. She introduced Harish as the new librarian of the centre and asked him to show them his private office. Unflustered by Kamal's seniority, the young man stepped out from behind his desk to shake Kamal's hand, his grip firm and confident, before leading him behind the desk and towards a door cleverly recessed into the wooden panelling so as to be invisible from the front, unless you knew exactly what you were looking for. He put his fingers against the edge of the door and pushed gently, creating a small gap through which rays of artificial yellow light streamed out brightly, eager to escape confinement. Harish inserted his fingers into the gap and pulled the door open, which slid noiselessly back on its well-oiled grooves, granting access to the room within.

Kamal moved into the room, close on Harish's heels, his eyes drawn to the mantelpiece and the ceiling fan that he had seen in the pictures. His eyes searched upwards from the mantelpiece, taking in the two paintings hanging on either side. Beautiful as they were, unsurprisingly, neither of them were the Roerichs that he was looking for.

Kamal thanked the librarian and asked Priyanka to escort him back to Abhijeet's room. How had the paintings left this room?

# Chapter 37

28 March 2010
Kappar
9.45 a.m.

Abhijeet jumped up as Kamal entered, a triumphant expression on his face.

'I have found the entries, Sir. The paintings were gifted to us on 15 June 1948 by Mr Rajesh Kumar, who was the district collector at the time. The artist's name is recorded as S. Roerich, and the description is similar,' he said, pointing to a lengthy entry in the register as the words poured out of him in a barely coherent torrent. 'There is no deletion in the consolidated register, so they are still owned by ICAR. I have also seen the last report by the auditor, which confirms that the paintings were on display as of 31 March 2009. Did you find them, Sir?'

'No, Abhijeet. Two paintings are displayed there but they are not the ones we are looking for.' To satisfy himself, Kamal took the register and read through the descriptions, which, however boring, as one would expect of an accountant, left no doubt that they were about 'Silent Night' and 'Valley of Flowers'. He also read through the auditor's report, satisfying himself that the code used by the auditor was the same as the code allotted to each painting in the register. 'So we did own them,' thought Kamal, 'and we had them till at least April of last year. Yet, for some reason, they are no longer there.'

'Could the paintings have been moved elsewhere, Abhijeet?' he asked.

'No, Sir. As per regulations, my written approval is required for any shift and I have not given any such approval.'

'Then where are they?' asked Kamal, a warning in his voice. 'They were here—the photos and registers make that clear but are not here any more. If you have not shifted them, how have they disappeared under your watch?'

'I don't know, Sir,' said Abhijeet, his voice quivering with the realization that he could be held accountable, even though he knew nothing of the issue.

'I think it is pretty clear. Either the auditors are incompetent and did not do their job properly, in which case, it is possible that the paintings went missing sometime before April 2009. I do not think that is likely. Or else, the auditors are involved in the disappearance and are covering it up, which is even less likely, given the consequences of being discovered. Alternatively, someone has stolen them from the centre after April 2009 and no one here has any idea of the theft, which I think is most likely. Which is it, Abhijeet?' thundered Kamal.

Abhijeet stood there, head bowed, perspiring profusely as the fear sunk in. 'I really don't know, Sir, I had no idea,' he mumbled softly.

A tough but honest officer, Kamal felt a pang of sympathy—he believed that Abhijeet's despair was real and that he really had no idea, either of the existence of the paintings or of their disappearance. He was just in the wrong place at the wrong time and though there was little, if anything, he could have done to prevent it, he would certainly still bear the blame, whenever it was finally assigned. A scapegoat would be needed, following the inevitable inquiry, which would conveniently conclude that he should have been aware of their existence and, limited budgets or not, he should have better secured the centre's assets. Any visit made by him to the librarian's office would confirm his guilt, regardless of whether he had registered the existence of the paintings or not. As sympathetic as he felt, Abhijeet's career was not Kamal's problem. He needed to focus on his own job, which was to recover the paintings, now resting comfortably at Sotheby's.

# Chapter 38

22 December 1948
Kappar
12.15 p.m.

Asif had risen earlier than usual to get dressed in time for a visit to the agriculture ministry's local centre. Roerich had insisted on this visit, claiming that it was the second most beautiful place in Kappar after the collector's house, and definitely worth a visit. He had spoken with Vivekananda Raju, the director, to secure permissions to visit the centre that was otherwise closed to the public.

Asif and Nagma were joined by his sister Mehroonisa and her husband Nazir, who had also accompanied them to the celebration in Kappar. As per Roerich's instructions, the group arrived at the agriculture ministry's centre at precisely 12 p.m. They were full of admiration as they drove in through its high wrought iron gates. Hundreds of deodar trees lined the gravelled driveway leading up to the main building. The temperature, even by the pleasant standards of Kappar, dropped noticeably as the car travelled down the driveway. The thick canopy took the sting out of the afternoon sun, allowing sunlight to filter through only intermittently. Located at the edge of a cliff, the centre, painted a pale yellow, stood out against the background of the beautiful Himalayas.

As they reached the porch, they saw a smartly dressed gentleman sitting on a bench, obviously awaiting their arrival. Their assumption that this was Vivekananda Raju, the director of the centre, was confirmed after introductions were made. Following a cup of tea, Vivekananda excused himself, directing the group to a subordinate, but promising to meet them for lunch once their tour of the centre was complete.

The designated guide began the tour, explaining the objectives behind the setting up of the centre and outlining the steps that were being taken to achieve them. He showed them the seed room, where scientists sought to breed new varieties of higher-yielding seeds. They visited the vault where various varieties of seeds were stored under sterile conditions, an insurance policy against any event that threatened the existence of any of those important species. The library followed—the pride of the centre, stocked full of academic journals from across the world. It was entirely occupied by staff peacefully reading. The subordinate then guided them to the fields at the centre, where the laboratory conducted its experiments in field conditions; the cycle of testing and further refining was aimed at ensuring that only healthy and high-yielding seeds were released into the Indian market. Finally, they walked through the forests that stretched to the boundary walls of the centre, their guide naming the dozens of varieties of trees and fruits that grew on the fertile slopes of Kappar. They were then escorted to a table set at the cliff's edge, offering views of the valley spread out below them on one side and the magnificent forests of the centre on the other.

The table was a permanent structure—clearly, they were not the only people to have enjoyed this experience. On it were laid the accoutrements of government hospitality—cheap, rose-patterned china; water glasses, which once transparent, were now permanently stained by the minerals in the local water; and hideously grimy steel spoons. A small bouquet of fresh flowers was placed on the table, their beauty contrasted by the ugly brass vase in which they had been placed.

Water was served to the guests, the long walk at that altitude having dehydrated the residents of Bombay. As they gratefully sipped the fresh mountain water, so different in taste from the metallic water they drank in Bombay, they were joined by Vivekananda. The group spoke at length about the centre, Vivekananda explaining in depth the work they were doing to guarantee India's food security. Asif, always looking for stories that could be transformed into movies, was transfixed by Vivekananda's lesson on the history of famines in India and the economic toll they had taken on the country, which extended well beyond the immediate human suffering. They discussed at length the ills of the feudal system, which lined the pockets of an elite few while forcing millions into poverty and birthing the many ills of female infanticide, child marriage, illiteracy, malnourishment and crime, all of which already plagued India's march to economic prosperity, and would continue to do so for decades to come. Asif would eventually be inspired by this conversation to create one of India's most iconic films, *Ma Bharat*.

They ate while they spoke, steadily working their way through the meal put together by the canteen that serviced the permanent residents of the centre.

'I noticed you have several paintings. Some of them are absolutely beautiful,' noted Asif.

'Ah, yes. That speaks of the generosity of people like our common friend. A few good artists, including Svetoslav, live in and around Kappar. In a community this small, everyone knows everyone and given the years I have been here, I am happy to say that I consider most of them my friends. Most of the paintings are gifts from the artists or their patrons, and we feel that displaying them is the deepest form of appreciation we can offer for their generosity.'

The conversation dwindled till it was obvious that the guests were overstaying their welcome. Asif sought permission to leave, thanking Vivekananda profusely for his time. Ambling along the pine-strewn path, the guests returned to their cars and left for Sommerville House, to attend the Christmas Eve celebration being hosted by Roerich and Devika.

They were to leave on Christmas Day for Bombay. Asif and his family had declined all of Roerich's and Devika's entreaties to stay on till at least New Year, explaining that Mehroonisa and Nazir needed to return to Lahore urgently to address some issues at their farm. Their hosts had grudgingly accepted but had immediately planned a grand Christmas Eve party to bid them farewell in style.

# Chapter 39

28 February 2010
Kappar
10.15 a.m.

Kamal formulated a plan of action and methodically commenced working on multiple fronts simultaneously. He had the relevant pages of the registers scanned and then emailed them to James, clearly stating that the registers were irrefutable proof of the ICAR's ownership of the paintings, thus reiterating the ICAR's claim over the paintings. He also stressed that the paintings had likely been stolen and that the government intended to file a police complaint to investigate their disappearance, promising to forward a copy of the complaint to him when possible. Given the likely theft, he warned James not to proceed with the auction and requested confirmation that the paintings would be withdrawn.

That done, he emailed an update to his minister from his phone, informing him of the mail sent to Sotheby's and his intention to have the centre file an FIR with the local police.

He asked for permission to initiate an inquiry to understand the lapses that had led to the disappearance of these paintings so that any further thefts could be prevented. Lastly, he recommended that the Ministry of Law be involved at the highest levels, given his expectation that recovering the paintings could entail a long-drawn legal process. The necessary steps thus taken, Kamal turned his attention to the most pressing need—involving the police.

Knowing that cooperation from the police would come through more swiftly if the right people in Delhi encouraged them, he called a friend in the Home Ministry and requested him to let the local superintendent of police (SP) know of his intention to visit the police station within the next thirty minutes, promising to answer all of his friend's questions later. He walked to his vehicle, Abhijeet in tow, and instructed the driver to take them to the police station.

Twenty minutes later, they were impatiently awaiting the SP's arrival, the message from Delhi having earned them the privilege to wait in his private office. Kamal and Abhijeet looked up as SP Tushar Misra's vehicle pulled up, siren blaring, all constables snapping smartly to attention, as the most powerful representative of the law in their small town strode into the station.

Tushar looked like a policeman. Tall and slim, he wore an immaculately starched uniform stretched out over his broad shoulders and narrow waist, the lean muscle in his arms evident; the moustache adding gravitas to a young face. He walked up and saluted his civilian seniors smartly. Introducing himself, he apologized for keeping them waiting and requested them to take their seats.

Kamal had googled Tushar while they had waited and was impressed with what the young SP had already achieved in his short career. A 2005 Indian Police Service officer, who, despite having been ranked fifth in the UPSC examination, had opted to join the IPS, instead of the more powerful Indian Administrative Service or the more enjoyable Indian Foreign Service. He was well-educated and had trained in law at the reputed National Law University in Jodhpur and the highly acclaimed Indian School of Business in Hyderabad, and had, despite the multiple opportunities that must certainly have come his way, chosen to work in public service. He had been awarded the President's Bravery Medal for his crusade against a liquor mafia, a battle that had cost him the lives of both his parents—killed by a bomb meant for him. He had taken charge in Kappar recently, where he was already battling the timber mafia, responsible in a large part for the destruction of the state's forests and the illegal sale of timber.

Apologizing again, he explained that he had actually been en route to a suspected illegal logging site when he got the call from Delhi and had turned around immediately to meet with them. 'Please tell me, Sir. What is the matter?' asked Tushar, addressing Kamal, the most senior official in the room.

'Thank you, Tushar. I am sorry for approaching you in this way but the matter really is of utmost importance.'

Tushar nodded, waiting for Kamal to continue. Kamal took a moment to compose his thoughts before narrating the sequence of events as they had transpired, starting from the time he had received the email from Sotheby's.

'To me, it's clear,' said Kamal. 'The paintings had been at the centre from 1948 till at least April 2009. Our registers, Sotheby's documents and the auditor's reports make that absolutely clear. I cannot be certain that the auditors are not guilty, but I have dealt with hundreds of auditors in my career, and I cannot believe they are in on it. The only explanation seems to be that the paintings have been stolen sometime after March 2009, and have somehow made their way to Sotheby's in London.

We have already written to the law ministry to update them in case we need to initiate legal proceedings to recover the paintings. But even in that case, our best chance is to find out how they disappeared and who is responsible. Of course, we want to catch them, but if we can't, we must at least be able to produce substantive evidence of the manner of their disappearance.'

Tushar sat quietly through the narration, mentally absorbing, reordering and dissecting the information. While he instinctively agreed with Kamal, he could not jump to any conclusions. He would need to conduct a proper investigation, which meant chasing every possible line of inquiry, eliminating one possibility after another, till he found the one that was most likely. 'I understand what you have told me, Sir. In order for me to investigate, the ICAR will have to file an FIR with us. Once that is done, I will personally oversee the investigation and find out what happened to these paintings. I will, of course, need copies of the registers, all documents from Sotheby's and the auditor's reports from the time that the paintings were gifted to you. I also expect that I will receive full cooperation from all employees at your centre.'

'Of course, Tushar. Abhijeet will file the FIR with you right now. Photocopies of all the documents will be delivered to you before lunch today. Abhijeet will also ensure that every employee extends his full cooperation. Please call me if you face any difficulties at the centre,' said Kamal. He reached into the breast pocket of his shirt, pulling out his card and wrote his cell number on it for Tushar.

'Thank you, Sir,' said Tushar. 'Let me have the FIR filed right away.' He sent for a constable and the FIR register. Once the constable was ready, Tushar dictated the FIR, summarizing the complaint from the centre, his clarity of thought coming through as he spoke without stuttering or stammering. The constable rushed to keep up with the flow of words, shaking his aching hand whenever Tushar stopped to take a breath. The dictation complete, Tushar read out the complaint to Kamal and Abhijeet, both of whom nodded, more than satisfied with its contents. Tushar had Abhijeet sign the FIR and handed him the complainant's copy for their records.

The three finished their tea, keen to return to work. Tushar escorted Kamal and Abhijeet to their vehicle and saluted the senior officers as they closed the doors behind them. Once they returned to Abhijeet's office, instructions were issued to send across the photocopies that Tushar required. Kamal also had Abhijeet's secretary scan the copy of the FIR and composed another email to James.

Dear James,

Further to my previous email, please find attached a copy of the police complaint filed by the ICAR. The paintings are now the subject matter of a criminal investigation and it is our every intention to press criminal charges against the persons responsible for depriving the Indian government of these assets.

I reiterate the Government of India's claim and request your confirmation that these paintings will not be included in the auction.

Based on the evidence already provided to you, please let us know the next steps for the recovery of these paintings from you and their safe return to India.

Kindly also let us know the name of the seller and his purported claim to the paintings so that we may conclude our investigation and make available this information to the relevant investigation agencies.

Regards,
Kamal Maheshwari

He forwarded the email to the minister as well, updated him on the police complaint and then retired to his room.

He lay in bed, puffing thoughtfully at his cigar, concluding that there was nothing more for him to do in Kappar till Tushar finished his investigation. It would be best to return to Delhi to meet with his minister and coordinate efforts with the law ministry to recover the paintings, as well as with the external affairs ministry for their diplomatic assistance, should Sotheby's refuse to return the paintings.

He called Sandeep to have his return flight rescheduled for that evening, electing to utilize the time to work on the book he was authoring on preparing for the civil services examination.

'It really is up to Tushar now,' he thought, noisily eating the lunch that had been served to him on his private balcony. 'Would he be able to find out what happened?'

# Chapter 40

28 February 2010
London
10.15 a.m.

While standing in the Tube on his route to work, James read each word of the email from Kamal as carefully as he could, feeling sick to the pit of his stomach at their implications. The registers clearly showed that the paintings were gifted to the ICAR and the auditor's reports established that the paintings hung at the Kappar Centre at least till 2009. These were government records and would constitute important proof under British law, especially if the auditor's reports over the years consistently established that the paintings had hung there.

He didn't want to believe it, but this could only mean that the paintings had been stolen from the ICAR. He had seen it happen often enough to understand that it was possible, especially with two paintings that had not exchanged hands for decades. With the police complaint being filed and enough doubt being cast over their ownership, it was no longer possible for him to include them in the auction. He would have to get the catalogues amended and find two other items to include in the auction in their place. That, at least, would not be a problem—Sotheby's owned hundreds of priceless objects that it had purchased over the years in the expectation that their value would appreciate.

He forwarded the emails to his chairman, along with a brief summary, recommending that the paintings be withdrawn from the auction and requesting permission to include two replacements instead. Wanting to ensure that it received the urgent attention it warranted, he called the chairman's secretary to instruct her to convey printouts of his email along with all attachments to the chairman, wherever he was in the world.

Only the most unpleasant task remained. He now had to inform Abbas Ali that he had been deceived and that the paintings appeared to have been stolen from the ICAR. Abbas was going to be livid to learn that he had been cheated, and was certainly not going to be happy at being told that not only would the paintings not be included in the auction but that as per the law, they would be held in the protective custody of Sotheby's till their rightful ownership was established through appropriate legal proceedings. This could take several months. He could not afford to lose Abbas's business and needed to ensure that Abbas didn't blame Sotheby's for these circumstances which were beyond their control. The unpleasantness would have to wait till he heard from his chairman—unlikely as it was that the chairman would allow the Roerichs to be included in the auction—which gave him enough time to get to his office before he had to email Abbas.

With the kind of money that was at stake, both parties would undoubtedly fight over ownership and Sotheby's was going to get dragged into the legal battle, whether it liked it or not. They had to start preparing for what lay ahead to ensure that their most cherished asset—their reputation—was not hurt in the process. He needed to bring his legal team up to speed and wrote to the head of the department, requesting a meeting as soon as possible.

By the time James reached his office, the chairman had responded, mincing no words while expressing his disappointment at the loss and the legal trouble that was bound to follow, but granting his approval to withdraw the paintings from the auction and include two other artefacts in their place.

He stormed through the automatic doors of Sotheby's and whizzed past his secretaries, not bothering to return their greetings. He went straight to his computer and sat down to write emails to Kamal and Abbas.

Dear Mr Maheshwari,

Please let me express our sincere gratitude for your prompt action. I have reviewed the documents shared by you and have also discussed them internally.

As per British law, if adequate documentation is provided to us to contest ownership of any object due to be auctioned, Sotheby's is obligated to stop the auction of that object. It is our view that your documents show that the Government of India has a strong claim to 'Silent Night' and 'Valley of Flowers'. Accordingly, neither of the paintings will be included in our auction on 10 March 2010, nor in any other auction, till their ownership is established clearly.

However, Sotheby's is unable to hand the paintings over to the Government of India till such time as (i) the person currently claiming ownership waives his claim to them, or (ii) a court of competent jurisdiction upholds your ownership and directs us to release them to you.

Until such time, the paintings will be held in our custody. The costs of storing, protecting and preserving these paintings will have to be borne by you in case the current claimant withdraws, or by the party to whom these costs are apportioned by the court, in the event of a legal contest.

With respect to your other query, the paintings have been made available for sale by Mr Abbas Ali, who is among the foremost art dealers in the world. However, under applicable law, we are not at liberty to disclose details of the supporting documentation provided by him and are therefore unable to make the same available to you.

We will speak with the current claimant and revert with his decision regarding the withdrawal of his claim within the next 48 hours.

Please do keep us updated on any developments at your end and do let us know if there is any way we can be of assistance to you.

Yours sincerely,
James Mitchell

The easier communication handled, James now set about composing the delicate email to Abbas, thinking through every word carefully, fully cognizant of the need to balance legal compulsions against Sotheby's business objectives.

Dear Mr Ali,
I trust this finds you well.

Unfortunately, I bear the burden of bringing bad news. As you know, protocol requires us to inform the foremost experts and art buyers about the proposed sale of 'Silent Night' and 'Valley of Flowers', and to seek objections, if any.

We received an adverse observation from one of the foremost experts on Svetoslav Roerich in the world, who made available to us certain photographs which suggested that both paintings had been on display at the Indian Council of Agricultural Research Centre in Kappar. We discovered that the ICAR is part of the Ministry of Agriculture of the Government of India and accordingly, contacted the Ministry of Agriculture to confirm that they had no claim over the paintings.

We have heard back from the ministry today. Unfortunately, they have provided several documents that suggest that they have a strong claim over the paintings. The Government of India has also asserted their claim and has initiated a criminal investigation into the unauthorized displacement of these paintings from the centre.

As per instructions given to me by our chairman, Sotheby's will, as per the requirements of British law, withdraw the paintings from the auction and hold them in custody up to such time as their ownership is unequivocally decided. You, Sir, as the original claimant, may choose to either waive your claim over these paintings, in which case we will promptly hand them over to the Government of India, or, alternately, you could choose to contest ownership in a court of competent jurisdiction, in which case, we would continue to hold the paintings. We would be very grateful if you could please let us know your decision within the next 48 hours.

Mr Ali, while I am barred from sharing the documents that the Government of India has provided, given our longstanding relationship, I would like to inform you that in Sotheby's opinion, the Indian Government's claim over these paintings seems irrefutable. Based on my own experience, it seems likely that they may have been stolen and the chain of ownership has been fabricated. Not to put too fine a point on it, but it appears that you have been cheated.

We do hope that you appreciate the position that Sotheby's finds itself in. As always, we will remain available to offer any assistance that we can.

Yours faithfully,
James Mitchell

A mighty storm was imminent for Sotheby's, caught in the middle as the Government of India collided with one of the richest men in the world over Roerich's paintings. The only way for them to emerge unscathed was to take no sides and for this, they would have to keep to the letter of the law.

Now all that remained for Sotheby's to do was to wait and watch. Until then, it would have to be business as usual. James buzzed his secretary on the intercom and asked her to bring in the catalogue of Sotheby's owned assets.

# Chapter 41

1 March 2010
London
2.15 p.m.

Abbas had returned from Geneva in the morning after his meeting with representatives of the Swedish royal family to discuss their interest in the auction. The meeting had gone extremely well and Abbas was confident that the family of avid art collectors would bid at the auction, eager to add the paintings to their private collection.

He boarded the Swiss Air flight from Genève Airport, delighted that the pieces were falling in place. He had not heard back from James, which, in this case, was reassuring. With just three days till the Indian Government lost its opportunity to claim ownership, another success was just around the corner. He had done all he could and believed that the paintings would sell significantly higher than their base price, possibly even generating 80 million pounds each. 160 million pounds, after deducting all commissions and expenses, would still mean over

1500 crore rupees, enough to arm the Jaish with unlimited capability to attack India from multiple fronts.

The first-class attendants knew Abbas well, since they had flown frequently with their premium customer. The Swiss, with customary efficiency, had accommodated his preferences on even this short flight, providing his favourite breakfast and tea, prepared the way he liked it. There was little to do till he returned to London, so Abbas spent the duration of the flight thinking back to the events that had led him to this point.

Born in Bombay, Abbas had been brought up in a joint family. Despite the poverty that had plagued India under British rule, Abbas and his family had lived well, his uncle Asif's production house generating enough money to keep the entire family living in style. Life began to change with his father's involvement in the movement for a separate state of Pakistan, his proximity to Jinnah becoming a source of severe friction between him and Uncle Asif, the patriarch of the house. Abbas remembered the heated arguments between his father and his uncle, and while he was too young to understand the argument itself, he was old enough to feel the charged emotions. Despite his uncle's best efforts to keep the family together, Abbas's father had eventually decided to leave Bombay for Lahore.

Abbas had been forced to move too, leaving behind a life he loved. He found life in Lahore to be lonely, unable to identify with the children of his own age group, all of whom were driven by a strong communal ideology. Desperately lonely and a huge fan of Devika Rani, like every other adolescent, he had begged to accompany his parents to her wedding and was heartbroken when his family had refused.

He had waited impatiently for his parents to return and thereafter, spent days forcing them to recount every detail of the wedding and the celebrations in Kappar. He had nearly come to believe that he had actually made the trip to India, attending in his imaginary world the wedding in Bombay, the celebrations in Kappar, the journey from Bombay to Kappar and back to Lahore, and all the places that his parents had visited while they were in India.

Within weeks of their return, Nazir had passed away, followed closely by Mehroonisa, who had been unable to deal with the grief of losing her husband. Abbas had been shattered and had struggled to come to terms with the unjust world. He had immersed himself in his schooling, mastering his lessons. His teachers, the religious scholars, had taught him about the unique mission that the Qaum had been allotted, by the one and only God. They had taught him the meaning of holy jihad and as his ideology had shifted, he made friends with other children similarly driven.

He had earned a Bachelor's degree in law from the University of Lahore and then a Master's degree in Oriental Studies from Oxford University. At Oxford, he had grown close to the scions of several elite Pakistani families and been introduced to the idea of India as the true enemy, the Kafir that posed the greatest threat to Islam.

On his return to Pakistan in 1963, Abbas joined the University of Lahore to teach law, while his new friends took up various positions in the government or launched new businesses that relied on governmental relationships. Abbas's radicalization had continued and gradually, he had even begun to express the stronger opinions that were taking shape within him, exchanging ideas with his closed circle on the means of inflicting maximum damage on India. The embarrassing defeat in the 1971 war had driven home the realization that Pakistan could never win a conventional war against India, and Abbas had begun to support the emerging strategy to bleed India with a thousand cuts.

His shifting ideology had not gone unnoticed. In 1973, he had been invited to a dinner at a friend's house, realizing shortly that the entire evening had been organized to enable Major Liyaqat to spend some time with Abbas. Liyaqat had made it clear, without ever expressly saying so, that he was ISI. As Abbas well knew, the ISI was far more than an intelligence service and was, in fact, the de facto ruler of Pakistan, exercising complete control over both the civilian government and the army, and significant influence over the judiciary.

Liyaqat and Abbas had spoken at length about Pakistan's strategy to liberate Kashmir by weakening India through a series of initiatives that forced the civilian government to spend disproportionately on defence. Abbas had recognized the conversation for what it was—a test. He had laid out his ideas to expand the strategy against India, advocating attacks against the civilian population in India's metropolises, in addition to the continued harassment of the armed forces—the combination designed to break the will of the civilian government. This could not be done directly by Pakistan, so they would need to create an army of unofficial soldiers under independent umbrellas, in theory, which would report to the ISI, in practice. The ISI would train these fighters and provide the logistical and financial support that they would need to terrorize India and to do so, would need to create an entirely separate source of funds that would not appear on any balance sheet.

Liyaqat had been duly impressed and over the next few meetings with Abbas, who had covertly joined the ranks of the ISI, they jointly created the financial strategy for the 'wet' funds that the ISI needed to create verticals for the smuggling of drugs and arms, as well as the sale of art and artefacts, each with its own 'business plan'. The ISI, impressed, had then asked Abbas to head its newly created Department of Art, which they felt was most suited to him. Abbas had accepted, setting up a dummy corporation in Pakistan, the fake history of which was provided by the ISI. Leveraging the antecedents of this corporation, small in scale but well-known in its home country, he had set up its London office in 1980.

He did not allow business to boom immediately, conscious of the need to create a cover so deep that it would be impenetrable. Abbas had started small, bringing a few less valuable artefacts from Pakistan, supplied by the ISI. As his income grew, he was able to show the purchase of more and more artefacts of increasing value. He had started with the smaller auction houses in London, his sole objective being the strengthening of the company's track record—the profit generated being a by-product of the need to demonstrate growth. Eventually, he had decided that the time had come to begin playing in the big leagues, bringing out remarkable lost works from noted Pakistani painters, including luminaries like Ismail Gulgee, Anna Ahmed and Ghulam Mustafa. One of the paintings had sold for nearly a million pounds, and suddenly, he was the toast of London, being invited to the parties that he had always needed to access and rubbing shoulders with some of the most influential people in art, as well as some of the wealthiest people in the world. Firmly entrenched in this world, he had finally begun to monetize his credentials, regularly bringing unique finds to the market, that had the wealthy salivating and clamouring for more. The ISI had been thrilled at his success, the tens of crores of rupees he earned them finding their way back to Pakistan, where they were gleefully laundered by the ISI through a network of charitable organizations to which the company generously donated. Business had become so good that the ISI had eventually set up a small division to support the activities of Abbas. This division was responsible for discovering an ever-increasing number of items of value that Abbas could sell, regularly looting the storage rooms of Pakistan's museums to procure what they needed or begging for contributions from Pakistan's wealthy in the name of liberating Kashmir. The division was also responsible for ensuring that the chain of antecedents was always clear, the ISI's experts producing a chain of masterfully doctored documents.

A patriot, Abbas loved his job and believed that he was making a significant contribution to Pakistan's national interest. He did not care for the money he now had, nor for the luxury that he now lived in, enduring both because they were expected of a man of his stature. He firmly believed that no single operation was worth risking forty years of effort and had therefore argued vehemently against the ISI's demand to sell the Roerichs, the knowledge of which he had been hiding up his sleeve for the last seven decades. His brows now arched in disgust as he recalled the orders from the chairman, better known to the world as Lt General Beg, the chief of the ISI.

Waking from his reverie as the plane touched down, Abbas was the first to disembark, walking through the immigration line reserved for first-class passengers and getting into his waiting car. The Roerichs were in play, for better or worse. He could now only hope that lady luck, for once, smiled on Pakistan.

His hopes were to be dashed in just over an hour.

# Chapter 42

As Kamal had promised, Tushar had received a *basta* full of photocopies from the ICAR by lunch on the previous day. He had spent the rest of the day studying the registers, struggling at times to read the handwriting squeezed into the impossibly small margins, as well as the auditor's reports stretching back to 1961, when the auditing process was probably first introduced, each report inordinately detailed and monotonous.

Reviewing the documents had taken him the entire day, at the end of which his office looked as if a tornado had ripped through it, leaving papers scattered in its wake. In his view, Kamal had summarized the situation perfectly. The paintings had undoubtedly been gifted to the ICAR by Rajesh Kumar, the then district collector. The auditor's reports, covering the best part of fifty years, clearly established that the paintings had been hanging at the centre ever since. The registers had been signed by dozens of officials as they came and went in the course of their duty, including twelve different directors of the ICAR and also by fifteen different auditors. It was impossible that the rot ran so deep that all of them had either been too lazy to verify that the paintings actually hung in the centre or conspired in their disappearance. Clearly, the records were accurate and the paintings had indeed disappeared sometime after March 2009.

Wanting to get a feel of the processes at the centre, he stationed himself outside the centre at 9 a.m. this morning, waiting unobtrusively behind a tree near the tea stall outside, watching dozens of officials trickle in. He had already observed that other than the disinterested chowkidars at the main entrance, the centre posted no guards near the main building itself, and people were free to come and go as they pleased. Surrounded by acres of thick forests, it would have been child's play for anyone to walk in when they pleased, by simply climbing over the six-foot-high brick wall that surrounded the compound. Well, that made it easy—it meant everyone was a suspect!

He walked in through the main entrance once he saw Abhijeet arrive, the chowkidars not even bothering to ask him for identification. Sauntering into the main building, he found his way to Abhijeet's office, seeking directions from various members of the centre's staff and utilizing the opportunity to observe the centre's layout. He introduced himself to Abhijeet's secretary and was ushered into Abhijeet's office soon after. The customary cup of tea and biscuits ordered, the two sat down to talk.

'Thank you for the documents. I studied them yesterday and agree that it is most likely that the paintings disappeared sometime after March 2009.'

Abhijeet nodded miserably as Tushar spoke.

'Here's what I need from you. I want to see the room where the paintings hung and then I want to interview everyone who has any reason to be in that room. I may want to speak to the rest of your staff as well, in due course, but first, the staff with access to that room.'

Abhijeet nodded and buzzed Priyanka in, asking her to escort Tushar to the librarian's office. Tushar nodded towards Abhijeet and rose to follow Priyanka. As they walked, he struck up a conversation with Priyanka, trying to put her at ease. He was sensitive to her nervousness, cognizant that she probably knew of him from the newspapers. By the time they arrived at the office that Kamal had visited only yesterday, he had learnt that she was single, twenty-five years old, originally from Delhi, had only been at the centre since October, had tremendous respect for Abhijeet, but was already thoroughly bored of her job. Now at ease, she walked confidently into the library, introducing the bespectacled librarian, Harish, to the SP.

Tushar asked the librarian to escort him to the private office, taking in the room and the two paintings that now hung there as he walked in.

'How long have you been the librarian here?' asked Tushar.

'Since 1 November last year, so about five months,' came the reply.

'Have you seen any other paintings in this room?'

'No, sir. Just these two.'

Tushar walked around the room, looking for any signs of another place where a painting may have hung—a nail that didn't belong, a hole in the wall hinting where a nail might once have been, or a dust outline that suggested a painting may have hung there. He found nothing. Clearly, the stolen paintings had once hung where the two paintings were now displayed.

'Who else has access to this room?'

'Sir, just the head librarian, unless the director approves otherwise.'

'Isn't that unusual—for access to be so limited?'

'Not really, Sir. Everyone can access the library during working hours. Only access to this office is limited because we store the centre's research papers in those filing cabinets over there. Some of them are very important and need to be protected. Also, no one is required here—I can provide whatever papers they need.'

'What about housekeeping?'

'They are also allowed only if I'm accompanying them.'

'Don't they have a key?'

'No, Sir. I lock the library when I leave for the day and the key stays with me.'

'So if anything is removed from here, it can only be with your permission?'

'Or the director's, Sir. But I would certainly know if anything is removed from this room.'

Tushar thought about what Harish had told him, his sincerity convincing him that he was telling the truth and knew nothing of the theft. In that case, the paintings had hung there in April 2009, when the auditors would have performed physical verification, and Harish had not seen any other paintings since the time he joined on 1 November 2009. So then that meant that the paintings had disappeared sometime between those dates.

'Who was the head librarian before you?'

'I'm not sure, Sir. I never met him. Priyanka?' he queried, turning towards her.

'His name is Kaka,' chirped Priyanka, happy to finally be able to contribute to the conversation.

'Kaka?' questioned Tushar.

'No . . . not Kaka. I'm sorry. I mean, that is not his real name, Sir, but that's what everyone called him. He was the head librarian for over ten years and retired in September last year.'

'How did you know him then? Didn't you join only in October of last year?' asked Tushar.

'Yes, Sir. That's right, Sir. He had retired before I joined. But he used to hang around here a lot, reading books and spending time with his old friends. We all felt very sorry for him. His wife was in a coma, I think, and he had no one else. He was sweet and never got in anyone's way, so everyone just let him be.'

'Is he here now? Does he still come here?'

'No, Sir. He stopped coming around after October, I think. From what I heard, he had admitted his wife to AIIMS in Delhi and had moved there.'

'Get me his file once we go back,' Tushar told Priyanka.

'It has to be Kaka,' thought Tushar. He fit squarely in the window within which the paintings appeared to have vanished, and had left Kappar soon thereafter. He would need to go to Delhi to find Kaka.

# Chapter 43

Tushar returned to the station and sat studying the centre's file on Kaka. Abhijeet had confirmed what Harish had explained—access to the librarian's office was indeed limited and the only people with permission to enter at their own discretion were the finance department and the auditors, that too only once a year. Abhijeet himself had visited the room only once and Kamal and he were the only outsiders to have visited that room in the last five years, at least to Abhijeet's knowledge. But when pressed, Abhijeet could not guarantee that the head librarians had not allowed anyone else into the room and had eventually agreed that given the centre's lax security, it was not impossible that strangers could have been allowed in.

Tushar read through the lean file containing Kaka's resume, interview transcript and annual confidential reports. Kaka's name was Jiten Singh and he was a resident of Bharatpur,

Rajasthan. He was one of seven sons of a former tehsildar in British India, but after his father's early death, had worked as a painter, an usher and a daily wage labourer to put himself through school, and then earned a scholarship to complete his Master's in English from Rajasthan University. He had come to Kappar to work in his uncle's business, married a local girl and continued to work with his uncle till his death. At a loss for what to do next, on the advice of a friend, he took a Diploma in Library and Information Sciences before finding employment at the centre. As Priyanka had said, he had been the head librarian for ten years before retiring in September 2009.

The file had only a singular mention of Jiten taking time off to admit his wife to the Kappar City Hospital but contained no further mention of her illness. Tushar called the hospital administrator, whom he had met a few times before, and within a couple of hours, learnt from him that Jiten's wife had indeed been admitted into the ICU for a brain aneurysm, which, while sparing her life, had left her comatose. After his retirement, Jiten had her discharged from the hospital to admit her to AIIMS, Delhi; the last record available with the hospital mentioned that an air ambulance had been organized to fly her out of Kappar on 19 October.

'What was the cost of keeping her in the hospital?' asked Tushar.

'It should have been very little. We are funded by a charitable trust, so he would have paid only for consumables. I can check the billing, but I cannot imagine it being more than Rs 15,000 a month for a case like hers,' replied the administrator.

'And the cost at AIIMS?'

'Well, that is hard to say. She would have needed the ICU there as well. I don't know for sure, but my guess would be less than 1 lakh a month.'

'And the air ambulance?'

'About 15 lakh.'

Tushar thanked the hospital administrator, requesting him to send over the files on Jiten's wife to him, and ended the call.

Jiten would not have been eligible for such exorbitant costs under the Central Government Health Scheme, so from where did a head librarian from a poor family get that kind of money? Was this his payoff for stealing the paintings? It was time to leave for Delhi and get these answers from Jiten Singh himself.

# Chapter 44

1 March 2010
London
3.30 p.m.

Abbas was driven straight to his palatial home from Heathrow Airport, the journey taking just over an hour. He strode into his study, inputting the series of passwords required to unlock his computer and access his emails, which he had been unable to do yesterday due to his hectic schedule. Abbas never used a smartphone—by the time they were invented, he knew that the actual capabilities of law enforcement far exceeded the public's grasp, including the near impossibility of guaranteeing the privacy of mobile phones. He preferred his privacy over the convenience of a mobile, and therefore, carried just a normal mobile phone.

He read his emails in the order in which they had arrived, responding to those that needed answers. Emails had come in from across the world to congratulate him on the acquisition of the Roerich paintings, several senders promising to be present— at least through a representative if not in person themselves—at the auction. Elation turned to frustration the moment he read the email from James. How could the Indian government have moved this fast? Was Pakistan's luck so poor that their plan would need to be scuttled because they had run into the only hard-working bureaucrats in the entire country?

The sale of the Roerichs at the Sotheby's auction was now out of the question. In fact, those paintings would never be sold through him again, for he knew he would lose the judicial battle if he chose to fight it.

He had, however, anticipated the unlikely contingency and now put Plan B into action. He replied to James, expressing his shock at having been cheated and his deep disappointment that these marvellous paintings would not find a loving home through Sotheby's. However, as James would appreciate, he could not just let go of two of the world's most valuable paintings, at least not until he had made further inquiries. Till such time, he would not relinquish his claim.

Having replied as Sotheby's would expect him to, he moved to update the ISI. He wrote out his message on a piece of paper and retrieved a copy of Salman Rushdie's *The Satanic Verses* from the bookshelf to code the message, using a combination of page numbers and word numbers to numerically code his message. This was amongst the oldest and hardest-to-crack coding techniques in the world as it offered no clear pattern which the decoders could work off. The only way to break the code was for the codebreakers to identify the book being used. They had selected *The Satanic Verses* for just that reason—no one would expect a devout Muslim to refer to the blasphemous book that had earned its author exile.

The ISI received the message a short while later, bounced from around the world using a series of VPNs, so as to make it impossible to trace. The message was decoded on priority and sent through to General Liyaqat, one of the five men in Pakistan who knew of Abbas's real role for the ISI. General Liyaqat spoke with General Beg, seeking permission to extract their man from India immediately, before he was identified and captured, as was likely now that a police investigation had been initiated. General Beg agreed and General Liyaqat called Harish's handlers, instructing them to warn Harish and ask him to disappear immediately. General Liyaqat had not been altogether surprised when the handlers failed to reach Harish, surmising that Harish was already aware of the impending threat and was on the run. If he had already been captured, then all was lost in any event. No matter how much he resisted the interrogation, he would, like every person on Earth, eventually break and disclose that he worked for the ISI. The ISI would deny it, of course, but their days of stealing art from India would be over.

But if Harish was on the run, he would need the ISI's help to get out of the country. Liyaqat knew the perfect man—Harish was no longer the only person looking for Suraj.

# Chapter 45

2 March 2010
Delhi
10.30 a.m.

Tushar had arrived in Delhi on the early morning flight from
Kappar. Yesterday afternoon, he had spoken to Ashish, his
batchmate from the IPS, and now a DCP with the Delhi Police,
to seek his assistance, which had been prompt and forthcoming.
Ashish was waiting for him outside Terminal 1 at the Delhi
airport and enveloped him in a bear hug as soon as they met.
They had been great friends at the academy and had stayed in
touch, though the pressures of their jobs meant that they spoke
less frequently than they would have liked, and were meeting in
person after three years.

Delhi was obviously suiting Ashish, who, once lean, thin and
muscular, had now developed a bulge around his middle. His
broad shoulders and thickly muscled forearms were reminders
of the once well-built frame, but his earlier chiselled face had

begun to show the effects of being deskbound for hours on end, its sharpness giving way to pleasant roundness.

The old friends caught up on their drive to AIIMS before Tushar shifted the discussion towards his investigation. Ashish's constables had already made inquiries at AIIMS and confirmed that Asha Jiten Singh was indeed in the care of the neuroscience department and was still comatose. Her records confirmed that she had been flown in from Kappar by an air ambulance arranged by her husband and admitted there on 19 October. Her husband visited her every day between 11 a.m. and 1 p.m. and spoke to her for the entire duration, not once receiving a reply. All her bills were paid on time and other than the husband, she never had another visitor. As Tushar had requested, the Delhi Police had made no efforts to question Jiten.

Thanking Ashish for his assistance, Tushar spent the rest of the journey explaining the case to him, hoping that another expert may grasp something he may have missed. Before long, they were at the entrance to AIIMS, the enormous hospital shining brightly under the blue summer sky. They drove in through the entrance on Yusuf Sarai Road, their siren clearing a path through the traffic jam at the entrance. They drove down the driveway, packed with ailing humanity, the cars parked on either side transforming the once two-lane road into a barely navigable one-way. Not even bothering with the public car park, Ashish's driver drove straight into the parking reserved for the hospital director's guests, the otherwise haughty guards backing away meekly at the sight of the police jeep.

Ashish was familiar with the labyrinth of AIIMS, having been here dozens of times on business. The massive complex, spread over one hundred acres in the heart of Delhi, comprised thirteen buildings, all interconnected by a series of corridors and walkways. Despite its complexity, the hospital lacked adequate signage and with each corridor looking exactly like every other, Tushar would have been completely lost without Ashish. Ashish walked purposefully, finally pushing open the doors to the neuroscience department. A pretty nurse, dressed in a clean skirt, smiled as she saw Ashish, obviously familiar with the policeman.

At his request, she showed them to the private room occupied by Asha Singh. The old woman was alone, dozens of wires and pipes protruding from her body, connecting her to the machines that beeped and whirred tirelessly to keep her alive. Tushar and Ashish stood there sombrely, feeling sorry for the old woman, till the nurse asked whether they wanted to meet her doctor as well.

Tushar shook his head, deciding that the doctor could add nothing but technicalities to the unfortunate reality that lay before him. He asked instead to see her file, following the nurse back to her station. He flipped through the thick folder, verifying again, though he did not really doubt it, the dates that Ashish had confirmed for him. He also had a close look at the bills for the last three months, discovering that the administrator at Kappar had not even been close in his estimate and Jiten was actually incurring a monthly expense of nearly Rs 3 lakh to keep Asha there.

He nudged Ashish towards a corner, away from the ears of the nurse, and explained that he was keen to catch Jiten by surprise. The last thing he wanted was for the suspect to think that the police were waiting, and disappear once again. Ashish nodded, walked back to the nurses' desk and briefly explained the situation to her; she was delighted at the unexpected excitement. She showed them to an empty room, where the two men sat down to wait for Jiten.

# Chapter 46

2 March 2010
Delhi
11.30 a.m.

Tushar and Ashish had been waiting for an hour, but Jiten had not arrived, even though it was past his usual time. Both looked at their phones for the millionth time to check the time. Ashish knew what Tushar was thinking—after all, the same thoughts were running through his head. Could his visit yesterday have tipped off Jiten or could someone have warned him that the police were lying in wait? Was it inconceivable to believe that some of his payoff had been used to buy the cooperation of the hospital staff?

Tushar had begun to impatiently pace around the tiny room and Ashish was concerned that he might leave the room. As soon as he stood up to calm the restless Tushar, the nurse opened the door, her eyes opened wide in excitement, signalling wildly that their quarry had arrived, her head bobbing up and down.

'Where is he?' whispered Tushar.

'In her room,' replied the nurse breathlessly.

'Does he suspect we are here?'

'I don't think so. He greeted us like he always does and walked straight into her room.'

Tushar rushed past her and ran into the ICU, Ashish trailing in his wake. Jiten, startled, jumped out of his chair as the two officers barged in, closing the door behind them. He looked at both of them, mouth agape, consternation on his face, his brain unable to process why these two strange men were there.

Tushar recognized Jiten from his file photos. Deciding that his best chance at a confession was aggression, he stared straight at Jiten and spoke, 'My name is Tushar Misra and I am the Superintendent of Police at Kappar.'

Jiten stared blankly at Tushar, unable to understand a thing. Finally, he spoke, 'Yes Sir. I am Jiten, Sir. What can I do for you?'

Expecting the old man to fold under pressure, Tushar decided to adopt the direct approach. 'Where are the paintings?'

Jiten stared at Tushar vacantly, struggling to make any sense of the question. 'What paintings, Sir?'

'Don't play dumb! Tell me! Who did you sell the paintings to?' yelled Tushar, taking a menacing step towards Jiten, the old man backing into his chair. Scared witless, Jiten burst into tears and put up his hands protectively.

Tushar and Ashish exchanged a glance while they waited for Jiten to finish sobbing, both agreeing on the next step without speaking a word. Playing the role of the good cop, Ashish walked up to Jiten and gently placed his hand on Jiten's shoulders, sympathy writ large over his face. He consoled the weeping man, poured him a glass of water and spoke to him gently till he finally calmed down.

'Just tell us what you did with the paintings,' said Ashish gently.

'What paintings?' repeated Jiten, looking at both officers beseechingly.

'The ones you stole from the ICAR,' growled Tushar.

'I have no idea what you are talking about, Sir. I have not stolen any paintings.'

'Don't lie to me! Tell us the truth and I will do what I can to ensure that you serve as little jail time as possible.'

'I am telling you the truth, Sir. I have not stolen anything,' whimpered Jiten, a quaver returning to his voice, his fright apparent to both officers.

'I'm talking about these paintings,' said Tushar, stepping forward and holding up pictures of 'Silent Night' and 'Valley of Flowers'. 'The ICAR has filed an FIR about the disappearance of these paintings. Just tell me what you did.'

'I didn't do anything,' replied Jiten meekly. 'I know these paintings but I have not stolen them. I swear I have nothing to do with them.'

Tushar banged the table hard in exasperation. 'Do you think I am a fool? They were hanging in your office till you left, but are no longer there. Who else could have taken them?!' thundered Tushar.

'I don't know, Sir, but I didn't take them. The paintings were still hanging in my office when I left. I swear on my wife, Sir. I did not take them.'

'Liar! How else did you get the money to bring her here!?'

'I sold my mother's house,' said Jiten quietly. 'I had to sell it to take care of her.'

Something in his tone made his words ring true. Jiten looked straight at them, his posture regaining some dignity, confidence returning to his voice. 'Sir, you can check. I sold it to Madhav Menon at the end of September 2009. The sale is registered. You can call Madhav and check,' he said, getting up and offering his cell phone to Tushar.

Tushar took the phone, pulled up Madhav's number and stepped out of the room to make the call, signalling to Ashish to stay and guard Jiten. The phone was finally answered after eight rings, a breathless man yelling into the phone. Tushar introduced himself and explained why he was calling. Five minutes later, he walked back into the room and returned the phone to Jiten.

'Madhav confirmed everything,' said Tushar, answering Ashish's unspoken query. 'My office is checking with the sub-registrar in Jaipur. We should know soon.' Hearing Tushar, Jiten relaxed, knowing that his story was true.

'You have six brothers. How did you sell the house?' asked Tushar.

'They are all dead, Sir. My nephews and nieces agreed to let me sell the house so I could take care of her,' he said, pointing to his comatose wife.

'Why did you leave Kappar in such a hurry?'

'Sir, I didn't leave in a hurry. I left only after I had retired, even though she was in a coma long before that. Even then, I had to wait to sell the house before I could bring her here.'

'Are you sure the paintings were still there when you left?'

'100 per cent *pakka*, Sir. They never left that room while I was there.'

'Yet the new librarian says they were not there when he joined. Can you explain that?'

'I don't know, Sir. When I retired, I gave the keys to the director. I never entered that room again after retirement. I went to the library sometimes to meet with my friends and to read while I waited for the sale to come through.'

'Are you saying the director stole the paintings?'

'Oh no, Sir. He would never do that. Perhaps someone took the keys from him?'

Tushar took out his phone and called Abhijeet, the director answering on the first ring. He put his phone on speaker so they could all hear the conversation, explained what he had found so far and asked him whether anyone had taken the keys from him after Jiten had left. Abhijeet was adamant that those keys had remained in his office locker—the only time he had taken them out was to hand them over to Harish when he had joined.

'Shit!' exclaimed Tushar.

It wasn't Jiten that had stolen the paintings. It was the man who had lied so smoothly to him.

# Chapter 47

2 March 2010
Delhi
12.15 p.m.

'It had to be Harish,' said Tushar, dialling as he spoke. 'This is Tushar,' he said as soon as the phone was answered by the duty officer at the police station in Kappar. 'Take Harish in for questioning right away in relation to the theft of the paintings.'

He then called Abhijeet and asked him to ensure that Harish did not leave the premises till his team had arrived. 'Ask him to bring you some files,' yelled Tushar at Abhijeet's stupid question on how he should do that.

While they waited to hear from Kappar, Tushar apologized to Jiten. He jotted down Jiten's number and address in Delhi, and asked him not to leave Delhi without checking with Ashish first.

The two returned to Ashish's car and rolled down the windows to let the trapped heat escape. Both men sweated copiously while they waited for the car to cool, the air conditioning straining to alleviate the heat even on its maximum setting. Tushar answered his phone, his face transforming into a scowl as he heard the news from Kappar.

'Put out an alert straight away. Make sure that we have men covering the airport, railway station and bus stand. Circulate his photo to every policeman in the state and put it up in as many places as possible. Put up *nakabandi* on all roads leading out of Kappar. I want him caught,' said Tushar urgently.

'He's already disappeared?' asked Ashish. Tushar just nodded, acutely aware that Harish had had the better part of twenty-four hours to leave Kappar. Harish had not come to work and was not at home. The police were questioning his neighbours, but it was improbable that would lead to anything quickly. For all they knew, he had simply left yesterday. He had been so close to catching the real culprit, but his gut had let him down and Harish had duped him. 'Fuccccckkkk,' screamed Tushar, denting the dashboard as he put his angry fist into it.

Ashish waited for his friend to regain his composure. As long as Harish hadn't left the country, they could still try and find him, difficult as that would be, but if he was already beyond Indian borders, there was no real way for them to bring him back. Once Tushar had calmed down, Ashish expressed his thoughts to him.

Tushar nodded. They could only hope that he was still in India. Even if they could find a way to keep an eye on all legal routes out of India, there was little chance that they could stop Harish from traversing India's porous borders through the dozens of illegal routes. An exercise of that scale was well above his pay grade, requiring a level of coordination between multiple law enforcement agencies across the country that only a political nudge could provide. Though Tushar didn't believe he would get the required support—the matter was simply too small in the larger scheme of things—he could think of only one person he could ask for help. He picked up his phone yet again and dialled, hoping that the man would answer.

# Chapter 48

2 March 2010
Delhi
11.30 a.m.

Harish had arrived at the Inter State Bus Terminal in Delhi—the ISBT as it was better known—earlier in the morning, after boarding a late-night bus from Kappar. He had stayed in Kappar much longer than he had liked after stealing the paintings and had spent the entire journey cursing his boss, who had insisted on him staying till they had stolen two more paintings from a timber merchant in Kappar. He had managed, with great difficulty, to maintain his equanimity, first in front of Kamal and then in front of Tushar, but the brief interaction with Tushar had convinced him that it was time to leave. Everyone in Kappar knew of Tushar's reputation and Harish was no exception.

He had wanted to leave as soon as Tushar left his office, and it had taken every ounce of self-control to stay and continue doing his work, just in case Tushar had posted watchers outside the centre to keep an eye on anyone who behaved suspiciously, such as anyone who left earlier than usual. He had spent the rest of the day in the library, cowering behind the counter, one eye constantly on the entrance, waiting for Tushar to reappear to arrest him.

He had practically run out of the centre as soon as the clock had struck six, eager to get out of the city. He had congratulated himself on his decision to stay when he walked out of the centre and his trained eye spotted the policeman posted outside the gates, trying to blend into the populace in plain clothes. His training had taken over, restoring calmness to his frayed nerves. He had matched his pace to the others, looking to the world like any other tired office-goer leaving at the end of the day. The cop had given him a quick look, decided that he was of no interest and turned his attention to the rest of his colleagues, as they poured out at 6 p.m. Having avoided the trap, he had headed to the bus stand to book a ticket to Delhi, finding one only for the last bus, given the rush of the tourist season. With the ticket in his pocket, he had proceeded to Sukhna Lane, the hub for all taxi and car rental services, hoping to either hire a taxi to Delhi or rent a car he could drive. He had gone from shop to shop unsuccessfully, all options already booked or rented out. Left with no choice but to wait for the late-night bus, he had gone home. He had spent the time pacing up and down in his small house, counting the seconds, looking anxiously out of the window, expecting to see the police storming his door any time. Close to panicking, he had eventually decided to leave home— even if the police pieced the story together, he wouldn't make it that easy for them to catch him.

Invigorated by the decision, he had shoved his bed aside and pried up the loosened tile to expose the small hole that he had gouged out underneath. The plastic bag lay where he had left it, cash and his real passport resting safely inside. He pocketed the

cash and passport and packed a light backpack, looking like just
another traveller, and hoped to blend into the tourist crowd of
Kappar. His preparations completed, he had walked to Pihu's,
his favourite restaurant in Kappar, to take his last meal in the
city.

An uneventful meal later, he had returned to the bus stand
and waited restlessly, chain-smoking till it was time to leave. He
sat nervously till they were out of Kappar, before finally relaxing
enough to take a nap. He had slept fitfully on his utilitarian
metallic seat on the bus and was sore and tired by the time he
arrived in Delhi.

Having had time to think, Harish knew that he had an
enormous problem. If Tushar had already visited Kaka in Delhi,
he would have concluded that Harish was the thief—knowing
Tushar's reputation, it was likely that he had boarded the first
flight from Kappar that morning and gone straight to AIIMS
to find Kaka. In that case, the police would already have tried
to find him and raised the alarm when they realized he was
missing. The first thing they would have done would have been
to scour the airport, train and bus stations and the car rental
agencies, to discover whether he had already left Kappar; the
confirmation of this would be received from the CCTVs at the
bus stand. They would know that he had boarded the bus to
Delhi and likely assumed that he would take an international
flight from the capital, seeking to get as far away from the hands
of the law as he could. Tushar would certainly have made every
effort to alert all ports of international departure, starting with
Delhi and then expanding outwards, before his target had had
time to leave India.

Harish calculated that setting up the alerts would take some
time, but, all things considered, he decided not to risk a flight
from Delhi. In fact, the more he thought about it, the riskier the

proposition of leaving through a legal route seemed. He thought about hiding in Delhi, but dismissed that idea as well, fearing that the police would start tightening the noose and make it impossible for him to escape a manhunt in Delhi. That left him with one option—he had to get to Jaisalmer and find Suraj. The man had taken the paintings out of India with little difficulty, and Harish hoped that he could smuggle him back into Pakistan just as easily.

He needed to leave Delhi while the police were focused on international departures. He gobbled his breakfast and hailed an auto to take him to the New Delhi Railway Station, agreeing to pay the small fortune demanded by its driver. He intended to board the first train out of Delhi that he could get on—if it took him to Jaisalmer, well and good, else he would board one that got him as close to Jaisalmer as possible and then make his way there himself.

Thirty minutes later, they reached the station, Harish parting with a 500 rupee note, the driver grinning at successfully extorting that amount for the few kilometres they had travelled. He walked to the booking office and joined the queue for tickets, his heart thudding faster against his chest with each passing minute, as adrenaline pumped through him in the fear that the hunters were about to start closing in on him, erasing any hope of escape.

# Chapter 49

2 March 2010
Delhi
11.45 a.m.

Harish had been waiting at the same spot for the last fifteen minutes as some idiot at the front of the queue was fighting with the station staff over something. The heat was stifling and sweat poured down the faces of the hundreds of people that resignedly waited their turn. The booking office stank of sweat and unwashed bodies, of spit and urine, and of decay, all of which combined to create a nauseating mix that sickened him to the pit of his stomach. It was only his desperation that kept him in line, shuffling uncomfortably from one foot to the other.

He had discarded his mobile in Kappar, wanting to make it inconvenient for Indian law enforcement to track him. Most people believed that a phone, once switched off, could not be tracked, but Harish knew better. Not only could it still be located, but the unique signature of each phone was tacked on to each SIM card that was inserted in it, making it pointless to simply switch SIM cards. However, under stress, he had made a huge mistake, leaving behind the Gita into which key contacts were coded as a fallback for just this type of eventuality. Now, without his phone and the book, he was disconnected from his handlers, who would neither be able to connect him to Suraj nor provide any other assistance. He would just have to make his way to Jaisalmer and find Suraj by himself.

The line finally began to move once the Railway Police had removed the offenders, their protestations and threats of dire consequences when their allegedly powerful parents heard about the incident ignored by the four burly cops who dragged the young men out. A few minutes later, he reached the counter and purchased a ticket for the unreserved compartment of the next train to Ahmedabad, which, as per the schedule displayed on the electronic board above the ticket counter, was the next train going towards Gujarat.

Ticket in hand, he moved towards the washroom, holding his breath, as he walked into one of the dirtiest places in India— the only place at the station without CCTV coverage—the toilets. He walked over to the auto driver who had brought him to the railway station, parting with an additional 500 rupee note in exchange for the ticket that the man had bought for him, for Jaipur. Eyeing his baseball cap, Harish pointed at it, the driver holding up another five fingers, this time to signal the exorbitant price for the tattered baseball cap.

He exited the bathroom, baseball cap pulled low to hide as much of his face as possible from the dozens of CCTV cameras installed in the main concourse and on each platform. Trained to avoid CCTV surveillance, he carefully watched their movement, before picking a route that brought him into the line of sight of only two cameras. He had not tried to avoid the CCTV at the ticket office, wanting his pursuers to see the time stamp to identify the ticket that he had bought, knowing that there was no way for them to know that he now held a second ticket. Hopefully, they would not look at the rest of the CCTV footage as carefully once they knew which train he was supposed to be on, and he would be able to buy himself some time while they chased after the red herring.

He strolled towards Platform 2 to board his train to Jaipur. Given the extensive surveillance at the railway station, once his pursuers found that he had never boarded the train to Ahmedabad, they would no doubt revisit the CCTV footage and discover that he had travelled on the train to Jaipur.

But, hopefully, by then he would have been able to get to Jaisalmer and, with a little luck, found Suraj and made the arrangements to be smuggled back across the border.

# Chapter 50

2 March 2010
Delhi
12.20 p.m.

Kamal was in a meeting of the Planning Commission, the entire ruling political establishment and the top echelons of the central bureaucracy assembled under one roof for this three-day marathon. They had been in a conference since 9.30 a.m., debating over means of minimizing leakages in a centrally sponsored scheme, so that the intended benefits actually reached the poor. As yet, not one person had had the courage to address the elephant in the room—the sticky fingers of the responsible minister and the avarice of his cabal of cronies who ran the scheme.

Kamal had sneaked a glance at his phone, vibrating to alert him of an incoming call, the name 'Tushar SP Kappar' flashing across the screen. He knew that the call must be urgent as Tushar had chosen to call him directly on his mobile, but there was no way for him to step out of the meeting without irking some of the politicians. Kamal rejected the call with a text message saying that he was in a meeting and would call back.

He looked at his phone when it buzzed yet again. Barely able to contain himself after reading the message, Kamal waited impatiently for the lunch break to arrive, jumping out of his chair and moving with alacrity towards the exit as soon as the chairman adjourned the session. He called Tushar back and listened carefully as he explained everything that had happened and how Harish had escaped. He heard Tushar's request for inter-agency cooperation to facilitate a lockdown, but unsure whether he could arrange for it, he had asked for time to see what he could do, asking him to use whatever contacts he had at his disposal in the meanwhile to ensure that Harish did not leave the country.

He thought of approaching his minister but decided against it. By the time his minister actually did something, it would be too late. He looked around the room where the most powerful people in the country were assembled, realizing that he had not one true friend amongst them. Suddenly, an idea, albeit a long shot, occurred to him.

The chief of intelligence, one of the three men in India who could lock down the country in a matter of hours, was from his alma mater St Stephen's College, Delhi University. While he had been a couple of years senior than Kamal and they hadn't been friends, Kamal did have access to him through the Stephanian alumni network, reputed globally for its willingness to support other Stephanians. He was confident that the network would introduce him to the CI, and that the chief would listen simply because of the St Stephen's connection.

He called his friend Pankaj, also a Stephanian, and now the special Secretary in the Home Ministry. Kamal requested the introduction, explaining that he was short on time. His friend of thirty-five years, Pankaj trusted Kamal's judgement and knew he would never have asked if he did not believe the matter to be of paramount urgency. Wasting no time, he promised to organize the call.

Three minutes later, Kamal's phone buzzed again, this time with a message from Pankaj. Kamal typed out a quick thanks, opened the message and clicked on the number Pankaj had shared. The call was answered on the first ring; Kamal, being as concise as he could be, briefed the CI on the theft and Tushar's investigation, and conveyed his request to lock down international departures before Harish could escape.

The CI, who had taken the call out of courtesy, had perked up on hearing about the stolen paintings appearing for sale in London. His first thought was that this could be the connection to the 'artist in London' that Abdul had informed him about, and he decided to help the police capture Harish, wanting access to any information that Harish may have.

Expecting to be turned down, the matter being treated as irrelevant to national security, Kamal had been surprised when the CI agreed to help, asking for Tushar's number to coordinate with him directly. The CI also asked Kamal to come and meet him at his office in South Block, promising to provide more information when he got there, before disconnecting the call.

Kamal, his curiosity piqued, left for South Block immediately—the politicians would just have to carry on with the rest of the charade without at least one officer who wanted to perform his duty.

# Chapter 51

2 March 2010
Delhi
1.30 p.m.

Amitabh and Kamal arrived at South Block at the same time. As Kamal walked towards the CI, he was stopped firmly in his tracks by two armed men, part of the CI's security detail. Phone pressed to his ear, the CI noticed the minor commotion from the corner of his eye, recognizing Kamal. He signalled the security men to let him pass, continuing to whisper into his phone while Kamal waited.

After ending the call, he turned to the smartly dressed young man standing quietly by his side, introducing him to Kamal as Yash, his chief of staff.

'Has the lockdown protocol been activated?' asked the CI.

'Yes, Sir, as soon as we received your call. All international airports are on alert and his picture has been circulated to immigration. The same is being done for all ports and international border crossings right now,' replied Yash.

'Good. Let's start locking down domestic travel as well. Send his picture to all airports, railway stations, bus stands, taxi rentals and shared cab services. CCTV from Kappar showed him boarding a bus to Delhi last night, so let's start with Delhi. Maybe he hasn't left Delhi yet, if he actually did come here. Then widen the lockdown area as quickly as you can—focus on the Pakistan and Nepal borders since they are the closest.'

Yash was already on the phone, implementing the CI's instructions, as both Kamal and Yash turned to follow the CI, striding towards his office. A minute later, Kamal found himself in an underground bunker under South Block. Having been in the government for thirty years, he had been posted across multiple ministries, several headquartered at either South Block or North Block, the two massive stone-block office structures that guarded the way to the Rashtrapati Bhavan. And yet, not only had he never seen the bunker, he was not even aware that it existed. He looked around hurriedly, struggling to keep up with Amitabh, who was walking purposefully towards a glass door at the end of the cavernous hall. Reaching the door, Amitabh removed his spectacles and peered into a retinal scanner, the door hissing open a few seconds later to permit the three men into the situation room.

While Amitabh and Yash headed straight to the bank of monitors on one wall, Kamal looked around in amazement. The room looked like it was from the future. Most of it was dimly lit and packed with electronic equipment, of which Kamal recognized only the computers, into which dozens of technicians were peering, their fingers clacking on their keyboards. Despite the number of people inside, the room was eerily quiet, the silence broken only by the constant hum of the electronics, the keyboards and occasionally, whispers exchanged between the occupants. As he walked through, he caught glimpses of the computer screens—aerial views of cities on some, dangerous-looking men on others, and a stream of text messages on a third. He eventually made his way to Amitabh, who was supervising a team that was scouring through CCTV footage of a railway station. As each person appeared on screen, the images were overlaid by graphics that measured the facial features of each individual, throwing up the names of each person as the analysis was completed.

Kamal was mesmerized—he had seen similar images in a recent article about China's surveillance systems and recognized that he was looking at a facial recognition software. Despite his seniority in the government, at that point, he had not had even an inkling that India not only had access to but had also deployed a mass surveillance system of such calibre.

'The Israelis developed it for us,' Yash whispered into Kamal's ear, answering the unasked question evident in his astonishment. 'We hacked into the CCTV recordings from Delhi's railway stations and uploaded Harish's image into the software. The software is now checking if he was at any station in the last twelve hours.'

Kamal continued to stand there, hypnotized by the rapidly moving images. The supercomputers powering the system analysed gigabytes of data each second, the images on the screen appearing as if on fast-forward. Five minutes later, the computer pinged, isolating one image from amongst the thousands, and displaying it on the screen. The image showed Harish standing in line to buy a ticket, the time stamp showing 'New Delhi Railway Station 11.47 a.m.'

'There is no way he is still at the station,' spoke Amitabh. 'Analyse the rest of the footage, see what train he boarded. Pull up the list of departures from NDLS today,' he instructed, two technicians nodding their heads in acknowledgement.

The first technician keyed in additional instructions and the images began to move again. Another brought up the departure schedule and displayed it on one column of monitors for all to see. Without being asked, he was displaying departures only between 11.47 a.m. and 1.52 p.m., the current time. A few seconds later, the machine pinged again, showing a man in a baseball cap on Platform 2 at 12.15 p.m. All eyes turned towards the board, locking on the seventh row, which showed the train leaving near that time—the 12.30 p.m. Makranti to Jaipur.

'Continue searching. Make sure that wasn't a decoy and he is indeed on the Makranti. Get access to live footage and keep looking.' The technician nodded again, his fingers flying over the keyboard.

'Yash, get the railway police to man every stop between Delhi and Jaipur. No one knows we have this capability and Harish would likely be expecting us to take a lot longer to discover where he has gone. I don't think he will get off before Jaipur, but let's take no chances.'

'Get me the police commissioner in Jaipur,' he signalled to another aide. The police commissioner was on the phone a few seconds later, being briefed personally by the CI. Harish was to be nabbed at the railway station and held informally by the Rajasthan Police till Amitabh's representatives reached Jaipur. The team tasked with nabbing Harish was to be dressed in plainclothes and was to use a private vehicle and a safe house. No formal record was to be maintained and no government facility was to be used. Instructions issued, the CI disconnected the call.

'Yash, that train takes four hours to reach Jaipur. It is now 2 p.m. Get a team on a helicopter to Jaipur, but wait till the police have done their job. Ask them to fly the same route as the train, so we can divert them in case he decides to get off earlier.

I will be in my office. And someone please find out who this Harish really is!'

Final instructions issued, he asked Kamal to follow him. 'I know I promised you more information. But for now, I need to focus on catching him. Perhaps, you could wait?'

'Of course, Sir,' said Kamal, recognizing that the CI wasn't really giving him an option.

'Excellent. We have a waiting room. My staff will show you to it. Now, if you would excuse me, there are other matters to deal with.' Not waiting for a response, Amitabh turned and left, walking towards the other fires that he needed to put out.

# Chapter 52

2 March 2010
Delhi
2.15 p.m.

Kamal was resting comfortably in the CI's waiting room. It was more a suite than a waiting room, containing a bedroom, a sitting room and a private washroom, comfortably larger than his son's apartment in Mumbai.

He was already bored. With little to do and, as always, unwilling to waste time, he decided to learn more about Roerich—after all, it couldn't hurt to get to know more about the subject that had triggered such frantic action at the highest levels of the government. He sat at the computer console in the sitting room to google Roerich and see where the research took him.

He started with 'Valley of Flowers' and 'Silent Night', reading more about the paintings, their supposed provenance and their expected value in the upcoming auction. While he knew that the paintings would not be auctioned on the tenth, Sotheby's had not yet made an official announcement of the same and the art world, therefore, had continued to speculate, with estimates ranging from the floor price of 20 million pounds, extending all the way to 100 million pounds for each painting. While he knew that art sometimes sold for extraordinary prices, to be this closely associated with works which could set new records for the most expensive paintings ever to be auctioned, was quite exhilarating nevertheless. If the ICAR could recover both paintings and sell them, they could have an additional 2000 crore to spend. It would sort out all of ICAR's financial problems in one fell swoop.

He began reading about Svetoslav Roerich, starting with his Wikipedia page. He learnt that Roerich was born to famous parents; his father, Nicholas, a renowned painter, and his mother, Helena, a significant promoter of India's Vedic knowledge. The family had fled to India to escape Lenin, making a home for themselves in Kappar. Roerich had taken after his father and began painting at an early age. He soon began to find fame and gather what would eventually become considerable wealth.

In 1948, he had met and subsequently married Devika Rani, the doyen of Indian cinema in that tumultuous time. He found some articles that delved into their fairy-tale romance, several highlighting that they had first met in Kappar while Devika was there shooting a film, describing the grand wedding in Bombay and the reception in Kappar. The couple had lived in Kappar till early 1961, after which they migrated to Bangalore. They had sold Sommerville House and purchased a fifty-acre estate in Bannerghatta on the outskirts of the city, soon becoming the leading lights of the emerging cultural hub of Bangalore, regularly appearing at and hosting parties. The marriage had ended with the death of Svetoslav at the age of ninety-three, Devika following a year later, both buried next to each other in the gardens of their estate.

Kamal read, with disgust, the consequences that followed their deaths. Without legal heirs, their will, which passed on the estate to their housekeeper, had been found to be a forgery. While the investigation was ongoing, the housekeeper had disappeared, taking along several treasures from Svetoslav and Devika's personal collection, supposedly including ancient manuscripts that Nicholas had discovered, as well as negatives of movies which had not been released to the public by Bombay Talkies, the production house that Devika had founded. The government had, thereafter, taken over the estate and, unsurprisingly, mismanaged it, failing to protect the destruction of dozens of Roerich paintings that lay within, from the heavy rains in Bangalore.

His curiosity piqued as he read about their fascinating journey, Kamal decided to delve deeper into the movie that had brought them together. Pulling up a list of movies starring Devika, he painstakingly collated information about each movie from a multitude of articles, finally concluding that she had starred in only one movie that had been shot in Kappar. While he had never heard of *Beintehaan*, the movie had been a tremendous success, elevating the career of those associated with it to much greater heights. He read more, learning that it marked the first time in Indian cinema that both leading characters died in the movie, amazed at the risk-taking appetite of a producer in the 1940s, when even in 2010, the whiff of even one of the leading characters dying was generally enough for a movie to tank. The producer Asif had backed the brave ending back in 1948, and been met with great success.

Impressed, he decided to learn more about Asif. It appeared that Asif had been active till the early '60s, having produced over forty films, almost all fairly successful and only three considered flops. He had retired wealthy and enjoyed retirement till 1983, when he finally died of old age. In addition to an incredible legacy, he left behind a lot of real estate in Mumbai, which, despite his will, had become the subject matter of legal dispute as various factions of his family fought over them. The case, not unusual in Bombay, had made national news only because Asif's sister's side of the family, despite having moved to Pakistan just before Partition, had staked a claim, creating myriad jurisprudential issues.

Absorbed in this historical battle and keen to understand how the issue was resolved, he began to grapple with the case itself. He read the various opinion pieces that had appeared in the media around the time, thinking how much higher journalistic standards had been before the emergence of the twenty-four-hour news channels. Finally, he decided to read through the judgment of the Bombay High Court to understand the legal principles that the court used to deny the claim made by the Pakistani side of the family. While Kamal already knew the facts from the media articles, his meticulous nature drove him to read through the facts as they had been presented to and understood by the court, before jumping to the resolution. He was scouring through the pages swiftly, leveraging all of his experience from years of reading files, when a paragraph caught his eye. He re-read the paragraph more carefully a second time, as it laid out the entire family tree and the relationship of each member to Asif. And there, towards the end, were the words that had caught his eye.

He read them again . . . 'and Mehroonisa's son, Abbas Ali.'

Could it be? Was this the link between knowledge of the paintings' whereabouts and their appearance in London? Mehroonisa was Asif's sister and Asif was very close to Roerich, courtesy of his relationship with Devika. Was it too hard to believe that either Abbas's parents or his uncle knew of the paintings hanging at the centre and had, at some point, told Abbas about them? Of course, there would be a million Abbas Alis in Pakistan, but how much of a coincidence would it have to be for some other Abbas Ali to have stepped forward to auction paintings that were connected to the Abbas Ali mentioned in the judgment?

'Surely, that would be too much of a stretch,' he thought and switched his attention to learning all that he could about the man from the case. There were thousands of articles about Abbas, who, it turned out, had built an enormous fortune as a leading art dealer in London. Some articles spoke about his emigration from Pakistan in 1968, but he could find nothing about his early life. As far as the media was concerned, his was a spectacular story of an immigrant making his way to a land of greater opportunity and finding success through intellect and hard work.

Kamal had scribbled some notes as he read. It was only when his stomach growled that he realized he had lost all track of time going down the peculiar rabbit hole, and it was already past 6 p.m. Tired but feeling as though he had traced the link between the appearance of the paintings in London and their disappearance from Kappar, he typed out a succinct note for the busy CI, printing a copy and exiting the room to find Amitabh and tell him what he had found.

# Chapter 53

2 March 2010
Jaipur
4.45 p.m.

Harish had hated the journey from Delhi. It had been so hot in the general compartment that one winced in pain the moment their hand touched any metal surface. To compound the heat, the compartment was overflowing with people, several of whom smelt like they hadn't bathed in several weeks. He was disgusted by their filthy clothes, their unshaven faces and the stench of sweat and urine coming from them. He had tried to create a bit of breathing space around him but had given up the fight under pressure from a heaving mass of people which seemed to grow at every station.

He had considered deboarding at each of the stops on the train's laborious journey for a breath of fresh air, but had decided against it each time, choosing the little comfort of the privilege of being seated, rather than being forced to stand for the rest of the journey. Having carried no water with him and unwilling to accept the water offered by his stinking neighbours, by the time he finally arrived in Jaipur, his throat was dry and he was famished. He opened his eyes at the announcement of their impending arrival in Jaipur, the thought of a fast exit evaporating the moment he saw the tumult that had ensued, people jumping off the train even before it had halted. Instead, he had shrunk back into his seat, lifting his feet off the filthy floor and on to the berth, and waited for the bogey to empty.

He stepped on to the stone floor at Jaipur Junction and took note of the direction in which the crowd was moving, recognizing that as the main exit. Rather than following them, he walked towards a water fountain and washed his face with the warm water, careful not to drink any of the likely unfiltered water. He wiped his face with his handkerchief and strolled to the closest food stall, procuring a cold drink and samosa, relishing the moisture as it revitalized his parched throat and the feeling of hunger dissipating. The platform was empty, save for a few coolies lounging around and a few people waiting for their train to arrive. Relaxed by the fresh air, samosa and cold beverage, he was lost in thought, thinking about his next steps, and so, failed to notice the four men surrounding him till two of them grabbed an arm each and yanked them back painfully, constraining them with zip ties behind his back. As he sucked in a deep breath to scream, a third man stepped in front of him and punched him hard in the stomach, knocking the wind out of him along with his capacity to alert anyone at the station. Harish doubled over, his eyes turning bloodshot red with pain, spittle falling out of his mouth, his lungs burning to draw in the air that had just been expelled so violently from him. The men holding his arms marched him forward, supporting his body weight with their muscular arms, as Harish tried desperately to keep his feet on the ground. The other two men walked directly in front, blocking the view from the few people on the platform, most of whom were scurrying away from them anyway.

They climbed the stairs towards the exit, more or less carrying Harish out of the station, and bundled him into the back of a waiting van, his head hitting the steel floor hard as they forced him inside. Before he could sit, a cloth was shoved into his mouth as a gag. He shook as violently as he could to free himself, but was unable to, with his hands tied behind him and his back pressed flat against the floor of the vehicle. He tried to sit up but was rewarded with a powerful punch that broke his nose. He finally collapsed in pain, unable to breathe through his mouth and finding it increasingly difficult to breathe through his bloody nose.

The vehicle drove away unmolested, most people failing to notice the abduction and the rest not daring to intervene. Harish lay on the floor, wondering who these men were and why they had grabbed him. His brain, with its full capacity directed towards helping him breathe, was unable to provide an answer. Confused, breathless and in tremendous pain, Harish finally surrendered and passed out.

When he woke up, he was in a helicopter, once again lying bound on the metallic floor, with two men he had never seen before glaring down at him. He tried to speak, only to find that the gag was still in his mouth, held firmly in place by tape that he could see from the corners of his eyes. He tried to move but found that he was restrained more firmly than earlier, his arms behind him, his feet held together by two zip ties and his head chained to the floor. He panicked, the primal urge of flight suppressing all reason. As he struggled against his binds, one of the men pulled out a syringe, removed the cap to reveal the needle and plunged it into Harish's arm to deliver the contents of the syringe into Harish's bloodstream. A few seconds later,

Harish was fast asleep, though the two men kept an eagle eye on the sedated prisoner.

The helicopter landed at Delhi's Safdarjung Airport forty minutes later, whipping up a dust storm underneath, the deafening roar of its rotors forcing the people waiting on the tarmac to cover their ears. Situated in the heart of Delhi, the Safdarjung Airport was used primarily by India's intelligence services for some of their more delicate operations. Over time, the government established a firm perimeter to prevent unauthorized entry and even got the New Delhi Municipal Corporation to erect opaque barricades on the flyover that overlooked the airstrip, to guarantee its privacy. The two guards jumped out of the helicopter and undid the chain holding Harish captive to the floor, lifted his comatose body and placed it in the back of a waiting ambulance. The ambulance's attendant took his seat next to the 'patient' and the driver made off instantly, setting a course for South Block, where interrogators from the CI's office awaited Harish.

The next time Harish opened his eyes, all he saw was a bright light that forced him to squint. He could hear people moving around him, speaking in whispers. He tried to move but once again, was unable to do so since his legs, hands and torso were bound with leather straps to the chair he was seated on. Understanding his predicament, he simply gave up the struggle and let his body relax, preparing mentally for whatever it was that was coming his way.

Amitabh took this as his cue. He stepped forward and stood in front of Harish, who recognized him right away. While the CI made every effort to keep a low profile, he was well-known to the ISI. All agents of the ISI were schooled in identifying important targets within the Indian government and the CI's name ranked high in that list. The pieces fell in place for

Harish as he grasped that he had been captured by Indian law enforcement, his mind working furiously to work out how they could possibly have caught him so soon.

'How . . ?' stammered Harish.

'That is no longer relevant. The question is, what next? You obviously recognize me so I will leave the decision to you,' said Amitabh, speaking softly.

Harish's mind was in a whirl. He had no doubt that they would use increasingly painful means to extract the information they needed, till he capitulated. There was no Geneva Convention in the real world, at least not in the world of spies. There was no mercy either. And yet Harish, indoctrinated for years by the ISI, was unwilling to give in. He simply glared at Amitabh, defiance written across his face.

'That's unfortunate,' said Amitabh, recognizing the look on Harish's face. 'Take him away,' he said to the man standing in the corner.

# Chapter 54

2 March 2010
CI's Headquarters, Delhi
8.30 p.m.

It had taken the interrogator only a few minutes to break Harish. He had not bothered to build up to the 'enhanced interrogation'—the diplomatic term used to describe the most awful forms of torture—and instead, had directly adopted the method he knew to be most effective. Harish's head was tilted back and held firmly in place by the strong hands of another interrogator. A cotton cloth was placed over his face, letting in just enough light to allow him to see shadows.

He saw one shadow move to the water dispenser, calmly filling a jug with water. Harish's eyes widened in terror at the realization that he was about to be waterboarded, the technique perfected by the American armed forces. He tried to shake his head to loosen the iron grip that held it in place but ceased his exertions at the sight of the jug being tilted towards his face. He caught one last breath before the cold water poured into his nose and mouth, the unending stream continuing to drown him long after he had expelled the last dregs of air from his starved lungs. At the count of twenty seconds, the interrogators stopped, allowing Harish to sputter out as much of the liquid as he could. Just before he could suck in another breath, his head was jerked back in place and the stream of water poured once again on to his face, this time for a count of thirty seconds.

Starved of oxygen, his brain shut down all non-essential functions, redirecting the remaining oxygen to fuel the systems on which his survival depended. His body was a cacophony of panic, unable to deal with the sensation of drowning. His vision had begun to cloud over as his brain refused to process any information other than the demand for air from his screaming lungs; the rest of his body was paralysed as all motor control became focused solely on his mouth and nose in a desperate effort to get them to draw breath.

The interrogators took another brief stop, allowing just enough oxygen to return to his body for him to retain consciousness and for his brain to recover some functionality. The pauses had been scientifically refined to guarantee the cooperation of the subject and the interrogators had enough experience to know that anyone unwilling to die would eventually cooperate.

Just as his brain began to reboot, the waterboarding was reinitiated, this time continuing for forty seconds. The sudden reversion towards death short-circuited the parts of his brain that dealt with deep cognitive reasoning, transforming it, albeit temporarily, into a state in which it was willing to trade all rationality for survival. The men removed the wet cloth from his face and waited for Harish to catch his breath.

'Shall we continue?' asked one of the interrogators.

Trembling with fear, Harish shook his head, staring at the interrogators in terror.

'You should have known better. Are you ready to go back to the other room?'

Harish nodded in mute agreement and was carried back to the room where Amitabh was waiting. Amitabh looked up from his phone, waited for Harish to be placed on the ground in front of him and then took his position.

'I really am sorry that it had to be like this, but you left me no choice. I hope we don't have to do it again. Will you answer my questions?'

Harish nodded resignedly, desperate to avoid another waterboarding.

'Who do you work for?'

'The ISI,' responded Harish without hesitation. Amitabh's eyebrows arched in surprise at the revelation.

'Why would the ISI steal paintings from India?'

'They sell them to generate funds. The ones that are not recorded in any budget.'

'How long has this been going on?'

'I don't know. I have been doing this for four years.'

'Who is Abbas Ali?'

'I don't know who that is.'

'How did you know where the paintings were?'

'The ISI knew. They told me to steal them.'

'How did you get the job?'

'The ISI provided fake documents. The interview was not difficult.'

'How did the ISI know about the paintings?'

'I don't know.'

'How were the paintings taken out of India?'

'I don't know for sure. The ISI sent a man called Suraj to steal them. I helped him steal the paintings. He smuggles them over the Jaisalmer border.'

'When were the paintings stolen?'

'30 November.'

'How do you get in touch with Suraj?'

'I don't. The ISI coordinates the meetings. Suraj gets in touch with me.'

'How?'

'He came to Kappar to take the paintings on the day we had agreed.'

'How were you planning to leave India?'

'By finding Suraj in Jaisalmer.'

'How?'

'I am not sure. I would have found him somehow.'

Amitabh believed every word. Harish was just a foot soldier, and apparently a very good one, but the ISI had, as always, played the game well by keeping the various parts of the operation segregated from each other. The only questions that really mattered to him now were who was Abbas Ali and how had he come across paintings stolen by the ISI?

He looked at Yash for any follow-up questions. Seeing Yash shake his head, he waved his fingers, sealing Harish's fate to spend the rest of his life in a prison he could never escape.

'I want to know everything about Abbas Ali and whether he is connected to the ISI,' said Amitabh, looking at Yash, who simply nodded.

# Chapter 55

2 March 2010
Delhi
10.30 p.m.

Kamal managed to get some dinner at the cafeteria in South Block, which remained open twenty-four hours to provide sustenance for members of the government machinery who worked late into the night more often than the public could have imagined. While the meal had been insipid and oily, it had provided him with the energy to continue waiting for the CI, who was in a meeting that he could not leave.

Exhausted, Kamal had nevertheless continued to wait, wishing desperately that he had carried a cigar. After watching the news, he decided to take a walk in the garden outside South Block, letting the CI's staff know where to find him. He called Mira, his wife of thirty-five years, to let her know that he would be late, refusing, as he always had, to answer her questions about his work.

Eventually, he felt a hand on his shoulder and turned around to see Amitabh. Despite the long day that the CI had had, he looked as cool, composed and in command as he had earlier that day.

'Abbas is ISI,' said Amitabh, making no effort to acknowledge Kamal's long wait. 'Harish confessed that the paintings were stolen to generate funds for them. The R&AW office in London has had their eye on Abbas for a while and suspects that he is a front for the ISI. You must have been wondering why I got involved and I promised you an answer—it's because we had intelligence that funds for an unimaginable attack by Jaish were being generated in London through some connection to an artist. The paintings were stolen by the ISI and given that they were being sold through Abbas, it is likely that the R&AW's suspicions about Abbas are correct. Harish was just a pawn of the ISI, who are effectively the masters of the Jaish. Where the ISI is unable to provide funds directly, it provides logistical and organizational support. That's what they did here—providing a man to steal the paintings, means to smuggle them out of India and a front to sell them. No doubt the money would have found its way back to Pakistan and from there, to the Jaish.'

As Kamal heard the CI out, all his research made sense. This had to be the same Abbas Ali whose name had appeared in the court case. An art expert, he had known the value of those paintings and had, when his employers needed the money, found a way to have them stolen from India.

'He already knew about the paintings,' said Kamal, handing over the note he had prepared. Amitabh read the note, not insulting Kamal's intelligence by asking questions about the source of the information.

'So, what now?' asked Kamal. 'Can you have him arrested?'

'On what grounds?'

'For theft of national treasures, of course!'

'And how do we prove that he had them stolen? The only people who can make that connection are in Pakistan and are certainly not going to help plead our case.'

Kamal was quiet, thinking through the CI's point.

'Kamal, what happens to the paintings now that we have made a claim?'

'Sotheby's has already confirmed that they will withdraw the paintings from the auction. But, they will not give them to us unless Abbas relinquishes his claim over them. If he does not, a court will have to decide who the owners are.'

The CI contemplated the information and finally spoke, 'I think I know how to get the paintings back. Best for you not to get involved,' he added before Kamal could ask what solution he had come up with. 'You carry on pursuing our case for recovery of the paintings and I will see what I can do. If anyone tells you not to pursue it, please tell them that the instructions came straight from the PMO and they should call there to confirm, if required. I will reach out when the time is right. For now, thank you. You have done a great service to this country.'

That said, Amitabh walked off again, without waiting for a response. One of his aides appeared magically at Kamal's side, escorting him gently towards the car which had materialized on the side of the road.

'The car will take you home, Sir. Good night,' said the aide politely but firmly, shutting the door closed behind Kamal. Too tired to argue, Kamal let himself be driven home to rest, ready to wake up the next morning to serve his country again.

# Chapter 56

2 March 2010
London
5.30 p.m.

Aastha had rushed out of the shower, dripping wet, to answer her phone. That particular ringtone was for one person only and there were very few circumstances in which that ring could go unanswered. Still naked, holding the phone slightly away from her wet ear, she focused hard on the instructions being issued by the quiet voice on the other end.

The instructions were, as always, crystal clear. Terminating the call, she finished her shower, postponing her hair day to another. Wrapping herself in a towel, she went looking for her husband to inform him that she had been called in for a work emergency and that he would, once again, need to watch their six-month-old in her absence.

She stood before the mirror and took a moment to admire her lithe body, the hard work she had put in after the birth of her son visible in the tautness of her skin and the lean muscle in all the right places. She noted the little fat that remained around her belly, committing to herself that she would get rid of it before the year was out. Five minutes later, she was dressed in the attire of an Indian defence attaché in London—a knee-length skirt and silk blouse covered by a jacket designed to show off her curves. She kissed her husband goodbye and cuddled her baby, holding him close for a few seconds before reluctantly setting him down in his crib.

She spent most of the thirty minutes of her drive on calls, organizing what she needed, before arriving at India House in Aldwych, the office of the High Commission of India. While she was familiar with the guards who secured the building, she was stopped and her car was searched meticulously, checking as she well knew, for hidden explosives. She checked her phone while a golden retriever sniffer dog slowly circled the car, taking its time examining the various smells emanating from the car, its tail wagging happily. The precaution had become standard protocol across all embassies, the global diplomatic corps having learnt the hard way of the need to protect themselves against car bombings, the devastating tactic pioneered in Asia, which was now being employed across the world from Beijing to Guadalajara. Finally, the dog finished, its tail still wagging happily, and her identity card was returned. The guard signalled the booth to lower the steel barriers at the entrance and she was waved through. As a mid-ranking defence attaché, she did not have a designated parking spot and had to drive around to look for one.

She leapt out and walked speedily to the elevator to make up for lost time. She placed her palm on the biometric scanner and announced her name into the microphone, waiting as the High Commission's software reconciled her print and voice against its database. Verification complete, the lift ascended to her office on the fifth floor, where her team was already assembled. The men stood up as she entered, acknowledging the arrival of their boss. The head of operations moved to her side and explained to her the steps that had already been taken.

Teams of watchers were setting up base outside the target's home and office. From now, a twenty-four-hour vigil would be maintained on both premises by rotating teams of two agents working in six-hour shifts. A separate team would follow the target's vehicle till they managed to place a tracker on it. A team of analysts had been taken off other assignments to staff the operational base created in the Indian embassy—they had to combine research with analysis of surveillance footage from the on-ground teams to provide all the information the boss may want. Additional resources drawn from the technical team were allocated to ensuring exhaustive electronic surveillance of the target and working to hack into his phone and Internet network, while the on-ground team prepared to tap his fixed line.

Satisfied, Aastha asked for the taps to be patched to her laptop and withdrew into her office to update her boss, the Chief of Intelligence for India.

Codenamed 'Pumpkin', India's highest-ranking spy in England had just cast an invisible surveillance net around Abbas.

# Chapter 57

3 March 2010
Delhi
11.55 p.m.

The surveillance had gone off as well as he had expected from the highly trained team deployed in London. The mobile pursuit team had been able to place a tracker on Abbas's Bentley while it was parked at a traffic signal, enabling them to give up the pursuit of the vehicle and instead support the watchers, thus further reducing the risk of them being spotted. They had been unable, so far, to bug his home office as the security was a lot tighter than they had expected it to be. The team had sought permission to undertake a risky operation to achieve this objective, but unwilling to allow even a hint of their activities to come to Abbas's notice, he had refused, instructing them to avoid risk of exposure and propose an alternate strategy.

A big success had come from the technical team, who had successfully tapped Abbas's wireless Internet connection and piggybacked on it to gain access to his computer and mobile phone, so that they could see the activity on each device in real-time. They downloaded his entire hard disk and mobile storage on to a remote server, which analysts in London and Delhi were now combing through to unearth any information relating to the impending attacks on India.

Most importantly, the team had intercepted two emails, which they had forwarded to him. The first was from James Mitchell:

Dear Mr Ali,

Thank you for your email.

On behalf of Sotheby's, I note your decision not to waive your claim to the two paintings, 'Silent Night' and 'Valley of Flowers' that you had submitted to us for the auction on 10 March. As per my previous email, under law, the paintings will be held in our custody till their ownership is decided by a court of competent jurisdiction.

I would also like to inform you of another development that has come to light. As you would know, given the importance of these paintings, our verification department had, out of abundant caution, also subjected the frames to an X-ray analysis, the report for which has come back today. The analysis has unexpectedly revealed a small bulge of paper hidden in the frame of Silent Night. This envelope was removed during the analysis, and remains, like the paintings themselves, in our custody, to be handed over in accordance with the court's decision. While we have not opened the envelope and do not know what it contains, the envelope itself has upon it a seal depicting two elephants standing on their hind feet, holding up a flag. Though our team has so far been unable to recognize the seal, we wanted to share this information with you (and will also be sharing it with the Government of India) in the hope that it may allow for clarification of the chain of ownership. A picture is attached for your reference.

Once again, I express our deepest disappointment at being unable to proceed with the auction and hope that you understand our constraints.

Humbly yours,
James

His eyes opened wide in disbelief as he read the description of the seal. As CI, he was deeply involved with Kashmir and was well-versed in the history of the state, including the former kingdom that the seal represented. He had heard of the legend that a document had been signed secretly between Raja Jai Kishan Singh and a representative of Lord Mounten's at the time of the accession of Kashmir; a document said to contain a secret so explosive that it could shake the geopolitics of the region. He had never really believed that it existed, as no reference to it had ever been found in the papers belonging either to the raja or Mounten and surely, if the document was as important as legend suggested, at least one of them would have left a clue to its whereabouts. In the absence of any leads, he had not actively hunted for the document but had always kept an eye open for any clue that may verify its existence and provide a lead to get to it.

Now, when he least expected it, a document bearing the seal of the Kingdom of Kashmir had appeared, hidden in a painting stolen from India. Everyone who had studied the raja knew that Nicholas Roerich, the father of the artist behind the two paintings, had been a close friend of his. Was it possible that this was the document from legend? It was certainly plausible—given their friendship, the raja may well have entrusted the document to Nicholas, who was, perhaps, more importantly, an outsider who did not bear the burden of Partition and had no stake in the Kashmir conflict. If Nicholas did indeed have the document, was it really too much of a stretch to believe that he had hidden it in a frame his son had used?

No one knew what the document contained; hearsay from history had clouded the truth. But, if it did indeed contain an explosive secret, he reasoned that it could only have to do with the accession of Kashmir. In that case, it was vital that he recover the document to understand its implications, and then decide what ought to be done with it. His primary goal would now be to procure that document.

He opened the second email from London, containing a series of numbers, interspersed with single spaces. He recognized the coding tool, having employed it himself in Pakistan, and sighed unhappily, realizing that without knowing which book Abbas was using as a reference to code his message, there was no way for the code to be broken. But at least the use of code confirmed that Abbas was a spy, and unfortunately for him, one who had succeeded for far too long.

Amitabh leant back, wondering how he could recover the document which was undoubtedly secure in the vaults of Sotheby's. He didn't know it then, but he wasn't the only one grappling with exactly the same question.

# Chapter 58

3 March 2010
Islamabad
8.30 p.m.

General Beg, General Liyaqat and Colonel Abdul were assembled around General Beg's conference table, a copy of the decoded message placed in front of each of them. Abbas's latest email had come in a few minutes ago at the address reserved for communication between him and the ISI, and the officer on duty had, as per protocol, decoded the message on priority and sent it through to General Beg.

General Beg's reaction had been nearly identical to Amitabh's. The ISI, unlike the CI, was aware that this document actually existed. In a final stab to India's heart, Mounten had informed the Pakistani government of the contents of the document. Knowing that it would damage their claim over Kashmir permanently, the ISI had secretly searched for the document for the last seventy years, but had failed to find it. They had suspected that the document had been stolen by Charan Singh, but by the time they had mounted an operation to find him, he had already died in an accident. In desperation, they had tortured his wife for its location but eventually concluded that he had not confided in her.

The secret of the document's existence was guarded very closely by the ISI, who had decided long ago that preventing the knowledge of it from getting out was paramount, even though it meant that the ISI was never able to dedicate the resources that it would have liked to hunt for it, forced as they had been to obfuscate the truth under the mountains of lies.

Now, incredibly, it seemed that Allah had finally smiled on Pakistan, rewarding the ISI's benevolent support of the Jaish's celebration with a far more rewarding discovery. Like all senior ISI officers, General Beg was well-versed in the history of Kashmir and the characters who had moulded its future during Partition. He, too, was aware of the friendship between the raja and Nicholas, and because he knew that the document existed, he had no hesitation in linking the paintings to the document.

He summoned Liyaqat and Abdul urgently and swore them to secrecy before revealing the secret to them, deciding that he needed their motivated involvement if they were to move fast enough to recover the document that could change the current geopolitical equation forever. General Liyaqat and Abdul sat transfixed as General Beg narrated the history and the chain of events which he believed had led them so close to having it in their possession. Like the CI, he too had decided that procuring the document took precedence over everything else.

'I need that document,' he said, looking in turn at both Liyaqat and Abdul.

Both men nodded but remained quiet, their minds working furiously to draw up plans to recover it.

'We need to steal it from Sotheby's,' said General Liyaqat.

'With all due respect, General, we don't have the time,' said Abdul. 'Sotheby's is one of the most secure buildings in the world and has never been robbed. We would need months of work to plan such an operation and even then, we can't be certain that we would succeed.'

General Liyaqat nodded. 'So, if the document cannot leave Sotheby's and we cannot steal it, what do you think we can do, Abdul?'

'Whoever said it can't leave Sotheby's? It just can't leave with us,' smiled Abdul. 'Here's what I think we should do . . .'

A few minutes later, he had outlined a simple plan. While it required rapid deployment, it also offered a high probability of success and a negligible probability of the effort being traced back to the ISI. General Beg thought it over for a few minutes before nodding.

'Go ahead, Abdul. Make the arrangements.'

# Chapter 59

4 March 2010
London
3.30 a.m.

The black Ford Fiesta stopped 200 metres from its destination after having covered 500 metres with its headlights turned off. Three men, their dark clothes invisible in the night, exited the car and fell into formation, hugging the shadows as they made their way up the slope towards their target. Each of them kept a trained eye out for any bystander who could potentially witness their actions, talking softly to each other through their wireless earpieces. They had launched the operation at 3.30 a.m., the darkest hour of the night, to minimize the probability of being spotted. And even though it was the easiest assignment they had ever undertaken, they were thorough professionals throughout to minimize the chances of any error or interruption.

The electronics expert was the first to get to the main door, his companions keeping watch while he performed his task. Within fifteen seconds, the expert had made a mockery of the alarm system, undermining the enormous amounts of money that its manufacturing company had spent touting itself as the best alarm one could buy. He opened the door silently, allowing his colleagues to slip in, before walking in himself and closing the door behind them. The electronics expert guarded the door while the others searched the ground floor. Seeing no one, the three tiptoed up the stairs to the first floor, finding the people they were looking for behind the first door they opened.

Two men walked to the side of the bed occupied by the snoring man, while one stayed on the side occupied by the woman. Coordinating with each other through gestures barely visible in the little light filtering in through the window, they shook the couple awake from their sleep, stuffing a gag into their mouths before they could gather their wits to scream. The leader pointed a silenced weapon at the couple, discouraging any resistance, while he spoke softly, asking both of them to get out of bed.

James and Janie, terrorized, complied and docilely followed the leader into the den. They sat in the seat he was pointing to with his gun, watching mutely as one of the other men zip-tied their wrists together. Quivering in fear, they failed to hear the leader speaking to them and were shaken out of their paralysis with a slap across James's face.

Having captured their attention, Shadaab removed his mask, smiling politely at the couple. He had received a call from Abdul, earlier that evening. It had taken him several hours to put the required pieces in place, and now, with the couple in his grasp, he was ready to execute the rest of Abdul's plan. When James and Janie regained their wits, he explained why he was there and what he needed James to do.

James was horrified at the request, unable to believe that they expected him to remove a document from Sotheby's without authorization, his entire being revolting against the idea of betraying his employer. The gag in his mouth making verbal communication impossible, he shook his head vigorously, leaving no doubt about his refusal. Shadaab, smiling wider, removed the gag.

'I won't do it,' sputtered James, swallowing large gulps of air. 'I can't.'

Shadaab nodded, stepped up to Janie and smashed his fist across her face, drawing blood from the nose he had just broken. James sat there, mouth agape, stunned at the violence. The gag was shoved back into his mouth by Shadaab, who then took a seat, waiting patiently for James to realize that he had no choice.

Janie passed out as James watched her with worry, concerned at the short gasps of breath she was drawing. A full minute passed before James finally turned to look at Shadaab.

'I can't get the document out. Not without leaving a paper trail. I will spend my life in prison if I steal it.'

'No, you won't. Not if you do what I ask you to do.'

James shook his head again. Annoyed, Shadaab nodded at his colleagues, who began to unpack and assemble the apparatus they had carried with them. Shadaab grabbed the unconscious Janie's hair and dragged her to the base of the apparatus, shackling her legs to its hooks. As one of the men turned the winch, her body was raised off the ground, till it dangled upside down like a carcass at a butcher's shop. Shadaab looked again at James, his eyebrows raised questioningly. James shook his head again, still refusing to do what they wanted.

Without hesitation, Shadaab removed a serrated blade from its sheath on his belt, assuredly puncturing Janie's jugular vein and allowing her blood to fall on to the floor, its patter reverberating through the quiet room. James struggled violently against his bonds, desperate to rescue his pregnant wife, his eyes growing bloodshot as he fought for breath under the gag, but was held down firmly by the third man. Finally, he quietened, nodding his head in defeat, watching gratefully as his wife was lowered to the floor, the flow of blood reducing in intensity.

Shadaab pulled up a chair in front of James and looked him straight in the eye. 'I don't really want to hurt her, but I will if I have to. Are you willing to listen to what I have to say?'

James began to cry, the gagged whimpers shaking his entire body. Shadaab waited, having witnessed the emotions before, knowing that composure would follow shortly. The sobbing eventually subsided, the question that Shadaab had been waiting for finally emerging from James.

'How do I do it?'

Shadaab smiled again, patting James on his knee. 'Thank you, James. Here's how we get what we want without you going to jail,' he began, spending the next few minutes laying out Abdul's plan. 'And, of course, James, should we even suspect that you have betrayed us, Janie will die. I promise.'

# Chapter 60

4 March 2010
London
9 a.m.

James left the tube station at 8.45 a.m., physically and emotionally drained, having spent the rest of last night and the entire morning considering his options. He had thought about approaching the police but had rejected the idea, certain that the intruders would have no qualms about killing Janie if they so much as suspected the police's involvement. He had considered approaching the chairman for help but had dismissed the thought as well, as it would have led to the same place—the police. No matter what he thought of, every idea seemed to lead to the death of his wife.

Unable to come up with a viable solution, before leaving home, he had made the decision to implement Shadaab's plan, rehearsing it mentally during the ride to Sotheby's. He exited the tube station and walked hesitantly towards his office, his feet increasingly leaden with each step. He checked the inside pocket of his suit jacket for the umpteenth time, reassuring himself that the vial that Shadaab had provided was still safe in its silk cocoon. Standing outside Sotheby's, he hesitated again, fighting the urge to run, reminding himself of the two lives at stake. He walked in, surprising the doorman with his unusually early arrival, and strode into his private office, ignoring the surprised salutations of his secretaries.

Shutting the doors behind him, he dialled Janie's handheld. The phone was answered by one of the guards, who turned on the camera to let James see his wife. Tears streamed down his face at the sight of her, battered and bruised, her hands still bound in front of her, looking distraught as she half lay on the sofa. She looked up at the sound of his voice, her eyes pleading for help, before the camera was turned down to the man's wrist, his finger moving from side to side, miming the passage of time. Without a word, the man disconnected the call.

His resolve strengthened and he set about executing Shadaab's plan. First, he pretended to work as he would have every day, replying mechanically to emails and staring blankly at the reports waiting on his desk. As the clock moved towards 10 a.m., he dialled his secretary, instructing her to bring up the document that had been discovered in 'Silent Night' so that he could examine the envelope in more detail. While he waited, James withdrew the vial from his pocket and emptied the contents into the glass of water on his desk.

The document was brought in a few minutes later, ensconced in the glass case in which it had been stored for protection, his secretary also carrying in a pair of gloves, tweezers and magnifying glass for him. While she placed the items on his desk, James took two large gulps from his glass, emptying it. James looked at the envelope he was going to steal, wondering what it could possibly contain to have brought such danger into his life. He thought about opening it but restrained himself, remembering Shadaab's instructions to refrain from opening the envelope under any circumstance. A few seconds later, he felt his heartbeat quicken, as Shadaab had told him would happen. The liquid that he had poured into his glass would mimic the symptoms of a heart attack without actually causing one, allowing him to exit the building in the hands of the paramedics that would be summoned to save his life.

James extracted the envelope from the case and placed it in the same pocket from which he had withdrawn the vial. Beginning to struggle for breath, he barely managed to press the button that summoned his secretary, before passing out on the floor. The secretary entered a few seconds later, running towards the desk at the sight of his outstretched body on the floor. She saw her boss gasping for breath, his face ashen and full of sweat, and concluded, as Shadaab had expected, that he was having a heart attack. She quickly pulled out her handheld and dialled 999, the emergency number.

Breathlessly, she explained the emergency to the woman that answered, who told her that an ambulance had been dispatched and would arrive shortly. Clueless as to what to do next, she sat by James's side, holding his hand, waiting for the paramedics, who arrived less than two minutes later. Expertly, they placed him on a stretcher and whisked him out of the building and into the ambulance waiting outside, its sirens blaring. The entire staff of Sotheby's exited their offices to see what the commotion was about, news of the heart attack spreading through the ranks.

Not one person noticed that the ambulance had arrived almost immediately after the call was made. That is, until the second ambulance arrived a few minutes later.

# Chapter 61

4 March 2010
London
9.30 a.m.

Pumpkin watched her team bind the men who had been left behind to guard Janie.

She had barely begun to plan Abbas's abduction on Amitabh's instructions, when he had called again. She had heard the new instructions, concluding that the CI had received fresh intelligence on which he was acting. Within forty-five minutes of his call, she had assembled her own assault team and made her way to the address he had given her.

Her team had watched from their concealed positions as the three men had entered James's home. They had watched the exits all night, wanting to make sure they knew how many people were inside. They had seen no movement till James had left earlier that morning, looking traumatized and dishevelled, accompanied by another man that none of them recognized. The assault team had made their move soon after the departure of James and the third man. Pumpkin had lobbed the tear gas into the chimney, the odourless, invisible gas designed to spread throughout the house. Fifteen minutes later, they had entered the house, carefully searching the ground floor rooms for any hidden threats, before making their way up the stairs to find all three bodies, fast asleep, where each of them had sat.

While she had no compunction about following the CI's orders as far as the two men were concerned, she was distraught at having to follow the order with respect to the innocent woman. For the first time in her career, she had challenged his orders but had been firmly rebuffed, the CI offering to replace her if she didn't have the stomach for what needed to be done. For a brief moment, empathy had pushed her to consider accepting the offer, but professionalism and self-preservation had prevailed, as the consequences of disobeying one of the most powerful men in India struck home. She had, coldly, promised to execute his instruction.

The fact that they were all unconscious made it a little easier. She nodded once at one of her team members, confirming the kill order and left the men to finish their task. She waited outside, permitting herself her first cigarette since her pregnancy.

She tried to comfort herself in the knowledge that a man like Amitabh would never have issued the order to kill the innocent woman, unless he absolutely had to. She had killed before, but she knew then that this one would stay with her for a long time.

# Chapter 62

4 March 2010
London
10.07 a.m.

The ambulance, siren blaring, drove out of the Sotheby's compound, making a right up Sotheby Road towards A1201, which would lead it to St Nicholas's hospital. But as soon as it had crossed the next signal, the ambulance turned off its siren and began cruising silently towards its real destination—the third floor of the parking lot at Avenell road.

Arriving at the lot, the ambulance drove to the corner where Shadaab was waiting. The 'driver' and 'paramedics' exited the ambulance and made their way out of the parking lot, intending to hail a cab to St Pancras station, from where they would board the Eurostar back home to Paris. When the investigation into the fake ambulance would be launched, while the CCTV footage would show the three men, the French police would not even try and find them once they had disappeared into the dangerous ghettos from where they had been summoned by Shadaab, no matter how many times the British asked.

Abdul's plan had gone off perfectly. James, believing that the liquid only mimicked a heart attack, had willingly consumed the poison that had painfully stopped his heart. The software that Shadaab's technical expert had installed on James's phone had allowed them to listen to everything happening in his office, thereby guaranteeing that their 'ambulance', parked just around the corner on Aberdeen road, arrived at Sotheby's before the real ambulance dispatched by emergency services did.

Alone, Shadaab opened the door to the ambulance and took the envelope from James's breast pocket, pleased that he had followed the instruction to store it there. He took one last look at the dead man, whose fate had been sealed the moment the men had entered his home, before he closed the door and walked out of the parking lot in time to keep to his rendezvous with Abdul.

Abdul was already on his way to St Joan's Catholic Church for his meeting with Shadaab. After receiving General Beg's approval of his plan, he had left for London to personally carry the document back to Islamabad. He had boarded a military jet from the Sargodha air base and landed in London earlier that morning, General Liyaqat making the necessary arrangements to ensure that Abdul's jet would be given permission to land, cooking up a story that the British, suspecting nothing, had easily accepted. General Beg and General Liyaqat waited in General Beg's office, in case any obstacles that appeared in Abdul's path needed to be removed, till the document was safely back in Pakistan.

En route to the airbase, he had explained the plan to Shadaab, the men agreeing to meet at the Church at 10.30 on the following morning. He had instructed Shadaab to eliminate the Mitchells to guarantee that the theft could never be traced back to Pakistan. He had then made one additional call to ensure that the last piece of the puzzle was put in place, sending a coded message, this time from his phone itself, just before his plane took off from Sargodha.

The two men met outside the church, hugging upon meeting each other after a long time. Shadaab handed the envelope to Abdul, confirming that any trail to Pakistan was now impossible. With nothing further to do, Shadaab returned to the shadows till he was needed again, and Abdul left to hand the document over to the man who was waiting for it.

# Chapter 63

4 March 2010
London
11 a.m.

Pumpkin and her team had returned to the Indian embassy, where the CI was waiting in the conference room. Amitabh had flown in earlier that morning, having 'borrowed' a private jet from the owners of a prominent business group. The plane had carried the elder scion of the family to Delhi earlier that evening and had been put at the CI's disposal upon request, the burgeoning mountain of data that his office had collected on the criminal activities of the liquor barons guaranteeing their cooperation.

Before Pumpkin could speak, the CI held up his hand, the group falling silent at the gesture. 'You need to trust me,' he said, looking straight at her, before ringing the bell under the desk and asking the attendant who appeared to bring in his guest.

Pumpkin's jaw dropped to the floor as the man walked in. His face was immediately recognizable to the entire intelligence community, especially to those in India's intelligence services, who battled him on a daily basis. She knew that the man had been responsible for the deaths and incarceration of several of her colleagues, but worse, the death of dozens of Indian civilians, and yet, here he stood, a guest of the CI.

'Pumpkin, meet Kanta, our highest-ranking mole in the ISI.'

# Chapter 64

4 March 2010
London
11.05 a.m.

The entire team stood in stunned silence, fighting the instinctive urge to wring their enemy's neck. Pumpkin was not easily confused, but at that moment, she had no idea what to think.

Kanta was responsible for some of the ISI's most successful operations against India and was among its most dreaded enemies. And yet, if he was here today, as a high-ranking mole for the CI, it could only be because the value of the intelligence he provided to India far outweighed the lives that he had been responsible for snuffing out. Given her own job, she thought sardonically, taking the moral high ground was out of the question, but could the intelligence really have been so good that it had been worth all the sacrifices?

Amitabh continued to watch Pumpkin carefully, expecting that she would attack Abdul. In fact, he had warned him that she may try to do so, owing to which, he now stood lightly on his toes, ready to move at the slightest sign of danger. She looked at Amitabh searchingly, hoping he would provide more of an explanation.

'Later,' said Amitabh, the wavelengths of the mentor and the protégé fully in tune. 'For now, we still need to get hold of Abbas.'

'I wouldn't worry about it,' spoke Abdul. 'Once the ISI understand what transpired and my role in it, they won't risk being accused of supporting a smuggling ring. They will simply disown him and without the ISI's protection, Abbas will be quite happy to come along with us—even he wouldn't risk the wrath of the madmen of the Jaish on his own. If you give it a few hours to let him appreciate his situation and then take him, he will tell you everything you want to know.'

Amitabh nodded. No one knew the ISI and Jaish better than Abdul, and if he was certain that events would transpire in the manner he had laid out, then he was happy to go along with it.

He had a far more important task to perform—he needed to secure the invaluable envelope that Abdul had handed over to him, a short while ago.

He asked Aastha to find suitable accommodation for Abdul, now a guest of India and under the protection of their team till he was conveyed to India safely. Once the group left, he gently tore open the envelope that so many people had laid down their lives for, and gently massaged the document out of it, reading through it slowly, memorizing every word. The legend was reality, right there in front of his eyes, the royal blue ink used by the flowing hand of the raja and his signature at the bottom. If anything, the legend had understated the explosiveness of the document, which would, without question, permanently resolve the Kashmir issue and impact the geopolitics of the Indian subcontinent in a way which would have ramifications for the entire world.

He requested the Indian ambassador for access to the embassy's safe to secure an important document. The ambassador, happy to help, escorted Amitabh to his office, using the help of his secretary to move the large desk below which the safe was hidden. He entered the code to unlock the safe—rather carelessly, thought Amitabh, noting the combination as the ambassador keyed it in and making a mental note to have the ministry issue protocols to secure the access to the embassy safes. Amitabh laid the document there gently, the secret finally in Indian safekeeping.

His work done, Amitabh excused himself, promising to return the next day to collect the document. He made his way to the residential quarters where Pumpkin had found a room for Abdul. He found the two and took them to lunch in the ambassador's private dining room, the meal prepared by the excellent chef that Taj Hotel had lent to the embassy.

Finally alone with his protégé, he brought her up to speed, starting with Abdul's warning to the Indian government about the impending attacks by the Jaish, the discovery of the stolen paintings and the plan that they had put together to recover the document hidden in the paintings. Finally done, he had asked Pumpkin to ask him any questions she had.

'Why is that document so important?'

'You know we are on a need-to-know basis. And in this case, you don't need to know, at least not yet. All you need to know is that this document is more important to national security than anything else we have previously done and we need to get it safely to India.'

Aastha, expecting to be refused, just shrugged her shoulders. 'I have just one more question,' she said, turning to Abdul. 'Why did you betray your country?'

'You don't need to answer that, Abdul. It's none of her business,' said Amitabh, glaring at Aastha.

Abdul shook his head. 'It's all right, Amitabh. I don't need to hide it any more.' In the next twenty minutes, he explained to Aastha how his life had been shattered by a bomb that had killed his son and maimed his wife. He had sought justice for his family, asking for the perpetrators, members of the Lashkar-e-Taiba, to be tried in court. The government had refused, prioritizing the protection of its homegrown monsters over the lives of the families of its government officers, willing to die for the country. It was at that point that Amitabh had reached out to Abdul, having learnt of the injustice through their common friends in the CIA. The CI had provided the funds that Abdul needed to keep his wife alive, the two of them collaborating closely to fabricate the story to explain the funds. Amitabh had provided a way for Abdul to undermine the homegrown terror groups that had escaped the control of their creators, and he had gladly helped, providing information that allowed the Indians and the Americans to strike repeatedly at them. Yes, he had had to hurt India to rise through the ranks at ISI, but he had also provided the intelligence that had allowed India to foil dozens of attacks and save the lives of thousands, each weakening the threat from Pakistan's rabid dogs a little more every time.

Aastha listened attentively as Abdul described the various operations that the ISI had conducted, the manner in which they dealt with, and protected some of the world's most wanted terrorists, and their relationship with Dawood. As she listened to the width and depth of his knowledge, she understood why the CI had allowed him some victories over India, even at the cost of Indian lives.

As Abdul finished, Amitabh took over, drawing their attention back to the unfinished task of getting hold of Abbas. Aastha, who had already been planning the operation from the time the CI had first called, laid out her plan, made easier by Abdul's inputs. The plan was simple yet thorough, and neither Amitabh nor Abdul had any questions. She looked at Amitabh for his final approval, and received a nod of assent.

The operation was a go. Another ISI asset would soon be in Indian custody.

# Chapter 65

4 March 2010
London
11.30 p.m.

The entire premises were asleep, both Amitabh and Abdul had been provided quarters within the embassy itself. Aastha had returned home to be with her family and the ambassador was at yet another dinner party, doing what he was supposed to do.

The thief had made it to the ambassador's office easily, knowing exactly where he had to go and how to bypass the alarms that guarded the building. He had avoided the prying eyes of most of the CCTV cameras. For those that he could not avoid, he had used a laser, the tool developed by his own country's intelligence services, to remotely put the cameras on an indefinite loop, even though they would appear to be functioning to the guards who were undoubtedly watching. Confident that his device worked, he had walked purposefully towards the office, using a key to open the locked door.

He made his way to the safe, moving the desk out of the way. The gloves ensured that he would not leave fingerprints for the investigation that would follow whenever the theft was discovered. He keyed in the combination and collected the document, slipping it into the pocket of his jacket. Having decided to position his intrusion as a larger theft, he proceeded to pick up several other documents, placing them in the other jacket pocket. Once his job was done, he quietly closed the safe, moved the table back and left the room as he had entered, locking the door behind him. He turned on the cameras again as he passed the line of sight for each, ensuring that the needle of suspicion pointed only in the direction of those who had had access to the office last.

Satisfied with the night's work, he returned to his bed, hiding the document in the jacket pocket of the book that he always carried on him. Those that he served would be pleased with what he had achieved that day. Perhaps, this could be his last job after all.

# Chapter 66

5 March 2010
London
4.30 p.m.

The team had returned from the makeshift interrogation room, though it was unfair to call either the sitting room that, or what they had just finished, an interrogation.

They had grabbed Abbas just as he had left Club Gascon, one of the Michelin-star restaurants that he owned in London. As Abdul had predicted, Abbas was already frightened out of his skin, sputtering incoherent nonsense when Aastha's team grabbed him, imagining that his end had come. To avoid a scene, the men had stabbed him with a hypodermic needle, the shot of hydroxyzine calming Abbas and making him amenable to the instructions issued by them. The CI had provided the hydroxyzine, the formulation developed by India's largest pharmaceutical company for the care of late-stage Parkinson's patients, but stolen by India's security apparatus and weaponized for just such a requirement.

The men had helped him into the waiting van and driven to Regent's Park to ensure that a British investigation into the missing businessman did not lead them to the Indian embassy. At the park, they had disguised Abbas and sat him in a wheelchair, Aastha playing the role of the old man's 'nurse', as she had walked him out of the park and into another waiting van. As far as the world was concerned, Abbas had just disappeared.

Back at the safe house, they had interrogated Abbas—or at least, they had planned to. As it turned out, Abbas had already concluded that he no longer had the ISI's protection and the moment he understood that his captors represented neither the Jaish nor the Pakistani government, but the interests of India, he had answered all of their questions, hoping for their protection. He had explained the story from the beginning, starting with his uncle's relationship with Devika, her marriage to Svetoslav Roerich, the party in Kappar, the gift of the paintings, his transformation into a front for the ISI and finally, the theft of the paintings.

Aastha had returned to the embassy to update Amitabh and seek further instructions, leaving Abbas in the safe house under the watchful eye of her team. Assuming that more than just the Roerichs had been stolen, Amitabh had asked her to escort Abbas back to India and hand him over to his team to continue the questioning to understand and close down the routes that were being used to smuggle valuable artefacts out of India to fund terror attacks. She was to stay on in India till Amitabh completed his remaining meetings in London and returned to Delhi.

The battle in London was over. All that remained was to ensure that the document was safely returned to India. With that thought in his head, Amitabh walked off to his room in the embassy to recover his clothes and the book that he carried with him wherever he went.

# Chapter 67

22 May 2010
New Delhi
3 p.m.

Amitabh stood in one corner of the VIP lounge at Terminal 3, watching Kamal, Tushar, Ashish and Abdul speaking to each other, thinking back over the events that had transpired from the time they had recovered the precious document.

General Beg and General Liyaqat had feared that something had gone wrong when Shadaab's team had failed to check in for two consecutive hourly updates. They had reached out to Abdul, who, unable to go himself, given his relationship with the ISI, had advised them to dispatch another team to the house to find out what had happened. The team, hastily assembled, had arrived a few hours later, and found police swarming all over the place, learning that the Mitchells' cleaning lady had discovered three dead bodies inside the house. The details of the triple murder made international headlines shortly after, the head shots making it clear that they had been terminated by professionals.

They had tried to contact Abdul in London to make sense of the news but found that his number was switched off. The embassy had confirmed that he had arrived, but had left for a meeting shortly after. They made inquiries at the hotel where he was scheduled to stay and with their networks in the British government but found no trace of Abdul, who had vanished into thin air. The generals eventually connected the dots; to their horror—Abdul had been the mole all along, his plan always being to snatch the document from Pakistan. Having struck a deep blow, Abdul had disappeared. They had sent their men to guard his wife, only to find that she had miraculously recovered from her coma and had been discharged. From the time she had left the hospital, accompanied by her nephew, they had been unable to find a trace of her.

Realizing that Abbas's cover was blown, they had simply closed his file, leaving him to his fate, the man having outlived his utility anyway. Jaish was informed that the fundraiser had failed and that the ISI would not be able to provide the money. They would just have to find another way, if they could.

Abbas provided Amitabh's team with the locations of dozens of artefacts that had been stolen from India, and the information was duly shared with the relevant departments to initiate their recovery. As part of his deal with India, he withdrew his claim to the paintings, paving the way for India's recovery of the two Roerichs. Abbas would spend the rest of his life comfortably under witness protection in Delhi, consulting for Indian intelligence on matters relating to art whenever they needed.

Amitabh used Abbas's revelations to dismantle the smuggling ring in the Indian subcontinent, coordinating with the Sri Lankan and Bangladesh governments to stop the looting of national treasures. He also provided a list of stolen artefacts to both governments, who were similarly pursuing recovery in various courts around the world.

Abdul's wife Salma was extracted from Pakistan using the same tunnels in Mandrake Gully that Abdul had often used to infiltrate terrorists into India. Her recovery from the coma so soon after his last mission for Amitabh had led Abdul to suspect that he had somehow fabricated her coma, but he had, prudently, maintained his silence. Both Abdul and Salma were made Indian citizens, living in comfort in Mumbai, under new identities.

Kamal was appointed home secretary at the CI's insistence and continued to serve his country with distinction. While not part of his remit, he continued to keep an eye on the recovery of the paintings. The Government of India succeeded in recovering the paintings, having negotiated Sotheby's costs, which is how the key players in the case of the missing Roerichs came to be in the same room together, waiting for the chartered flight from London to land, their excitement at seeing the paintings first-hand, palpable.

But not everything had ended well. The envelope that Amitabh had placed in the ambassador's safe had disappeared. With only the ambassador having access to the safe, Amitabh detained the ambassador and did the questioning himself, unwilling to believe the man's pleas of innocence. He asked to look at the CCTV footage to see who had visited the ambassador's office throughout the day, discovering that it was looped and had failed to record anyone in the corridor entering the office since late that evening. The ambassador was transported to India, where, despite extensive questioning, he refused to divulge the location of the document. Despite the protests of the Foreign Office, the ambassador was subjected to a polygraph test, which he had passed with flying colours—his experience as a CIA mole allowed him to tackle the awkward questions he was asked. The ambassador was released and wrangled a posting to America, where he enjoyed life with his old friends in the CIA. Amitabh, convinced that it was an inside job, launched an investigation against the entire staff at the embassy, one that was still ongoing. No matter what it took, they had to recover that document.

The CI answered yet another call on his phone, his face turning sombre as he heard the news. He faced the group, which, sensing that he had something to say, had quietened and turned towards him.

'The chartered plane carrying the paintings has just disappeared over the Arabian Sea.'

# Chapter 68

4 April 2013
12.30 p.m.
New Delhi

Amitabh and Kamal had just returned from Kashmir, having taken stock first-hand of the on-ground situation after the bombshell announcement by the union government. The state had been bifurcated into two union territories, which would now be administered directly by the central government; the special privileges accorded to the former state had been withdrawn.

The initiative had been conceptualized by the CI, who believed it to be the only way to protect India's national security interests. The political establishment, keen to be seen as a strong defender of India, had agreed, and things had moved quickly. Protests had broken out across the state, which was now effectively under martial law, with dozens of companies of paramilitary forces patrolling the streets to enforce a curfew. It would take time for the situation to stabilize, but both men believed that it eventually would and had reported accordingly to the prime minister.

On their way back from the PMO, as the two men discussed the situation, Kamal asked how the CI had found the additional 2000 crore that he had promised to his network of spies in the newly formed union territories, having never seen that sum appear on either the formal budget or on the slush fund ledger, which exactly eleven people in the country were privy to.

The CI smiled, finally deciding that he trusted Kamal enough to hint at the truth. 'As you saw, Kamal, the Jaish were not the only ones in need of additional money for their work,' he replied cryptically, leaving Kamal to draw his own conclusion.

# Epilogue

He was at the CIA headquarters in Langley, Virginia. Despite the heights to which he had risen, the number of years he had served the CIA, and the dozens of meetings that he had attended with them, he had never visited the headquarters before.

He had asked for the meeting, intending this to be his last job for them. At their behest, he had stolen the document from the embassy in London, using his knowledge to make the document disappear. As he had known would be the case, the thief had not yet been found and was never going to be found.

He was standing by the glass windows that overlooked the massive campus, waiting for Andrew, the director of the CIA, as he fingered the envelope resting in his breast pocket, having withdrawn it earlier that day from the book which he always carried with him. He was absolutely exhausted—the years of acting as a double agent had taken their toll.

Andrew finally walked in and shook his hand warmly, asking him to take a seat. He stuck his hand out and asked for the document, surprised by the hesitation at the other end.

'Andrew, I would like to offer you a deal.'

Andrew replied with a smile, 'Are you really in a position to bargain, after all you have done?'

'I wouldn't have made the offer unless I believed you would consider accepting it.'

Intrigued, Andrew decided to hear the man out.

'The document is far more useful to India than it is to you. I'd like us to keep it . . . so I must offer you something that you want even more than the leverage this would give you in the Indian subcontinent.'

'And what would that be?'

'OBL's location,' said Amitabh quietly.

Andrew sat up straighter. OBL, or Osama Bin Laden, as he was known to the wider world, had been on every American agency's most-wanted list for the best part of a decade, the country desperate to punish the man who had orchestrated the horrific attacks on the World Trade Centre twin towers. The country had spent hundreds of millions of dollars and lost hundreds of lives in Afghanistan in their effort to find Osama, with nothing to show for them. All of them, including the CIA, were under incredible pressure to bring him to justice and were authorized to do whatever it took to make that happen.

'You can't possibly know that,' he said finally. 'Even *we* can't find him.'

'India doesn't know. Only I do.'

'How?'

'Does it really matter?'

'No, it doesn't. Though I would like to know.'

'Well, that is not part of the deal. So it's up to you—OBL's location or the document. What will it be?'

Andrew stood up and walked over to nearly the same spot the other man had occupied, just moments ago. He had not risen to his position without being able to make quick decisions and now, standing there, he was ready to make the most important decision of his career.

'Keep your document, Amitabh. Tell me where he is.'

'Abbottabad. 34.1926° N, 73.2397° E. The only red-roofed house.'

Andrew memorized the information, eager to get a satellite over the coordinates as soon as possible to verify the presence of the world's most wanted man.

'Thank you, Amitabh. I am confident that as long as you remain CI, India is in safe hands and that the two countries will continue to share an excellent relationship.'

Amitabh nodded in quiet acquiescence, getting up from his seat to leave, to return to India and protect it as best as he could.

# Author's Note

This story, while inspired by, and based on, the fact of the theft of two paintings, is entirely fictional.

It is true that the Indian Agriculture Research Institute (IARI) owned certain paintings by legendary artist Nicholas Roerich and that two of these were indeed stolen, with the theft brought on record only when Sotheby's emailed the IARI to inquire about its claims on the paintings, which had been submitted to Sotheby's for auction by a Pakistani national, claiming they were family heirlooms. This book states that the stolen paintings were created by Svetoslav Roerich, which is a narrative device used for the purposes of this book's timelines and I am not aware if any of Svetoslav's paintings were ever owned by the IARI or were ever stolen.

While Indian law enforcement did investigate the matter, to the best of my knowledge, neither were the thieves identified, nor the date of theft ascertained. The IARI did lay claim to the paintings and the same were withdrawn from the auction a few days before they were slated for auction. A legal challenge was mounted by the IARI and experts on Roerich were called in from across the world to support the challenge, leading to the paintings being returned to India. All of the Roerich paintings owned by the IARI are now displayed in the Convention Centre of IARI at Pusa, Delhi.

It is true that Nicholas Roerich's son was Svetoslav Roerich and that Svetoslav married Devika Rani, who was a Bollywood superstar in the 1930s and 1940s. While it was never conclusively established, there was also evidence to suggest that the paintings were submitted for auction by one of the grandsons of a co-star of Devika Rani's, who had migrated to Pakistan.

The rest of this book is a work of fiction. There was never any secret document signed in relation to the accession of Kashmir. All conversations between the raja and Nicholas, his thoughts and the suggestion that they were friends are also a product of my imagination. While there are several conspiracy theories about the death of a former prime minister in Russia, to the best of my knowledge, his death was an unfortunate loss to India due to natural causes, and the entire chapter about the assassination of the prime minister is a creative narrative.

All descriptions of their lives or the conversations between or relating to the Roerichs or Devika Rani in this book are fictional as well. Further, while intelligence officers from various countries are characters in this book, all of them are fictitious characters and any suggestion of their involvement in the activities or affairs of another country or in the domestic affairs of their own country is fictional and the resemblance to any person, living or dead, is entirely coincidental.

# Acknowledgements

A lot of people have guided, nudged, encouraged or supported me in this journey, without whom this book would still be an idea in my head. While I will not thank each of you here, you know who you are and I just want to thank each of you with all my heart.

I do want to call out a few people, whose contribution has been immeasurable. First, to dad, for being full of stories, his love for narrating them and his ability to weave fact with fiction so adroitly that it is always difficult to distinguish between the two.

To mom, who, as always, selflessly and quietly made her invaluable contribution, painfully reading every draft to deliver the benefit of her own experience in reading the genre. And to my wife, without whose emotional support, belief and unstinting encouragement, this effort would have been abandoned before the first draft was complete. You deserve half the credit for getting us here.

To Vinay Sitapati, the brilliant author, who was among the first to read this draft. Honestly, given the distance that life had created in our interactions, when I reached out to you, I didn't expect you to put in the incredible amount of effort that you did. I doubt there would ever have been another draft but for your comment that evening over the phone, which I will never forget.

To Kanta, who despite the demands of his work and family, made the time to not only read but also ideate on this book. In my mind, you deserve credit as a co-author for this book. Without your incredible idea, this story may have remained bland, insipid and therefore, untold.

To Gautham and Freaka, whose unrestrained and honest criticism led to so much more work, but without whom the characters may never have been fleshed out and the gaps in the story never filled. To Andy and Manish, whose critical eyes helped plug in so many loopholes in the earlier drafts.

To Smita, whom I would hate to refer to as just my 'agent'. It would have been just as easy to say no when I reached out after a ten-year gap, but the warmth and welcome will forever be cherished. It's been real fun (with a little bit of luck along the way), and thank you so much for getting us here.

To Gurveen, my editor, without whom the plot would have had massive holes, thousands of unnecessary words and much poorer language. Thank you for hand-holding me through my first book, for the additional time when I needed it and for removing all laziness from the book.

As I begin writing my second book, I can only hope that all of you are part of the journey again.